Rendezvous

with

Armageddon

Book I of the Guardian Chronicles

Alex Taponi

PhoenixGate

ISBN: 978-0615660974

First published in 2012 by PhoenixGate

To my English Teachers, who always thought
my compositions were too long

Prologue: Windows

It was there, on its perch as it has always been in its sordid contemplation, still as what many of the entities it has watched over would refer to as a statue. Glowing orbs swirled around, windows to what can be, what has been, and that which is. The Order has never claimed omnipotence; for it understood that nothing could ever control the Rhythms that formed the basis of all reality. Steered, diverted maybe, but controlled, never. The Order was just wise enough to perceive and except that fact. Now as a window opened before its eyes, the Order saw yet another ending/beginning and yet as always those eyes watched with a curiosity those same watched entities would expect of children.

As with every beginning this one ignited in pitch darkness. Deep within the ovaries of a common woman, an extraordinary event was taking place --- life was being created, but not just any human life, but rather the likes of which has never been seen in an age and will likely never be seen again.

As flashes of electricity signaled the fusion of protein molecules and DNA, from within the womb a pulse reverberated across the magical world, sending a single message to all that could receive and understand it. A message that said three words: It is here ...

He wasn't sure why he was humming that tune or why it had chose that moment to pop into his head. Not that he minded, it was a rather pleasant tune, a complete reminder of the silly quirks and peeves that came with being a child of that era. A smile crept on his face. Ah happier times.

Then again, past times were always happier times because they were past and done. There were no reasons to worry about the past ---- those able to recollect the past, had overcome the obstacles and survived. The present and the future however were a different thing. One could adequately worry about the present and the future --- they still held uncertainties.

He was in his garden, his attention devoted to the Sheer Bliss roses that grew near the edge of the yard closest to the house. His hands just slightly above touching, sliding slowly down the barbed stem. Every other second or so those same hands would gently stroke the lush green leaves, sending tingles of pride, admiration, and concern. His humming resumed as he found the spot he wanted, placing the trimmers gently along side the stem before squeezing his hand all in one fluid motion.

"There, there that didn't hurt," he cooed to the plant. Two buds swayed gently in the breeze as if nodding in response. He looked up at the clear blue sky where the new afternoon sun beamed brightly. It was September, surprisingly warm and humid considering he was in the Pacific Northwest and not the Deep South where his family had (and still) lived for more than 200 years.

But it wasn't the unusual warm weather that was responsible for the warm simmering inside him; rather it was the tranquil stillness, a snug homey peace covering all in a soothing quiet carrying away any worries that may plague the heart and soul.

The silence however was broken by the thud of footsteps followed by a soft creek. Looking up he saw his daughter sitting on the porch swing facing the yard, the expression on her face was an all too familiar one and he immediately knew what had transpired to cause it.

"Your mother caught you using your magic again didn't she?"

She didn't answer him, at least not verbally, but the expression on her face said everything.

"I wasn't doing anything dangerous Daddy, honest! I just wanted to summon a morph to talk to. Nothing like the rose thing!"

He hoped his daughter couldn't see him cringe at the sentence. She had been six, her powers just manifesting themselves --- and she being her father's daughter had to try them out. She had heard her mother and aunt rambling on how beautiful blue roses were and how her father created a bouquet of them for their wedding. Knowing how her father felt about roses and desiring to give him the best surprise ever, the child used her powers to turn all his roses blue. Unfortunately she had failed to consider why it had been that her father turned cut roses blue and not the entire plant. Granted the rose bushes she had created were beautiful, however the change caused a serious shock to the plant's system. Just now were his roses starting to bloom in their natural colors again.

"I don't understand Daddy, how come you and Momma are able to use magic but I can't?"

"Trust me," her father laughed, "if your mother had her way, she wouldn't use her magic either." He cocked his head back and loosed a great laugh and as he hoped, the tears stopped flowing down his daughter's face.

Unfortunately her face was still set in a stony countenance that strangely enough left him feeling a tad bit unsettled, but no one could question its heritage. *Yep she definitely gets that from her mother.*

He sighed inwardly as he eyed his daughter. The flat, thin body along with pink overalls and barrettes said she was nine. Her facial and body expressions told a different story. He would joke that his daughter's average age was 15. Depending on the situation one would have thought of her being anything but nine. While possessing such a precocious child would be enough to startle any other parents, he and his wife took it merely as if it was an expectation. Besides, while his daughter may act like a teen half the time her interest in boys remained locked in that state of bewilderment and disgust that he knew would one day go away, thankfully that day had not yet come.

"It's not fair!" the girl whined, "I've heard so many stories about the Guardian and the Hands of the Order fighting demons, saving the world. Mother herself was barely older than I am when she started using her magic."

He sighed again, his daughter, a child of magic --- a suriana uchawi, one of the greatest natural wonders of the world and the most dangerous. "Yes and from those stories you know that wielding magic is not only a great responsibility but also a harbinger of great sorrow. Your magic will draw many dark and dreadful things to you."

The daughter merely averted her eyes toward the ground.

"Which is why you must learn to use it wisely," the father finished with a smile as he put down his shearers and offered his hand.

"Are we gonna have another lesson?"

The father nodded softly; moments later daughter and parent started toward the garden at the far edge of the yard. The warmth of the sun rinsing his face, his eyes closed as the warmth from the child's hand and the sun converged, all to the rhythm of a swinging arm and to the scent of sweet flowers and growing earth. *Yes, all for this, all for these things I live.*

His eyes opened and drifted toward his daughter. Their gaze meeting, the father closed his eyes, raining down a beaming smile. Though already excited and bouncing with anticipation, the child's smile widened.

For a moment, it seemed as if time had stopped, but he knew better. Rather time was retreating back to another year, in another place. Before he had a daughter named Brin.

The night was still and silent as he emerged from the foyer, feeling surprised and a bit terrified by the silence. His home city was known for being many things: seductive, entertaining, shocking, and dangerous among others but silent was never one of them. Then again every place has their quiet moments even New Orleans. Then again the silent calm usually preludes the violent storm and New Orleans was known for its ability to create a ruckus.

He stopped and eyed the building, the now familiar sensation pulsing through him. He gripped the cane he had been carrying, to the ordinary eye it was a simple walking cane, one that you could find it in any tuxedo store across the country if not the world. This was no ordinary cane though, it was the source of his magic, his power; a reminder of his curse and his obligation. He could see the white light shimmering within it, could already feel its energy pulsing through him, strengthening him, assuring him.

It's here. Resolve filled him as he stepped into the building.

He started up the stairs, his footsteps pounding the wooden stairs as he followed his instincts onto the third floor. He paused at the stairwell, searching for a clue of what direction he needed to head in when he heard it. A hiss, a soft yet frightening hiss. He turned to his left, advancing slowly when he saw it standing there in the darkness --- a demon! And not just any demon --- an archdemon!

"Guardian," it hissed. Its eyes burned with defiance and mock. Damien merely stood there unhindered, his hands gripping the white cane. He and the demon both knew that it was no match for his magical armor or might. He crept up slowly, waiting for the moment when he would unleash his magic. The demon growled, its huge wings slowly spread to their full length. Damien continued to advance, eyeing his opponent, bracing himself for anything that may follow when abruptly the demon crouched before spearing itself towards him.

"Serena! Serena, wake up!"

The teenage girl uttered a soft moan as she pulled off the covers and dragged herself to the window where the cause of her disrupted sleep stood.

"What is it?"

"What is it! Oh nothing; just a demon prowling in the park that's all!"

Serena sighed as she walked over to the dresser and pulled a Guess T-shirt. She wondered if all magical creatures were as moody as Morgoth or did it just apply to golden wolves that could talk.

"Serena come on!"

"I'm coming, I'm coming!" the girl replied as she pulled on her sneakers before climbing out the window.

"Now," she fussed when they were on the ground, and half way towards the park, "where is this so called demon that caused you to wake me up in the middle of the night."

Morgoth growled before galloping into a run.

"Hey remember Morgoth some of us only have two legs."

The wolf creature simply snorted before mumbling something about humans and limitations. Nevertheless he did slow his pace down, but not by much. Then again it wasn' t necessary, Serena was very fast on her feet and her style of running reflected her three years of track in middle and high school.

"Ok Morgoth where is it?" Serena inquired as they entered the park.

"Over there," the wolf hissed. His head pointing toward a clearing beyond the path, "Serena be careful."

"Am I always?" She ran at a stealth pace before a sudden sound caused her to stop. Her heart raced as she saw a dark thing standing in the clearing, slowly changing shape. It resembled something human yet more savage and sinister. Gathering her resolve she jumped through the clearing causing the demon to wheel around, its red pupil less eyes locked onto her. Serena summoned her magic. The tension in her mind loosened as she felt the magic gathering into a knot inside of her, a cocked force just waiting to be sprung.

The demon howled and with amazing quickness it was upon her, swinging its massive arms. Serena ducked, her head dropping just inches from where the claws swooshed around. She called upon her magic and could feel it responding, the warm tingling feeling that accompanied as it surged out of her. A scream came from the demon as the magic went to work. The creature gave a blood curling howl but despite its pain, it readied itself for another assault. Serena locked her eyes upon the creature's. Both froze; engaged in a battle of wills, each determined to emerge supreme. Serena focused, summoning all her might as she forced her way into the demon's mind. Suddenly a dreadful scream filled the night as the demon dropped to its knees. Its claws clasping its head as it collapsed onto the ground. Serena fell to her knees in exhaustion as she watched a shadowy mist rise from the remains.

"What kind of demon was it?"

"It wasn't an arch demon, but it wasn't far from becoming one either," Morgoth replied.

"God, he was powerful!" the girl panted as she continued gulping huge gasps of air. "It's never been that difficult before."

"From here on out they'll all be more powerful than the previous."

"Something is going to happen isn't it," Serena inquired as she slowly stood up. The pair eyed the black husk laying across from them. She had gone up against demons before, but recently things had changed. The demons were now much stronger than before. She had nearly all but destroyed herself in this battle but still this wasn't an archdemon. She had yet to face one and for the perhaps the umpteenth time she wondered the question: *would I prevail against one.* But before she could think any more on the matter, the world started to fall from beneath her.

"Serena," Morgoth hissed. "Come you must rest." The girl crawled onto the wolf's broad back and rested her head on his powerful shoulders. Relief swept through her as the softness of Morgoth's fur caressed her skin. "Rest Serena rest; for you have earned it." *And will need it.*

The window exploded with the demon's impact as it was flung across the room by the magic of his adversary. The Guardian raced to the window to see if his foe had fallen to the ground, but his eyes only saw shattered glass. He glanced upward to see a shadow disappear over the roof. He quickly ran up the stairs, stopping just short of the door leading to the roof. Slowly he turned the knob before kicking the door open and stepping through the entry. He grunted as a blow came to the side, knocking him to the ground as his staff skidded from his hand across the rooftop.

Clutching his side, he searched for his staff and saw it lying about ten feet away. He turned to see the demon advancing, his eyes displaying a look of triumph. The Guardian stretched out his hand and the demon stopped in its tracks, hindered by an invisible force of some kind. Rolling over, he grabbed his staff and brought it to bear upon the stunned demon. White lightning surged from the staff, knocking the creature about ten feet back. In an instant, the Guardian was on his feet and sent another surge of lightning into the demon. The creature tried to counter, but the lightning kept hammering it back, driving it closer and closer to the edge. The Guardian closed in to finish the demon off but before he could attack the demon, it gave a soft hiss and in one motion leaped over the edge, leaving him to watch in silent fury as it flew off into the night.

1 AM. A darkness drifts through a bedroom window, gathering in a swirling mist that rotated and twisted before compacting into a mass that shaped itself into a form. For a moment the form solidified as it took the shape of the Guardian. For a moment the ebony statue stood before a soft chink sounded and moments later the statue shattered into ash revealing Damien Parker bereft of clothes save his T-shirt and boxers.

Collapsing onto the bed, sleep quickly overtook him as he slipped beyond reality into the Resurrect Sleep. Drifting beyond ordinary reality into a place filled with so many different yet similar people. A place so close yet so far away. All hopes, dreams, fears, passions were within reach, all in one place, one time ---- the dream time.

He's walking not as the Guardian, but neither as Damien Parker. Rather he is a shadow, a dark husk of the identities he once carried. He stands in the cemetery, surrounded by a maelstrom of crosses and markers. He sighs as he walks on, but stops abruptly at a marker. For some reason the name he reads seems familiar but he can't remember when or where the name happened across his life. He sees five other markers, each with a name that rings with resounding familiarity yet he can t remember who they were or how they were involved in his life.

His eyes notice the sun rising in the distant horizon and he stares with awe. Something that once seemed so usual and granted, now seeing a sunrise was a luxury beyond the wildest of comprehension. He sighs again and continues walking when he hears a sound, one that he has not heard in a long time. He cautiously creeps towards its source and in astonishment he sees them: children, sitting beneath the remains of an old oak tree. Children of different cultures sitting beneath the tree engaged in an imaginary tea party of some sort. There were seven of them, each dressed completely in a different color. A faint smile forms on his face as he watches. Children ... hope. He looks up at the sun shinning brightly, illuminating the normally dark sky. So bright are its rays that he lifts his hands to shield his eyes. Sweat runs across his face as the sun seems to grow larger and larger, consuming the sky in its blinding glare. The heat starts to burn him and he collapses to his knees. Trees now catch fire and the world seems to disappear in swarms of red and yellow flames. He turns towards the children, yet they seem unfazed. They continue eating and drinking unaffected by the inferno that surrounds and engulfs them.

He screams as he feels his flesh burning. The sky is gone, in its place: fire and glares of the swallowing sun. He stares as a large face emerges from the flames and cackles a sinister laugh that chills him to the bone, but the face ignores him rather its leering, flaming face watches the children with lusting, fiendish eyes. He watches in horror as the face looms closer and closer, its mouth opening wider and wider until ultimately the children are within its jaws and with a malicious laugh swallows them whole. A malicious laugh that would be the last thing he ever heard as the flames consumed him.

Damien Parker jerked upright with a start. Sweat beaded his forehead and his breathing was in deep gulps of breath. He stared at the alarm clock on the dresser. 5:45 AM. He swung himself out of bed and walked over to the window. The sky was grey, the dawn just moments away. In silence he stared out at the rising sun, pondering, but he already knew what part of the dream meant. Someone is coming and evil is coming with it.

Friday
February 7th

Chapter 1

The bell ending first period had just rang bringing an end to the pacified hallways as they became congested with students scurrying to their next class. Damien Parker, however was in no rush as he walked slowly down the hall of John Ehret High, his mind still boggling on last night's dream.

Someone is coming

And evil is coming with it …

But who and what was he after? Or she as Serena would politely interject. Why couldn't it be a woman she would argue. Women are just as capable of evil as men are. He even knew that she would pause and display a wide grin before adding 'if not more.'

A smile formed on his face.

Serena Martin. They had been dating a little over a year now and it hadn't been an easy year that much was certain, but he wouldn't trade it for anything at the moment. It seemed as if they were meant to be together. Even the way they ended up together was the stuff of romance novels and T.V. movies, he thought as he reflected upon the previous year.

It was the start of his junior year, the thrill of anticipation could be seen flaring through the students like electricity. From the newcomers to the soon to be liberated seniors, expectations were high and outlooks positive.

It was with such expectations and outlooks that Damien Parker and his friends made their way through the halls of John Ehret High. While his friends chattered away on football and studies, Damien's mind was far from such novelties. Recently his life had gone through many complications. Granted a part of him had always believed in the possibilities of beings like elves, nymphs, and other creatures of magic. However learning that you were one of them, especially learning it from an entity, he couldn't even see! Yeah, it was definitely complicated.

He was still pondering how he had gone from an ordinary teenage kid to a Guardian of the Cross, protector of the city and its people, when his eyes noticed a beautiful figure floating down the hall. He wasn't enamored with her then, rather it was later at an academic team practice that he was stunned by her. She was tall, just slightly shorter than his five feet eleven stature. Her hair was dark brown, in a soft chignon style. She was slender but also blessed with curves that folded out, giving her a coke bottle figure and there was a smooth willowy sway in her walk that had him dumbfounded. Even then he couldn't summon the courage to tell her what he felt. He wasn't exactly Mr. Popular and his newly found ability to channel magic distanced him even further from the center of normalcy. Besides, Serena was too exotic for an abnormal person like him.

That all changed at the Homecoming Dance. He wasn't sure what made him do it, but something enticed him to pull her to the dance floor. Probably desperation.

Regardless she didn't resist and they had been together ever since.

It hadn't been easy though, his role as the Guardian was constantly a strain on their relationship, and he could see the effect it was weaving. Time and time again he thought of telling her, but how do you tell someone that you, a high school senior, was one of the focal points in a war that she probably wasn't even aware was happening. Until last summer, he had been unaware that it was happening! He laughed as he continued walking.

Serena closed her locker before she and Sara Winters started towards Mrs. Simon's Algebra class.

"You think you did well on that test?" Sara asked.

"I really don't know," Serena answered. "I think I made a B. You?"

"I'm not sure," the other girl replied, her voice carrying a tone of uncertainty. "I studied hard but I don't think I grasped that last part."

"Come on Sara, you're a math expert! I'm sure you did fine!" She smiled as she glanced at the girl beside her. She and Sara were best friends; when Serena transferred to John Ehret, Sara had been the first to befriend her. Warm, cheerful, and intelligent with an innocence and shyness that could easily be mistaken for naïve, Sara Winters was one of the few people with whom Serena Martin felt comfortable talking to, mostly because she, like Serena, was distanced from everyone around them. The only thing Sara didn't know was that she could do magic and the different world that ability placed her in.

They were near the classroom when Sara smacked straight into Andra Alexander, the female wonder athlete of John Ehret High. In her career so far at John Ehret, she had made All-Metro in volleyball, basketball, and track, led the Lady Patriots to 1 district title in volleyball, 3 in basketball as well as 3 trips to the state quarterfinals and beyond with the possibility of a fourth title and trip this year and was currently the state champion in the 100 and 200 yard dashes. Usually Andra was tolerable, but today she was in no mood for unnecessary disruptions especially from annoying nerds.

"Watch where you going?"

"Sorry," Sara replied shyly as she frantically tried to help her only to bump into her arm.

"Get away!" Andra hissed, knocking Sara away with a slight push.

"Relax Andra! She said she was …"

"Serena right? Look stay out of this."

"Andra we just."

"Look Serena what part of stay away from me don't you understand!"

Now Serena was boiling, there was only so much she could take and she couldn't watch Sara be humiliated just because "wonder woman" was having a bad day. "Now you listen heifer."

Andra quickly got up and faced Serena.

Oh yeah that did it.

"Heifer? No she didn't! Look just because you finally got a man doesn't make you all that." In a step she was in Serena's face. Serena didn't back down. She stared Andra straight in the eye, but deep down she was afraid of what might happen next. *Don't lose control, don't lose control Serena.* She could feel it slipping though and it was past the point of return for either of them.

"Now why you have to go and put me into this?" a voice inquired.

Both turned to see Damien Parker, and Serena could already feel the tension ease as he stepped in between them. "Andra, I'm sure you have bigger things to worry about than an accidental brush in the hallway." He didn't say anything more. The tone he had said it in was enough. Both eyed each other for a second before Andra glared at Serena, then back at Damien before walking around them continuing down the hall.

"Can't leave you alone for a minute can I?"

His voice was mellow and jovial and Serena could feel her cheeks flushing as she eyed the dazzling smile on Damien Parker's face. Smart, confident, and charming, he was known throughout John Ehret High. Captain of the Academic Team, award winning member of the debate team and president of two other organizations, everyone knew Damien Parker.

She was infatuated with him. His confidence, his soft deep voice, the way light seems to break with his smile. It was as if nothing could lower him from the

heights of achievement. *So eager to change and save the world.*
"Luckily I have you to watch over me."

"I suppose," Damien responded as he helped Sara
up. "You ok Sara?"

"Oh I'm fine," Sara interjected before walking
into the classroom.

"Don't worry about Andra," Damien replied, "she
really not a bad person. She's just been under a lot of
stress lately."

"That's no excuse!" Serena replied. "She isn't the
only one whose has a lot to deal with."

"Ok how would you feel if you had a sprained
arm that just got bumped into after playing 60 minutes of
basketball the night before? Wouldn't you be a little bit
cranky. Especially if your whole future is kind of
depending on that arm."

Serena's mind drifted back to last night and early
this morning and she started to see Damien's point.
"Ohmigod she has a sprained arm!"

"Not to mention that she's been playing with a
sprained ankle the last couple of weeks."

"Damien I didn't … I didn't know."

"I know dear. Only reason I know is because I
happen to get lucky and have my ears in the right wall at
the right time."

"But why? Why doesn't she rest?"

"The same reason people like you and me are in so many activities. Duty, desire, scholarships, pressure. Who knows."

"I'm glad you was there." Serena replied softly after a moment.

"Well it would look bad for one of the smartest students in the junior class to be suspended for fighting so late in the year."

"I suppose," she laughed before she noticed something in his eyes. "What's wrong? You seem kind of distant a moment ago."

Damien's eyebrows raised in surprise, his mind had drifted back toward the dream he had last night and he had hoped that the concern didn't show on his face. "Oh nothing just concerned about this composition for English class. I had a late night so I didn't get a chance to work on it much."

"I don't see why your compositions are always among the best in the entire school. Every English teacher from Ms. Stein to Mr. Nichols says so. But I know what you mean; I've been up racking my brain for this test in Algebra."

"I'm sure you'll do fine."

He always had confidence in her. She remembered last night riding Morgoth home, thoughts of him crossed her mind. He would have been so proud of her standing against that demon. She wished she could tell him, but he couldn't begin to grasp the concept and she didn't think she could stand being alienated from him should he ever learn of the wall that separates them, a wall made up of magic and demons. A pity really she thought, he would probably fit in a magical world because he was magical to her.

"Damien, Serena, you two better get to class!"

Damien smiled as he glanced at Mrs. Dunn before turning back to Serena. "I better get going." He pressed two fingers to his lips before softly touching them to hers. "See you."

Serena Martin watched until he disappeared around the corner before walking into the classroom.

Chapter 2

Traffic on Interstate 10 was a mass of commotion even for a Friday as Malagant made his descent. He sneered as he hovered above, watching them, reading their thoughts, feeling their fears, their prejudices, their hatreds. They were so pathetic. Ignorant and impoverished, so easily swayed, he wondered how they were even permitted to exist. Even now he was tempted to feed upon them, to manipulate their pathetic little lives for his own purpose. That however would interfere with his current task, tempting as it was. Part of him wondered why it even bothered with this alliance. It wasn't affected by responsibility or rules --- weaknesses that only lead to destruction. His purpose was one of survival. The destruction of humanity aided in his survival. That and only that secured his allegiance.

The demon noticed a figure leaning against the first E of the Green in the Green Wave Muriel that decorated the wall just off the highway. Malagant landed on the wall, breathing a long hiss as his eyes locked onto the tall, stern faced figure whose dark eyes never strayed from his. His coat swayed with a passing breeze, the only ripple in his smooth motions. His eyes displayed neither the fear nor caution that he noticed in humans whenever he terrorized them. Then again, the figure before him was just as twisted and evil as it was.

The figure stopped and stared at the massive beast that stood before him. His countenance was not disrupted as darklings jumped behind the wall and gathered around the both of them.

"Well Malagant?"

Another hiss drew from the demon as he crouched his head lower so that the two were practically face to face. A soft growl accompanied his snarled face. "It would seem that you were right. The seals are in the city."

"But of course!" the other replied, "Did you truly expect me to be wrong?"

Another hiss came from Malagant. "Do not assume victory so easily Magnus. The seals are there, but so is a Guardian!"

The chattering and hisses drew from the darklings at the mention of the word Guardian.

"Yes I am aware of Damien Parker! I have prepared for his presence should the occasion arise."

"I have battled this Guardian, Magnus, his powers are not to be ---"

"Fool! Do you think I have waited this long without anticipating the presence of the Order!"

"All I am saying is that I have battled this Guardian. Do not underestimate his power. It may be true that he is a ..."

"Maybe his powers are extraordinary, but there are ways of dealing with such nuisance." His face hardened as he turned toward the visible skyline of New Orleans. Welcome to New Orleans ... New Orleans, nexus of magic ... New Orleans, murder capital of the nation ... New Orleans, site of Armageddon.

The phone rang once, twice before Grant Pershing grabbed the receiver.

"Pershing."

"Grant Pershing with the New Orleans Times Picayune?"

"Who is this?"

"At the moment my name is not important. In these times one must protect our privacy."

"Sure. Okay. What's on your mind?"

"Your article on Judge Savoie and the Runner's Scandal, I read it."

"You and about a million other people in New Orleans. Look I'm kind of in the middle of some important things here."

"Yes I understand your endless crusade to change the world, Mr. Pershing. Or should I say your quest for a Pulitzer. I recently came across some information, particularly regarding city politics.

A brief pause followed.

"Mr. Pershing."

"I'm listening, talk to me."

"Oh talk I will, but not here, not now."

"Why not?"

"Not that I don't trust your confidentiality, but I am very discreet on who and how I give information.

Listen, be awaiting for my call at 3 pm and we will make an arrangement."

"Wait we can make an arrangement now! We can meet anywhere you lik ---"

"3 PM Mr. Pershing and don t bother tracing this call, I've played the game before, I know all the rules."

The phone clicked before a dial tone filled Pershing's ears. He looked at the row of numbers on the phone. He dialed several numbers before sighing. He was playing the game all right, but maybe there were some rules he wasn't aware of.

As usual, Enrica Bradley's mind was on everything but class. Serena couldn't help but smile as the 5'6" brunette put one of the boys, Glynn Turner, in his place.

"Now where were we before we were rudely interrupted," Enrica laughed casting a look in Glynn's direction. "Oh yes Mardi Gras."

"Yes Miss Enrica what are your plans for Fat Tuesday?"

"Plans? Who needs plans? Half the fun comes from not knowing for sure what you gonna do. Though I'm certain to end up in the Quarter after the parades"

"Going with Nick?"

Nick Thevanot was Enrica's newest subject in Boys 301, the only class that she excelled in better than Sara and Serena. Serena couldn't help but admire her a

bit. For a full figured woman who defied all the
stereotypes, Enrica had no problem in the social circles of
John Ehret High and she did it without having to be a slut.

Enrica gave a sly grin. "Don't try to make it like
I'm the one whose going to violate the girl's night credo.
I'm sure all your plans involve a certain guy with the
initials D.P.   I wonder who could that be?"

"Enrica!" It was the gleam of naughtiness in her
friend's eyes that bothered her, not the words.

"Girlfriend; its not my fault you guys make such a
nice couple. Too bad. If I would have known that the
shy, quiet Damien Parker in middle school would have
turned into the fine guy he is now. Well let's just say there
would have been one less guy available when you graced
us with your presence."

Part of her always wondered how Damien Parker
wasn't taken when she got to Ehret. She certainly wasn't
glamorous but then Damien was kind of unique. Not too
many could claim nerd status and still have some degree of
popularity. By now both she and Damien were use to
their "celebrity" status, at least that was how they joked on
the oohs and ahhs they seem to evoke from both faculty
and student alike. If she had a nickel for all the times she
had been told how cute she and Damien were as a couple,
she wouldn't need an education. And of course there had
already been a few who tried to "steal" Damien away.   On
one hand it was kinda of cool, but on the other hand it
was, well bizarre.

Enrica however was right, her Mardi Gras plans
did include Damien, however there was a complication,

like always.   Only this complication consisted of the gala
at the country club, late that Mardi Gras night. It was one
of those social events that her parents always had to attend
every year. She had hoped that lavish world that her
parents relished so much would be inaccessible when they
left Illinois. No chance. Her parents discovered the high
circles of New Orleans quicker than they found them in
Park Ridge. As usual she was forced to attend these silly
gatherings. Her parents would force her to go to the gala
that much was certain, so she considered inviting Damien,
but there were other complications. Serena sighed too
many complications.

The bell rang, ending the school day and Serena
walked solemnly to her locker after leaving a grinning
Enrica Bradley. She was about to open it when a loud
voice called her name. Immediately she wished she could
climb into her locker and hide, but being that she couldn't,
she braced herself for the annoyance she would have to
bear. He would be there in front of her right about …
now.

"Hey Serena."

Victor Morris. Victor was a senior like Damien,
played on the baseball team and really thought he was all
that and for some reason he had a thing for her. He was
bigger than Damien, but not as tall, nor as blessed with
looks. Damien Parker possessed a charismatic face
complete with a set of dimples, and while Victor wasn't
Quasimodo, there was something about him that just
made her want to vomit. He had one thing in common

with Damien though, he was persistent and stubborn. For the longest he has been trying to win Serena over. *Mostly when Damien is out of sight.*

"So what you doing for Mardi Gras?"

"Washing my hair."

Apparently he wasn't amused. "Seriously Serena. I thought you might like to go out with me to the Quarter this weekend. Then I could take you to the gala Tuesday night."

The mere fact that he said it as a statement and not as a question enraged her. That for the umpteenth time he was trying to come on to her while in the middle of a relationship, drove her over the edge. "Victor I have a boyfriend you know."

"Oh I know you have a boyfriend, but sooner or later you're gonna want a real man."

"Oh Lord!" Serena thought.

"Come on Serena, forget about Parker, he's a 4-F Wimp. You deserve a real man."

Funny, I couldn't get the time of day from you before I started going out with Damien Parker. It's something when you start dating someone.

"I know you don't want to hurt his feelings," he stepped closer to Serena. Too close. "He'll get over it."

"Look Victor. Read my lips. There is no us. Never have been, never will be." She slammed the locker shut and walked off.

Damien Parker was waiting at the end of the hall when Serena approached him, a look of relief filled her face as each step closed the distance between them. "Anything exciting happen last period," he inquired.

"Nah," Serena laughed as they walked. "Mrs. Cleaves was her usual self. Nothing but usual lab work."

"That's good to hear."

Serena glanced over her shoulder. Good no Victor Morris. The pair walked quietly through the courtyard toward where the buses waited.

"Damien."

"Yeah."

"What are you doing Mardi Gras night?"

"Probably just goofing in the Quarter or at home if nothing happens. Why? We had already made plans to go to the parades early that morning and afternoon."

"There's a gala at the country club that night and my parents are making me go. So I was wondering if you didn't mind ... being my escort."

Damien's eyebrows raised in surprise. "You sure your father will let you? He already wants my head on a stick."

"I'm serious," Serena laughed as they stopped.

"So am I? Your father doesn't exactly hide the fact that he hates my guts."

"But my mother loves you."

"Lot of good that has done me," Damien jested.

"Are you going to take me or do I have to endure torture by myself?"

"What do you think its going to be for me?"

"Misery is bearable with company." She stepped in front and placed her arms around his neck. "And I love your company."

"All right I'll go!" He laughed. "Just stop using those puppy dog eyes on me." He laughed again. "You better get on the bus before you get left here. Knowing your father he'll try to shoot me if I take you home."

Serena gave him a look before she kissed him quickly on the lips. "Call me later on. Bye."

"See you love," Damien replied before watching her board the bus.

Damien started back into the school, a smile on his face as he walked through the nearly vacated hall he noticed a boy and a girl were shouting at each other. His smile widened as he stood there listening as Achilles Harmon and Andra Alexander went at each other as they usually did. Everyone in school knew about their feud, but only few like Damien knew better. Their argument was just a front, deep down one of them liked the other and it wouldn't have surprised Damien Parker if it was vice versa.

By now the argument was really escalating. Achilles was holding his own against the athletic wonder, but Andra was determined to have the last say and there was no doubt that this would be a long one.

After having enough entertainment, Damien quietly walked between the two, who both were surprised to see him pop up between them and were about to start off on him. Fortunately he spoke before they could. "Look why don't you both just get a hotel and let me know the details."

Both looked at each other, then at the departing Damien Parker.

"What?" Andra exclaimed.

"That isn't funny Damien!" Achilles shouted before he started off after him. "God that girl!" he interjected once he had caught up with him. "Oh yeah thanks for save." He glance upward, "God what did I do?"

"Sounds to me like you like her."

"Humph," Achilles scoffed.

"How about you? How are you feeling?"

Achilles didn't have to ask him to elaborate. "Sorta better. Ain't it a bitch. Folks start talking divorce, start to get things back together and BAM! They're killed in a car accident." His face grimaced as he held back a sob, but his effort was not enough to conceal it from Damien. "I'm coping. What about you? What you and the ol' girl doing for Fat Tuesday?"

"She wants me to go to some fancy gala. Not by choice though. Her parents are making her go and well misery loves company." He stopped as he noticed a shadow beside him. He recognized the shape of it instantly. "Hello Victor."

"Damien Parker. I couldn't help but hear your plans for Mardi Gras. Women are a trip aren't they? Always asking us to be something we're not. Only to leave us for someone who we believe match their standards."

"But we play the fool for them anyways don't we?" Damien responded.

"Serena is a lovely girl, accustomed to having her way; her standards.   It's amazing you never worry about living up to the standards necessary."

"Amazing thing about standards. The less you worry about them, the easier and more enjoyable life is. We Parkers, we enjoy the simplicity of life. Don't need any unnecessary responsibilities like being on the Docking Board or anything like that. As for me and Serena, we wouldn't be together if we were worried about standards." With a grin of confidence he turned and walked away, followed by Achilles. He was about to open the door when he stopped. "A little friendly advice Victor, stop trying so hard. She's not feeling you and quite frankly it's really starting to look bad." He then walked out never seeing the annoyance on Victor Morris' face.

"Might I ask what was that about?" Achilles inquired.

Damien merely shrugged his shoulders. "Victor's been giving Serena a hard time about her choice of men. Apparently according to Victor she could do better."

Achilles scowled, "I don't remember Victor being interested in Serena before."

Again Damien shrugged his shoulders as he unlocked the chain to his motorcycle. "Like I said your guess is as good as mine. Victor could have any girl he wants in John Ehret High. Why he wants mine I haven't a clue."

"Maybe that's precisely his reasoning," Achilles replied as Damien fastened his helmet. "So what are you going to do about him?"

Achilles never got an answer for in that instant, the motorcycle roared to life and Damien Parker sped off.

She watched as he sped off the parking lot and disappeared around the corner. *He's young --- very young.* A pang of sympathy filled her heart as she pondered on what it must be like being thrust with so much responsibility at so tender an age. She sighed as she glanced around one last time as if she expected him to reappear. Finally she herself turned and walked away in the opposite direction.

Chapter 3

Grant Pershing glanced at his watch. 3:00 PM on the dot. *All right Cards in hand, stakes on the table, now …* The phone rang. "Hello."

"Ahh nice to see that you are still interested Mr. Pershing." A familiar voice answered.

"I think I've proven my commitment now its time for you to prove yours." Pershing quickly dialed a number on his cell phone. *Holden had better be there.* "So anytime you're ready, you can start talking."

"I admire your eagerness Mr. Pershing, but as I said earlier I am very cautious on how I spread information. To use the old phrase, walls have ears. You in your occupation should understand the necessity of such precautions."

"So you want to talk just not over the phone."

"Of course. Person to person is the best form of communication. Now Mr. Pershing listen carefully. Meet me on the southeast corner of Jackson Square at 5 PM sharp. Then you will have your information and trust me you will find it worthwhile."

"Who are you?" Pershing asked. "How do I know what to call you when we make contact? How will I even know its you? There could be hundreds of people in that area at that time!"

"You can call me Magnus. Everything else will take care of itself, goodbye."

Pershing sat in deep thought as he hung up the phone. It rung immediately. "Pershing here. Holden did you get him?"

"Get who? I've been trying to contact you for the last three minutes!"

Pershing ignored the last sentence. "Who?! Magnus! The guy I was on the phone with!"

"Grant there hasn't been anyone on this phone for the last fifteen minutes!"

"What, you're sure you're at the right location?"

Grant I'm at Claiborne and Tulane! Exactly where you told me to go!"

It was the place all right. "Damn! Are you sure?"

"I'm telling you Grant, no one's been here for twenty minutes now! Forget it pal, this is one guy who knows what he's doing."

Damnit! Pershing exclaimed to himself as he hung up the phone. Magnus had won round one and with it home field advantage. *Damn!* He glanced at his watch. 3:12.

5:00. Jackson Square. For all he knew this could be a wild goose chase, but his instincts were telling him different and they were seldom wrong. Somewhere in all of this was a story --- a big one and he was going to get to the heart of it one way or another.

The Oprah Winfrey show was the first thing he heard as he entered the house, an affirmation that his mother was home. He trudged into the 'sunroom' as it was called where his father was deep into the basketball section of the newspaper, occasionally glancing from the newspaper to the CNN station displayed on the television.

"Dag gone it. Houston did it to me again!" the older Parker growled.

Damien donned a sly smile. His father was a die hard Rockets fan, few things had pleased him more than seeing the Rockets win back to back NBA titles. Even more so because he disliked the Chicago Bulls, nothing against Michael Jordan or anything but it was just that he grew bored seeing the same team win over and over again.

At least he's not complaining about the 49ers.

Damien glanced away from the T.V. to the front page of Times Picayune. Slowly he reached down and picked it up from the coffee table. "Another protest?"

"Yep," his father answered following a glance at the T.V. "Another one. This time in front of the courthouse."

Damien sighed as he eyed the picture.

"It was bound to happen. Fischer dug his own grave."

"I suppose."

It all started when an ex Klu Klux Klansman named Thomas LeBleu was arrested for the rape and murder of 5 black women between the ages of 18 and 25. LeBleu had previously been in prison for a previous conviction of involuntary manslaughter of a black man named Ronald James, but only served 3 years of his sentence before being paroled by Judge Andrew Fischer.

Fischer already had a notorious reputation for his preference of white over black parolees but what really blew the fuse was Fischer's denial of parole to Darnell Coleman.

Coleman's story was the classic 'go to prison turn your life around' story. A high school dropout, Coleman had been sentenced to 15 years at age 21 for drug trafficking and illegal possession of a fire arm. During his first 8 years Coleman displayed exemplary behavior, earning his G.E.D and a college degree in sociology as well as participated in community events designed to help keep kids away from drugs and drug trafficking. All that seemingly wasn't enough for Fischer. The NAACP went on the rampage, the previous protest had been in front of the prison where was Coleman was being held – over 200 people showed up, nearly 100 were arrested.

"They're not holding back any punches this time," his father commented.

"How many were there?"

"About 500 people and it wasn't pretty either, they had everything from 'Free the Slaves' to 'Reel in Fischer: Dead or Alive.' The police apparently had to use tear gas – on national T.V. too. Police had to escort Fischer from his courtroom to his car and follow him home. I almost wish the 'Fischermen' luck."

"Dad!"

"Well it's either us or them. Dag gone it, they won't be satisfied until we're back in the cotton fields and with these crazed fools voting Republican they'll have the means to do so too. That's the problem with us we never see the writing on the wall. Damned fools. 'Look at me I live in a white neighborhood!' Next thing you know there's nothing but Negroes! What happened? I'll tell you what happened! Paul Revere comes a riding shouting 'The niggers are here! The niggers are here!' Next thing you know the Great White Exodus starts. They smile in your face the day you move in, next thing you know there's a For Sale sign in their yard. The next day his friends approach him at work. "Hey Joe I heard you moved outta your house." "Yeah! Damn niggers moved into the neighborhood."

"Dad!"

"Now granted son not all of them hate us, but enough of 'em do to get the job done if we're not on our p's and q's."

His father was in the middle of a statement about Reagan and his being elected because of how he dressed when Damien left the room.

"What is your father rambling about now?" a voice inquired.

"White people," Damien answered with a grin before kissing Marie Parker on the cheek. "So what's the scoop on today's Oprah?"

"Talking about how marriages can be more romantic." Her voice rose with the words 'more romantic.'

"I heard that!" her husband yelled back. "I can be romantic. I don't need Oprah to tell me how to be romantic!" His tirade on Oprah continued but had been reduced to mutters. However Damien and his mother could hear bits and pieces of it. "Why there'd never be a woman president ... Oprah this and Oprah that ... Crazy women taking advise on marriage from a woman who been avoiding it for over a decade ... Typical women always getting from someone they shouldn't be getting advise from ..."

He was flying and cursing the late afternoon traffic as he navigated across downtown New Orleans. Thank God it's the cellular age. He had called Clark Landon, the assistant investigation editor immediately following his meeting with Magnus. Clark had just returned from a meeting when Pershing finally got hold of him. His reaction was not all together surprising – Clark Landon was a cautious man so he ordered Pershing to bring in his evidence and the two would look it over before deciding anything.

Pershing already knew the story was going to make the front page. Fischer's acts on the bench had long since stirred tempers of all races, the Coleman situation had just brought it all to the forefront but even the Coleman situation had not brought this part of the story to the foray. Deep down he already knew that this was about to cause of firestorm, but those were the stories that won Pulitzers.

Chapter 4

His daughter was just sitting down in her usual place at the table when Carl Martin emerged from his study for dinner. Her mother, his wife, had just placed his plate upon the table. A shy smile accompanied her glance as she made her way to her chair across the table.

He caught himself as he thought of how lucky he was. Shad had been nothing but a blessing. She had helped him mend a heart broken by death, showed him how much from his heart he was still capable of giving. Most of all she had given him Serena.

Serena, his only daughter. True, he had children from his previous marriage, but there was something different about having a daughter that made the world – brighter. She was the apple of his eye, his little girl. Funny how fast all the years went by. How his daughter had blossomed into a beautiful young woman. She deserved the best in life, both of them did, and he was determined to give it to them.

He had been a working man all of his life but a few investments had paid off. He had the perfect house, plenty of money, and the ear of some of the city's most influential – many of whom had nice, handsome sons that would provide Serena with a life she deserved.

"Oh yeah Honeybun," he said using his nickname for Serena. "A few of us was talking at the meeting today and the gala came up and one of the men mentioned that his son didn't have an escort and since you still didn't have one yet, I thought it would be a great idea if the two of you paired up."

I'm sure you did, Serena thought with a sigh. They had been down this road before. Ever since they arrived in New Orleans, her father had been trying to set her up with whomever he considered to be a worthy suitor. His zeal was pushed further when he found out about her and Damien Parker.

"Well who is it dear?" her mother inquired, sensing her daughter's uneasiness.

"A nice young man and he happens to go to John Ehret with you."

"He goes to school with me!" Serena interjected. Everyone at John Ehret knew she was dating Damien Parker. Who would ...

"Yes," her father continued. "I think you've met him before since the man's son said he knew you. Victor I believe his name is."

Serena's heart dropped to the floor. No not ...

"You know Shad, John Morris' son."

Serena wanted to puke. She couldn't believe it. Her father had picked out some suitors but this one was the granddaddy of them all. "But I already have an escort."

The revelation led to surprise and shock on the look of her parents.

"I've already asked Damien Parker to be my escort and he agreed."

Carl Martin snarled. "Does Damien Parker know that this is a gala and not some hood party?"

"Dad he knows it's a gala. He knows he has to wear a tux and a mask, besides Damien likes partying about as much as you do."

"Humph," her father responded. "What is it that you see in this Damien Parker anyways?"

"Dear," his wife replied, "I've met this Damien Parker at one of Serena's academic tournaments, and I have to admit he is quite a talented and sophisticated young man."

"He may be nice, dear, but well its just that Serena could do a lot better."

In other words, Serena thought, *he's too poor for me.*

"Victor is a nice young man with so much to offer."

"Dad, all he has is money, and he's no where near as smart as Damien."

"He's very refined and has potential to move up in the world, Serena. He and Damien Parker are nowhere near each other. Surely you should see this, you go to school with the boy."

"Oh you're right Dad, Damien Parker is the captain of the academic team, the first Black captain in school history may I add. One of the best debaters and speakers on our speech team if not the state, has a 3.8 average and sings in the church choir and to top that off, he has a job. Victor Morris is just a sexually frustrated creep who drives a BMW and is heir to a trust fund. I'll take the poor gentleman thank you very much." She stormed off from the table, tears running down from her face as she collapsed onto her bed. 'Why couldn't he understand? No, he would never understand. No one could understand her. Her life was complicated by an ability to do magic that no one could grasp. Her life would never be normal.

She was six years old when her life was changed forever. She was back in Park Ridge, Illinois, her hometown, when it happened. She was sitting beneath an oak tree in the woods behind her home; just sitting there daydreaming when out of nowhere a voice came.

"Serena. Serena."

She recoiled sitting up, looking curiously in every direction, wondering who could be calling her.

"Serena… Over here."

She was certain it wasn't her mother and it was too gentle and serene to be her father.

"Over here Serena," the voice teased.

Her parents had taught her not to talk to strangers, but her curiosity won over caution. She followed, peering around the thick oak tree.

"Come closer Serena. You're almost there."

The girl looked around, but again no one could be seen.

"Almost there."

Finally she crept in between two bushes and she saw them: two of the strangest yet beautiful creatures she had ever seen. Both were tall and regal. The wolf like creature's golden fur sparkled and glistened in the afternoon sunlight. The other was beautiful, bathed in ethereal light; she was angelic only without the wings.

"Hello Serena," the golden wolf purred.

"Who are you?" the girl asked, her voice small and soft.

"I," the wolf started, raising himself to his full height, "am Morgoth. And this"

"You may call me Gloriana," the wingless angel finished.

"Do you live here?"

"Not all the time," Gloriana answered, her voice soft and gentle.

"How do you know my name?" the girl inquired.

"You're the reason why we are here. You are very special."

"I am?"

"Yes," Morgoth answered, a snarl hissing softly through the air.

"Why? What do you do? Why am I so special?"

"For one thing you can see us," the lady answered.

Serena couldn't help but be intrigued by her. She was so beautiful and radiant, even more so when the aura surrounding her changed colors from red to blue to green and back to red. "Can't everyone see you?"

"No only those who possess magic can see us."

"I can do magic?"

"Yes," Morgoth growled. "It is your heritage."

"Haratage?" the girl stammered slowly.

"Close enough."

"But where is my magic?"

"Inquisitive little thing isn't she," the wolf retorted. Suddenly he dropped on all four and the next thing the girl knew the golden wolf's face was inches away from her own. "Your magic is right here," he purred as he nuzzled his snout to her chest over her heart. "We just have to work on getting it out."

"Can I pet you Morgoth?"

"But of course! Just don't tug too roughly on my fur. Lymphs are very sensitive."

The girl slowly reached out and placed her hand upon the golden wolf's head and gently slid it along his neck and board back. The soft golden fur caressed her skin with each stroke, giving her a warm tingling feeling inside.

"What is a lymph?"

"The now relaxed golden wolf raised his head and eyed her with a stare that conveyed as much shock as it did surprise. "A lymph is what I am of course!" The wolf lowered his head unaware of the confused look that was upon the child's face, for while his response seemed explanatory enough to him, for her it didn't come close to answering her question. She was about to bombard him with many questions but luckily for the wolf, Gloriana's

angelic form moved near Serena, who in awe of the
gorgeous creature forgot everything else.

"Serena, your destiny calls for you to be a light
against the oncoming darkness." The fragrance from her
was soothing, refreshing and familiar. She recalled how
her mother had put some candles in the living room one
day; something about smells that make people feel good
about themselves. If she remembered right, this fragrance
her mother had called gardenia whatever that meant. Her
mother had been right though, it did make her smile and
feel good, reminding her of those times when her father
would take her downtown to that place with all the pretty
flowers. Their scents would fill the air with sweet
fragrances, which she would breath in deeply with delight
until eventually they made her sleepy. However, that
wasn't the case with Gloriana, her scent actually took her
there – to a place filled with nothing but flowers, sweet
beautiful flowers – and Gloriana's scent didn't make her
sleepy.

"You do not understand now," the lady
continued, "but through Morgoth you will understand
everything. You will have to be brave and very
courageous. Will you do this for me, my dear Serena?"

"Yes!" the child replied bravely, her words filled
with a conviction beyond her years.

Her life changed forever with those words, a
breach began to form between her and her family and
friends. None of them could grasp the magic that made
her different. She had tried to tell her parents, but they
dismissed it as figments of her imagination. Only her great
grandmother gave any merit to Serena's magical abilities as

she also used to see things that are hidden from the normal mind, but eventually, her age affected her ability to see the magical creatures of light and darkness cloaked now in a veil of obscurity that she is only aware of through memories of a far, distant past.

Her eyes slowly opened as a soft familiar ruffle came to her ears. A smile formed on her face as she started towards the window. As usual, Morgoth was there to support her. The golden wolf leapt inside and settled beside the bed. Serena laid back on the bed, one hand gently stroking the lymph's golden fur – even today his fur still brought that warm tingling feeling inside her.

Morgoth had always been a contrast of sorts; true he was a wolf but not like one you might find on the prairie or lurking behind a farm. Rather, he was more beautiful than any wolf you could ever see. There was the fur of course, but there was also his silver eyes that beamed like headlights even in the darkest shadows. At times he was so gentle that one honestly wondered how anything could be afraid of him. Then there was the fierce, stern Morgoth, fur flickering and glowing like a flame, lightning seemed to flash in his eyes as they peered deep into your soul, teeth snarling and claws gashing. Only the bravest dared move when Morgoth was angry. She had seen this side of him more than once while he was both protecting and teaching her.

With each stroke of her hand, the lymph purred, his lows seeped out of him like a flute beginning a musical piece, but there were times when even Morgoth's company was not enough despite the fact that he was her closest friend.   There were just issues that only a human could understand.

"Why do you humans argue so much?" Morgoth purred, arching his neck as the girl's fingers gently scratched near his ear.

"You mean you never argued with your father when you were little?" Serena laughed.

"In my 300 years, no!" the wolf answered. "I just listened as he instructed me on how to hunt and fight. My first 17 years were no where near as trying as yours."

"That's because lymphs don't try to dominate other lymph's lives."

"Of course not!" he snapped, showing a large set of silver teeth before shaking his head. "I suppose I will never understand humans," he sighed. "Thank the Creator," he added softly but Serena still heard him and he was right. There were just some things you could never relate to a lymph. You needed a human, a kindred soul. All these things she found in Damien Parker.

It was Homecoming, she had volunteered to pour drinks for the night. Why, she had no idea. Maybe because it was the only way she could get into the dance – no one had bothered to ask her. She merely watched as all around couples swayed and moved, joked and laughed, seeing the light of the rotating ball reflect off their faces. Even those standing by the wall were savoring the thrill of a 27 – 17 victory over Bonnabel High.

She noticed Damien Parker as he stood in a corner eyeing the dance floor. Every now and then a wide smile would show on his face as he said a word or two to friends as they passed by.

Damien Parker

Ever since that first academic team practice where she first laid eyes on him, she had a thing for him. His dark brown eyes, his thick eyebrows, the simplicit yet regality in his walk. That first day, his face held a sly, mischievous smile that suggested a joker rather than a team leader. However, as he sat down in the chair and took hold of his buzzer, his countenance changed – his brown eyes flared with intensity and his face displayed a confidence she had never seen before in anyone. Then and there you knew he was the leader of the team. What impressed her more was the depth to which it increased when he was in an actual tournament. In practice he was a team leader, in a real tournament he was a force. She had seen him by sheer will pull his team to victory. Damien Parker, fierce, determined, focused. Then there was the other side of him, the Damien Parker, funny, intelligent, charming, and understanding.

God, she thought wistfully as she poured a drink, in the corner of her eye she noticed Damien Parker eying her. Was he eying her? No, his eyes were on the dancers on the dance floor. God if only he was, it would be nice for something normal. She sighed as she tucked the dollar into the drawer. Her eyes rose in shock as she noticed Damien Parker coming her way.

"Sprite please," he replied, glimpsing the dance floor before looking back at her.

She said nothing as she poured the drink for him.

"Hey Damien," Ms. Stein replied as she walked behind the booth.

The music changed and a slow, smooth melody crooned across the gym.

"Serena would you like to dance?"

Serena didn't answer. She couldn't believe her ears. Before she could answer, Ms. Stein volunteered to watch the booth and Damien quickly grabbed her hand and gently pulled her to the dance floor. His arm went about her waist and his hands gently rested against the small of her back.

She eased closer to him, her eyes closing as she felt his arms tighten about her. The song was nearing its end when she dropped her guard and buried her face in his shoulder. Enamored in the reality of the moment. This one moment. For once she felt normal, hopeful, she didn't care if people were eying them, she merely kept her eyes closed and allowed Damien Parker to lead. She liked the warmth of his body and the way he smelled. She adored how he would glance at her every now and then just to make sure she was okay, and the words he murmured to her brought tingles.

When the music changed they remained locked in their slow dance, moving to a music that seemed theirs and theirs alone.

So sweet, Serena thought, her breaths soft and slow. She didn't care what happened, come what may, as long as he was holding her, everything was all right.

That had been a year ago, one blissful year. But
not even Damien Parker could break the wall of magic that
separated them. Serena wondered if he could, even if he
wanted to. Regardless he was a light in a cold dark place
and now her father was trying to take that light away.

Andra Alexander was accustomed to pressure and
pain, it came with the territory of being an athlete. Who
was she fooling, it came with just being a teenager, but she
had overcome pressure and odds before. Fear was a
foreign concept to her. She had her father to thank for
that. And yet she was edgy. Something, someone was
behind her, creeping up on her.

Get it together Andra. There's nothing out here.

She closed the door to her Ford Mustang just
outside teammate Michelle Michael's house and started up
the driveway to the front door. She had barely passed the
neutral ground when a sound caused her to turn and stop
in her tracks as she saw the deformed looking creature rear
its head; its yellow eyes locked on hers.

Chills ran down her spine as the thing leaped
toward her with bizarre speed.

"No!" the girl yelled, a scream that was half
defiance and half panic. Suddenly, a flash of light
appeared and from it stepped a horse saddled by a knight
dressed in tarnished and battered armor. The knight upon
seeing the creature drew his sword and urged the charger
forward.

Completely surprised by the speed at which the
creature closed the distance between them, all Andra could
do was duck and raise her hands to cover her face. At the
last possible moment the charger galloped in front of her
and another flash of light appeared.   Andra lowered her
hands and stood up to find herself unharmed. She glanced
around but both the knight and the creature were gone.

Chapter 5

It was a little past ten when the Guardian cruised down the interstate on his motorcycle. The city had just come to life, in more ways than one. The last two hours of the day spawned more than just pleasure seeking humans, it also spawned demons and other creatures who stalked the night destroying and devouring all that they could. Standing between them and their potential victims was he, a lone knight errand continuing a crusade that had been ongoing since the beginning of time. A crusade of light versus darkness, creation versus destruction, and all of it his responsibility, the weight of a city on his shoulders. *At least it's not the world.*

While there was only one Guardian of the Cross, there were other Knights of the Order, but not many and the burden each of them bore was a heavy one. Tonight though, the burden on Damien Parker, Guardian of the Cross, was not so heavy which brought feelings of relief but also ones of anxiety. Lately it had been quiet around New Orleans – too quiet. *The calm before the storm.* And then there was his dream, someone is coming, but who?

His mind tabled the question as he passed along the skyline and the looming view of the Superdome. Part of him wanted to check out the Quarter again, but he reconsidered. He hadn't detected anything unusual and nothing that the gargoyles couldn't handle. He stared at the tall towers of the crescent city skyline. Somewhere amongst the tops of those building, one or two of those winged monstrosities were gliding along the wind currents either on patrol or playing tag. While the creatures could easily be subdued by his magic, there was one thing that he would always envy them for: their natural ability to fly.

I may not be able to fly, but there are other ways one can actually have a little fun. He zoomed the cycle ahead faster and faster. He could feel the wind blowing through his cape, the potentially dangerous side drafts raging around him as the motorcycle flowed down the curve of the interstate with carefree ease, weaving in and out of traffic like a windy breeze. The Guardian was fully aware of how dangerous his acts were, but he never slowed down. It was only when a glimpse of a familiar figure caught the corner of his eye did his mind even considered slowing down. However, instead of slowing down he did something even more reckless. He leaned and executed a U-turn and guided the motorcycle weaving in between the oncoming traffic until finally he pulled to a stop on the side where a figure stood.

Achilles! It couldn't be?!

He turned off the cycle, kicked down the kickstand and took off his helmet before he slowly started toward his friend.

"Achilles?"

The boy didn't move. The Guardian crept closer, he was about five feet away when he noticed a large lump on the boy's back.

A netch! Great! Achilles was already confused enough from grief to contemplate suicide. *Daggone it Parker you should have known that he would be a prime target of a darkling, emotionally distraught as he's been. To it Achilles is pork roast.* The Guardian stopped, he had to be careful. If the darkling saw him before he was close enough, it might urge Achilles to jump. He knew he had to get through to Achilles, give him another voice to counter the crazed, mad ramblings of the darkling's.

"Achilles. Achilles it's me."

Achilles Harmon slowly turned his head till his eyes saw him, but his eyes didn't see the Guardian of the Cross, but his school mate Damien Parker. "Damien?" he answered, uncertain of the sight before his eyes.

"Yes it's me, Damien Parker. Remember we go to John Ehret together." *Just a little closer Damien.* "You know," his eyes glanced downward to the dark waters of the Mississippi that lurked below, "there's a better way to see the river. It's called the Riverwalk."

"I can't take it D," Achilles sobbed, "I need 'em."

"I know Killy Willy." *This would probably be the only time I'd be able to get away with calling him that.* "I know you miss them." *Just a little closer, Parker.* "But if you remember them then you will always have them."

"It's my fault D. I made them breakup, if they hadn't broken up they'd still be here."

"Achilles! No! You had nothing to do with the problems your parents had. Nothing. Your parents loved you very much – both of them."

"Maybe if I had been a little bit better, a little bit smarter. A little bit more ... like you."

Damien knew he had to read between his friend's words, all of his words possessed a grain of truth, but they were also laced with madness and confusion courtesy of the darkling. "Achilles, your parents loved you just the way you are." He could see the darkling clearly now, whispering its poisons into Achilles' ears. All he needed was a few more seconds, Achilles was only a step or two away.

"Look man, you remember how bad you felt at your parent's funeral? Do you want your grandparents to feel that way? Your friends at John Ehret? Me?"

Achilles turned toward him. "No," he answered softly.

"Achilles, take my hand. Everything is gonna be fine. I promise."

It was then that the darkling became aware of him, desperate it leaned over to whisper a final command, but Damien Parker quickly wrapped his arm around Achilles Harmon and with all his might pulled and lifted until both were huddled on the ground. Damien looked and felt for the darkling, but there was no sign of it. He exhaled a breath of relief and held Achilles Harmon in his arms and for the first time the flashing red and blue lights caught his eyes.

She sleeps, she dreams, she walks – where, she is not certain. A sigh draws from her as she surveys what she remembers as Uptown New Orleans. The sight she sees paralyzes her as she walks along what was once St. Charles Avenue. Her eyes close in remorse as she looks upon what once had been Tulane and Loyola Universities. Like everything else around her a crumpled heap of rubble

and ashes. Nowhere near the proud providers of
knowledge they had once been.

She moves on, trekking through what was before
Audubon Park, but instead of the serene song of laughter
and silence there is only hissing and gashing. Part of her
wants to turn and flee but she continues on. There is a
presence here, something dark and sinister – she could feel
it. She creeps softly, hoping to avoid the source of her
disposition, when she trips on a tree root, falling into the
grass. As she draws herself up, she sees it – tall, regal,
noble, yet also hideously evil. Her breath stops at the sight
of him, for in an instant she knows him for what he is –
the terror that she was attempting to flee, the on bringer of
the pillage she had witnessed around her.

His head turned as if he was aware of her
presence. Wanting to run, but paralyzed by fear she prays
for a miracle, for some kind of mercy. The red eyes stop
and all hope fades for she is certain that he sees her. She
eyes the blood stained blade where normally there would
have been a left hand. Reminiscing, she recalls the names
of all those dear to her anticipating her inevitable death,
but the monster does not move toward her. To her horror,
he sneers at her maliciously; his right hand lifts to show a
severed head in his talons. Her eyes widen with fright as
the face comes into view. *No, it can't be! Can't... can't be!*
Heart pounding in her chest, she trembles at the face
staring back at her; catching her soul in a clasp of terror.

Sara Winters almost screamed as her eyes opened
to the familiar surroundings of her bedroom, breathing
swift and hard. A nightmare, just a nightmare she told
herself. With a sigh of relief she let her head rest against
the pillow, but she could not stop the chills running

through her nor could she not forget the face she saw, a face she encountered almost everyday. A face whose presence in her nightmare only made it more horrifying. She closed her eyes, hoping the image would go away, but it didn't. It stayed with her, the image of that face, his face – the face of Damien Parker.

Saturday

February 8th

Chapter 6

They're dancing, their bodies moving to the tempo of the music; their hearts beating to its rhythm. How long had this moment been denied? Feelings suppressed, but it didn't matter – absence makes the heart grow fonder, and they were together now.

So good, so sweet.

Here away from the demons, the nightmares, no longer burdened with the weight of a crusade. No more secrets.

God, thank you for this moment.

She glances up at him, seeing him, her protector; her Guardian. She could feel his heart beating within his dark armor. She didn't know who he was; she knew who she wanted him to be. Her breathing grew soft as her eyes closed; then she heard the voice.

Serena.

She looks to her protector, but his body remains loose and calm. She hesitates, her mind in a state of confusion. Normally if she felt uneasy, he automatically sprung into action shielding her from harm – yet he did nothing.

Serena ...come to us ...

Once again she was confused. He had to feel her fear, her concern. Why did he not charge as he always did?

Serena.

She backs away from him and slowly moves towards the door before breaking into a run. Her eyes see nothing. "Where are you?"

Serena …danger.

She felt uneasy again, unsure. There couldn't be any danger – her guardian would have at least drawn his sword. "Who are you?"

Serena … danger … Beware of the Guardian … Beware of the Guardian.

What? The Guardian has always protected her – hasn't he?

Beware the Guardian

She turns not because of the voice, but because of the sound of a sword being freed from its sheath. Her eyes see him – her guardian and protector with his sword ready to strike.

"Yes Serena. Beware of me." Then he plunged the sword straight into her heart.

Serena opened her eyes. It was twice now – twice in the same night she had that nightmare. Both times she found herself in the arms of an armored knight, only to be killed by that same knight. What does it mean? Was this serious? She wished she knew. *Serena you're thinking too much of this, it's just a dream. Go back to sleep.* She laid her head back on her pillow and closed her eyes.

She didn't believe he was here, but he was. Now they're dancing. . .

"I sense you are distraught Damien. What is worrying you?"

Oracle's presence is perhaps the most bizarre complication that came with being the Guardian. Oracle had been his teacher when he first received his powers though it was strange to be tutored by an invisible apparition. Nevertheless, Oracle had ways of making herself known and always offered her two cents even when it was not requested. He had to admit though, her advice more oft than not had merit, which was part of what bothered him in hearing her now.

"Just reflecting on what you said about a Guardian having ties."

Silence. He wasn't surprised; the topic had always been the source of many arguments between the two.

"I recall saying something about you being a Guardian of the Cross," Oracle replied. "Ties such as friends and lovers only make you vulnerable. The Abyss knows who you are, where you live, and who you bond yourself to. It would only be a matter of time before its servants would attempt to hurt you through them." She pauses and looks Damien in the eyes. "May I ask what has brought this to mind? Usually on this subject you, hmm… how should I best put it… usually throw a hissy fit."

Damien wondered whether he should tell her or not. He had enough on his mind and really wasn't in the mood to hear one of Oracle's tirades of 'I told you so.' "I ran into a darkling tonight on the way home. It was trying to get this guy to jump off the bridge and commit suicide.

Turns out this guy goes to school with me." He waited for it.

Instead, a sigh seems to fall from a dark corner. "Now do you understand Damien Parker what I've been trying to tell you. This time it was a darkling just trying to feed and chanced upon someone you happen to know. You won't always be that lucky. What if it's an arch demon that is using your friends to trap you? This time it just happened to be an acquaintance. What if it is your father or your mother? What if it is Serena?"

Damien didn't answer. The thought of his parents or heaven forbid, his beloved Serena being attacked by an arch demon filled him with dread. Deep down he knew the Oracle was right, but he always pushed the issue to the back of his mind. Now because of the incident with Achilles, he could not easily ignore the Oracle's predictions. All this because he was a Guardian of the Cross ... one of the few beings capable of channeling significant amounts of magic as his predecessors had been all the way back to Simon of Cyrene, the man who supposedly carried the cross of Jesus. Unbeknownst to Simon, his act set into motion a change that would not only effect him for the rest of his life, but his descendants as well. Shortly afterward Simon became the first Guardian of the Cross, a task he served diligently until one day weary and exhausted he went to his youngest son and gave him his staff, supposedly made from the same cross that Christ had been crucified on, and instructed him to take it to Rome and deliver it to his elder brother.

Complying with his father's wishes, the son journeyed to Rome, found the elder brother and bestowed the staff upon him, completing the first rendition of the

ritual marking the end of one Guardian's tenure and the
beginning of the next, always a descendant of the elder son
of Cyrene receiving the charge from a descendant of the
younger son.   Fighter and Deliverer ... Champion and
Herald ... Guardian and Emissary.

        All of which would end with him, for supposedly
he would be the last. Perfect, as if being a Guardian wasn't
bad enough. Not only did he have the luxury of being the
last Guardian, but he also had the joy of being the suriana
uchawi, whatever that was. From what Oracle had
explained, it was the name given to a being able to channel
two different strains of magic. Magic ran strong in both
sides of his family. On his mother side, there was the
legacy of Simon of Cyrene. What kind of magic he
inherited from his father's side was a mystery, only that it
was very potent magic that usually only graced the women
of his father's family. Now it wasn't unusual for a human
to be born in families with more than one magical lineage;
that was really quite common. Usually though one magical
heritage would dominate over the other causing the
recessive magic to manifest itself in another descendant.
Rarely was there born an individual who had both magics
manifest. Supposedly being a capacitor for one form of
magic took a huge toil on a human body. Being one for
two, let's just say it was like setting off an atomic bomb in
a large crate and expecting the crate to contain it.
However every now and then such beings were brought
into the world, depending on how one defined every now
and then.   The last suriana uchawi was born nearly 770
years ago.

        *770 years, one heck of a gap. God must have been on a
roll when he was rolling the dice for my creation. So supposedly I'm*

the most powerful being in over 700 years.   Humph, great power. Great power only means greater responsibility.   Heck, I thought it was enough just to make it past high school without a jail record. True, he had defied the standard by keeping his ties with his family and friends, but he couldn't give them up, they were the catalyst that willed him to take on such a great task. His mind drifted while his eyes grew heavy as he struggled to stay awake. Drawing in breath, he fell back on the bed and the world went silent and black.

New Orleans, the Big Easy. Considered the heart of the South, the home of the Super Bowl – if there was such a thing. The man merely scoffed at the thought. The skyline was illuminated by the dawn's golden glow and he allowed himself a brief smile. Watching the sunrise always had that effect on him; it never failed to instill in him a feeling of hope even over a city of constant sin. The sunrise's magic didn't fail.

"Penny for your thoughts Reverend?"

Erther Eugene merely glanced at the driver beside him. Tall, athletic, and young, he was among those whose lives had been enriched by the enlightenment of the Lord's salvation. Once he had been among the lost, much as Eugene had been when he was young, *a tool being used and manipulated by evils beyond his comprehension. But look at him now, now he is an example to them all; a monument of the loving arms of the Lord.* "Do you know what one of God's greatest gifts were my son?"

"The sunrise," the young man answered. "It was the first thing you taught me."

"And do you remember why?"

"The sunrise represents hope. To be allowed to see a sunrise means God loves you and has a purpose for you to fulfill here."

"Ahh, you have done me proud my son. You remembered well."

"Do you think we can succeed Reverend?"

"New Orleans is one of the last bastions of darkness. Here sin and oppression run deep. However, I do believe we can succeed, for God will be with us. Know that though we go into the Valley of the Shadow of Death, we have hope."

"Let the Light of God be with us," his protégé said.

The older man smiled as the skyline of New Orleans grew larger with each passing second. *Yes oppression runs deep here. A fellow brother was in distress and Erthur Eugene would do everything to save him.*

He is sleeping; at least he believes he is sleeping. So why is he here? Wasn't he dragged from here just a short time ago? He eyed the murky waters below.

There's still time, you can jump!

He only stares, stymied at the words being said to him.

"Jump!" the voice hissed. "Join us there's still time!"

Us? Who is us? Jump? But wasn't he told jumping was bad.

"Come with us. There is still time." The voices echoed around him, surrounding him, pressuring him to their whim. "Jump! There is still time. You can join them, they are waiting!"

He steps forward, his thoughts lost, all he knew was one thing – the edge. Enslaved by their command, he takes another step. The chorus of their voices repeat in his mind until a skip occurs, a break within the rhythm of madness. It wasn't a long pause but just enough for him to break free.

"No!" It was more a plea than a declaration, but it was a spark. "NO!" He ran fleeing the madness, but it followed him; pursued him. "No!" He ran faster, his heart racing as his footsteps pounded on the pavement speeding away from the storm of chaos right behind him. He could feel them breathing down his neck. Their maddening cries seeking to destroy him. His mind froze as the maelstrom engulfed him. Barely recognizing his own scream, their horrifying thoughts and dark images overpowered him. His mind tries to close himself off to them, but they are too strong. Defeat filled him when he heard the voice.

"WAKE UP!"

He looked back, again they were pursuing him. Was there any escape?

"Wake up Achilles! WAKE UP!"

A flash appeared before his eyes opened to see a familiar face. "Wake up sleepy head," a kind voice requested.

Damien Parker. He's here, but where is here.

"Whoa! Hold up!" Damien scolded as Achilles tried to sit up. "Relax Achilles, relax."

"Where am I!" the boy exclaimed, struggling to free Damien's hands and arms from his shoulders.

"It's okay. You're in Tulane Hospital. You were brought in last night."

Achilles surveyed the room twice, hoping this was all part of a dream. Finally he accepted the reality of the moment and settled back into the bed. "You said I was brought in last night – by whom?"

Damien gave him a bewildered stare. "You don't remember? The bridge?"

"What should I remember?"

"It will be all right Achilles." A voice speaks in his mind.

Achilles wondered if his friend had meant to say that last line aloud. There was no denying that the voice was Damien's, but it was a question of whether it came from his mouth. Yet his mind processed the comment. *He's right. Everything will be all right.*

"Achilles?"

His mind snapped back to reality. "Hmm? What?"

"I was asking you how do you feel?"

"Like I just woke up from a nightmare. Why am I here?"

"You tried to jump off the expressway last night."

"So am I dead?"

Damien Parker shook his head. "No. No offense, but there's a lot of people I'd rather see when I get to the afterlife than you, but ..."

"All right I get the point. Stupid question. I'm alive. Okay where is everyone else?"

"Your Aunt and Uncle are talking to the doctor. She's cool, she's a friend of my mom."

"How long have they?"

"Will you relax!" Damien ordered. "They've been here since I brought you in."

"You! You were the one at the bridge!" Achilles turned away from him, clutching himself as he tightened into a ball. "Oh God! Ohmigod! What did I almost do?"

"Achilles your parents just died, and you were under a lot of trauma."

"Sto the shrink games D!" Achilles wasn't sure how but in an instant Damien Parker had somehow disappeared and emerged in front of his face. His brown eyes held him in place, and his face was terrible and awesome.

"Listen to me." The voice wasn't that of Damien Parker at least not the Damien Parker he knew. This voice was daunting and ominous, nothing like the circumspective, amicable voice that usually rang from Damien Parker. "Last night was not you. You probably didn't even know you were doing it."

The voice shook the very core of Achilles' being and in his eyes Damien Parker seemed to swell like a dark shadow covering the room with its presence.

"Now you have nothing to be ashamed about. You've been through a lot," the voice bellowed. "But you are not alone. You will survive this – understand me."

Surprised and frightened Achilles nodded his head. Even more frightening was that the instant afterward, Damien seemed to draw back, and his face returned to the familiar Damien Parker he had always known.

The door opened and Achilles' aunt and uncle started to enter, pausing when they noticed Damien Parker's presence. "Damien," they both started, "we didn't know."

"It's all right." the boy interrupted. "I was just about to leave." He walked past the couple and out the door.

"Damien! Wait!"

"Yes Ma'am."

"We just wanted to thank you again. I just shudder thinking of what might have happened had you not."

"It was nothing Ma'am," Damien replied interrupting her, "Achilles is a friend and I kind of understand what he's going through."

The woman smiled. "Thank you Damien."

Damien smiled. "Like I said ma'am; no problem. Least I could do." He turned and slowly walked around the corner and disappeared from the woman's sight.

He was debating which hallmark card he should pick when she approached him. "Well, well if it isn't Damien Parker. What's wrong? You're in the doghouse with Serena and need a makeup card. I have to admit I'm surprised; never expected you to fall below 5 star standards."

"Hello Andra," Damien greeted, his eyes never swaying from his potential choice of cards. He had known it was her before she even spoke. Damien couldn't really explain how he knew only that he did and it wasn't just with her, it was with everybody. He wasn't sure if it was because of the magic or what. Since he was six, he had this uncanny skill, or at least he was six when he first realized that he could do it. Until he became the Guardian, he had considered it nothing more than lucky guesses. Yet the funny thing is that he always claimed to never believe in luck. "Actually, it's for your sparing mate." He knew she was still mad about yesterday, and one didn't need magic to know that. The venom in her voice was enough.

"And who should I ask is that?"

Yep, she was still mad and even madder now. "Achilles."

"What's wrong with Achilles?" the girl inquired suddenly noticing the kind of cards in his hands.

His eyebrows raised, her voice had gone from mad to concern – genuine concern. "Why Andra I didn't know you cared? Could it be that you do have feelings for our boy?"

"Nonsense," the girl scoffed with a gruff humph. "My concern for Achilles is no different than it would be for any human."

Right "Well he's in Tulane hospital, trauma; about his parents and all."

"His parents?"

"They died in an accident about three weeks ago."

"Yeah I know how it feels to lose a parent," Andra replied softly.

Damien glanced at her. He had almost forgotten about that. "Think I'll go with this one." He set the other card back on the rack. "He's in room 310. Maybe you should visit him. He could use a little perking up," Damien teased, "and if you can't get him riled up, no one can," Andra Alexander scowled at Damien as he walked away. *Think you so smart Damien Parker; I just sympathize with the guy that's all. Imagine me and Achilles Harmon ... together! I mean, I can barely tolerate him; he's that annoying! Maybe we could be friends...but anything more than that ....* She stood there for a moment perplexed; not really sure how she felt about Achilles.

"I'm back!"

Silence answered Damien as he walked into the kitchen and opened the refrigerator. "I hope they went shopping," he thought as his eyes surveyed the near empty

shelves. His rummaging was halted by a knock at the door
– the back door.

Who the heck would be knocking at the back door? He
jerked open the door to find a woman standing there. She
was short, about to his shoulders, her hair was white but it
complimented her bronze skin. Her face suggested that
she was somewhere in her fifties at least. There was a vibe
of longevity that seemed to reek from her, that and the
look in her ebony eyes.

"Damien Parker?"

How does she know me? "Excuse me maam, have we
met?"

"Not till today but I have heard a lot about you."

*Probably knows my parents or one of my aunts or
something. That would explain it.* "Sorry, my parents are out
right now. They should be back sometime this afternoon."

"I'm not here to see your parents."

"May I ask who are you here to see?"

"Why you of course, Damien Parker, Guardian of
the Cross."

There was a sensation deep inside him that told
him the futility of playing dumb. She knew he was the
Guardian, very sure. *But how?* "How did you know?"

"There are signs. All who are of the Abyss or
understand the Order knows of you Damien Parker, last of
the Guardians; one of the Seven."

The Seven again. All he knew of the Seven was
that of all the human servants of the Order, the Seven

were the most powerful beings bestowed with magic, a
magic that elevated them above all others. Supposedly,
they represented the different choruses of the Order and
as the Guardian; he was one of them.

"So why are you here?" he replied, looking
beyond to see the inner depths of her soul.

"Ah, you can look beyond. Excellent! Yes, you
have fared well against the challenges you've faced thus
far, but there are still darker and more sinister evils that lie
over the horizon and the sleeper has yet to awaken."

Damien's face paled as he heard her last six words.
He moved out of the doorway and gestured for her to
enter. When she was in and seated, he softly closed the
door and turned to face her. "Now start talking."

Chapter 7

He could feel the spirits rising from the mist. Their spectre forms slowly trudged forward as if waddling in from the river. He drew towards them, half amazed at what he was witnessing. The ghosts began to dance, juking and weaving, each at a different chapter of a story. At times they seem to disappear, fading away only to return just when they were believed to be gone.

Concentrate

He focused; waiting for whatever visions they would show him. And then suddenly, a giant flash of white light fills his eyes, blinding him. His eyes open and a familiar face stares back at him.

"Grandmother?" inquired a frustrated voice. "Why do I keep having to do this? The spirits don't want to talk to me!"

"No my child, the Great Spirits wish to talk to us all. It is you who refuse to talk to them."

"I refuse to talk to them!" the teen exclaimed. "How is it I refuse to talk to them?"

"You must give yourself over to the spirits Seneca. You must feel the spirits flowing within you child."

"Why is this necessary? Why me of all people?"

"The time is nearly at hand – the time of the Guardians."

"Yes, yes Grandmother I know the story of the Guardians." Everyone in the tribe knew the story. The Great One had baked the four races of man within the forges of the earth. The white man he took out too soon and flung them to the Eastern continent, and they became the Europeans. The second time he waited too long, and the batch came out tall and dark. These he flung to the South, and they became the Africans and Bushmen. The third time, the Creator attended to the oven, but still they remained in the oven too long and were born bronze and red. These the Great One placed in the Central continent. In the final toil, the batch had come up golden brown, but they were hard. These he placed in the growing mountains of the West.

Originally the Great One had intended for men to be of one variety and in charge of the elements of creation, but the presence of the different races created a problem. To which race should be bestowed the stewardship of the elements – the white man, the black man, the red man, or the yellow man?

Knowing that to choose one race would promote disharmony, the Great One wisely divided the charge of the elements among the four races. Only by maintaining a balance of harmony with each other could the balance of nature be preserved.

Seneca often wondered on how disappointed the Great One must be at how man had bungled its sacred trust. He often wondered on the irony of how the Great One could give the charge of fire to the race that had cooked the least amount of time. Balance he guessed, just like the irony that the race that cooked the longest was given the charge of water.

Too bad the story has such a tragic ending. The flames of fire corrupted the white man, and instead of forging a balance, they sought to forge domination.

The Africans who had been placed in the desert and the rain forests were given the knowledge of irrigation and the cycling of rivers, but as their gift was exploited by others, they became bitter and shunned by the other races.

The Orientals of the West were given the charge of wind and received all knowledge that the wind possessed from its travels, knowledge that rivaled all others. The Great Spirits saw them as the conscience of the other races. However, their knowledge made them smug. Their superiority complex caused them to isolate themselves, but in isolation the light of their knowledge dimmed. In the end, they became slaves to lesser beings like fear and panic.

The saddest of all was the fall of his own people, the attenders of the land. His grandmother had often told him. *Once we were the link between Mother Earth and her children, the voice of the land. We were able to feel its growth, its blossoming; its pain. We were able to feel and draw the magic that dwelled within the earth. Now we exploit her with casinos and race tracks.* Even now, Seneca recalls his grandmother's final words as she would conclude the story at night by the fire.

The story is real. Mankind is slowly destroying itself — the harmony between the elements has been lost, shuffled aside in mankind's pursuit of greed. But the time is drawing near, a time when the harmony must be restored, or all creation will be tainted by the dark evil.

"But why me Grandmother? Why not Joseph or Kit?"

"Because you possess the link Seneca. You can do that which few of us can do. You can hear the cries of the land. You can feel its pain as none in our family have felt since the old age. But you must give yourself to the spirits; allow them to become one with you. You must not ignore them as your father has – feel it, let it take shape, control it but do not dominate it!

Seneca sighed. His grandmother always got carried away whenever she talked of the Guardians and the approaching darkness. Even though he thought the stories his grandmother told were nothing more than just tall tales, he knew he would continue to beat himself up trying to reach the supposed spirits beyond. He loved his grandmother more than anything else and for her he would do anything.

His eyes opened and his mind became aware that there was no feeling in his body; just utter numbness. As his mind gained consciousness, the plenary numbness was suddenly filled with pain. He could feel the pain ebbing in his body; ripping through him with agony. Willing his body to obey his command, he tried to move, but the pain attacked him anchoring him on the grass. Finally his will succumbed, and he fell flat with exhaustion. It was then that the reality of the situation began to set in.

The pain seemed to seep deeper and deeper with each breath. Death was certain. He noticed the burnt scars on his torso and arms. Torn, bloodied and burned, his mind contemplated the end. It was merely a question of whether death would come in seconds or in minutes. Regardless, he would soon be dead. His eyes drifted shut in exhaustion. For God knows how long he craved for rest, but his body had never been allowed to possess such a luxury. If not awake here, he was awake some place else.

No longer, now he would finally be able to rest. There were no regrets; he had done his best as a Guardian of the Cross, the entity he had once been. Names hissed from his lips. They were familiar yet he couldn't remember their significance. Wincing, he could feel death's icy grip choking him. He made one final attempt to relax his body so at least his last moments would be peaceful ones. His eye sight blurries, only shadows and haze fill his sight. Then abruptly, the darkness clears and he sees her.

That face ... there was something familiar about her. Her soft hands soothed his pain as they caressed his body. Her touch comforting, strengthening; yet not entirely healing him. He could hear her speaking to him. His eyes closing as the sweet melody of her voice enraptured him; easing him to peaceful sleep like a lullaby. As his consciousness faded into obscurity, he heard a few of her words singing to him. "The sleeper must awaken ... the sleeper must awaken."

Sleeper must awaken .. the sleeper must awaken. The words repeated in Damien Parker's head as he and the mysterious woman who introduced herself as Madame Fi La Reye stepped into St. Louis Cemetery # 1.

"Lady of the web," he thought to himself. She apparently had the gift of sight – an ability to see into the future or at least into a possible future.

"You said you knew about the darkness that is coming?"

"Yes," Damien answered.

"That someone is already here."

"I had a feeling he might be. Do you know who he is?"

"The vision was vague. The face of the person I am not sure of, but darkness surrounds this person. Much darkness. Come."

She was holding something back. Part of him suspected her to be the demon, but he sensed nothing demonic within her. And yet there was a shadow around her. There was more to Madame Fi La Reye than what she wanted to reveal and that alarmed every cautious fiber of his being.

Was it really Madame Fi La Reye that was causing these instincts to flare or was it something else? He paused, his senses processing the environment around him. There was something else here – an evil of immense power. A contained evil, but still he could feel the cruelty, the savageness crawling through him; pressuring him to succumb to it.

"So you can feel it as well."

Damien was about to reply when he noticed where he was, in that moment the presence of magic or even a disturbance in the magical balance no longer surprised him. Even from the grave, her magic was still a force to be reckoned with. Marie Laveau, the Queen of Voodoo, one of the more local famous persons in the struggle between the Order and the Abyss. "What was that?"

"A Maderan."

"A what?"

"A Maderan. A wild, evil creature – a berserker. Like other beings of the Abyss it feeds on the dark corruption of magic and nature, but unlike demons, it can generate that taint on its own. However, its hunger is never filled. It will keep destroying and killing until either nothing is left or it is stopped. Long ago such a creature pillaged this area. A group of French explorers and Indian shamans managed to imprison it, but their bond wasn't strong enough. The Maderan again terrorized New Orleans until the Voodoo Queen managed to imprison it again – trapping it. But there was a price, the effort cost her the bulk of her power. And to ensure its imprisonment, she had to sacrifice herself."

"But."

"Even the strongest of magic has a weakness just as the strongest flame flickers. Marie Laveau was a powerful force both above and beneath the water, but nothing is absolute. While it would take immense magical power to undo the workings of her magic – it is not beyond possibility." She sighed, "Alas, the Maderan grows stronger."

"How? What did Marie Laveau do to trap it?"

She didn't answer but sighed, and her height seemed to diminish as her white hair draped about her shoulder like a cloak.

"Look Madame Fi La Reye if I'm suppose to prevent this berserker from being unleashed I need some answers."

"Seek the paladin who longs for the dead who walks

    The Guardian who waits to be awakened

    Seek those who guard the land

      And the soul who guards fire

    Within the sleeper's heart lies the golden seal

      To find the silver and green follow the heart's
desire

      And together they walk as one on the Eve of
Penance."

    "What!" Damien exclaimed. "What part of
answer did you not understand!" He noticed his outburst
was for nothing because Madame Fi La Reye was no
longer there. *Where did she go?* He combed the cemetery
even though he knew it was a pointless endeavor. The
cemetery was a labyrinth of decaying tombs. A hide and
seek paradise – even Madame Fi La Reye could allude him
for a good while if she desired. After a few minutes, he
gave up. The Lady of the Web was gone for now, but he
had a good feeling they would meet again.

    Andra's heart had slowed to a crawl as she
followed the nurse. Her mind, however, was buzzing with
questions. What am I doing here? Why would Achilles
want to see me? Why did I listen to King Geek anyway?
She lost count of how many times she had tried to turn
around. She had approached the nurse's desk hoping he
couldn't have visitors. The nurse's words had made her
stomach fall.

    As the nurse left to return to her desk, Andra
willed herself to turn and run for the elevator. Resisting

her instinct, she slowly palmed the doorknob and gently opened the door.

His eyes opened with the click of the door as it closed behind her before locking on to her. Time seemed to stand still as they both eyed each other.

"Ohmigod! I did jump, and I was sent to Hell!"

"I see you still have your disturbed sense of humor," Andra scoffed.

"Let me guess, the Devil told you I was in here, and you came to finish the job."

"No!" Andra exclaimed. He paused as she glanced away before looking him straight in the face. "Look Achilles, I know how it feels to lose a parent."

"Come on Andra, are you trying to …" He stopped as he gazed into her eyes. "You're serious aren't you?"

Andra turned away and walked over to the chair near the far wall. "I was nine. Wasn't much to it, just an ordinary day. I watched my father leave for work as he had done countless times before. I waved goodbye to him like I always did." She paused and faced him for a moment before finally collapsing into the chair. "He didn't come home that night, but I wasn't too bothered by that. Sometimes he would work late or go visit friends, but he'd always be in the living room the next morning. Only he wasn't. I went to school; came back that evening. He still wasn't there. Another day went by and another and still he never showed up."

"What happened to him?"

She lifted her head towards the ceiling; a soft sniff escaped her. Her eyes closed as she lowered her head back towards the floor. A moment of silence passed before she faced him, her eyes red, flashing one moment with rage, sadness another, and confusion the next. "We don't know. He never came back."

"What! You mean the police, nobody could find …"

"You don't understand Achilles, he's not dead or missing or anything like that. He just never came back."

Achilles found himself speechless as the reality of her statement sank in. "You mean he … he abandoned you." The thought of this made Achilles feel sick in his stomach.

"Yeah," the girl answered softly. "God, I don't even know why I'm telling you this."

He had never seen the "Athletic Wonder" this vulnerable before. He didn't know it was possible. For almost nine years she had to deal with that gruesome transgression and the implications it spawned. It had to be hard, the impact that such an event could have on a person, on their psyche. "I'm glad you did," Achilles answered.

"How long are they going to keep you here?"

"Until this afternoon. The psych squad thought it would do more good for me to be surrounded by familiar faces and surroundings than being in a mini prison."

"It must be rough. I mean I was lucky to have my mom to help me deal with the absence of my dad. God knows how I would be if I lost her."

"God, Andra," Achilles sobbed. "I keep hoping that it was all some terrible nightmare but it isn't. God knows I can't explain it: one moment I'm looking at pictures of my parents in our family album – the next thing I know I'm on the expressway. If Damien hadn't passed …"

"Yes, Damien Parker with another accomplishment to add to his resume – Guardian Angel."

"Yeah, he is a good guy."

"Humph, he's also the Devil that told me you were here. And you're a nice guy to say such a thing about him especially after that snide comment of his yesterday."

"Yeah. I still have to deck him for that."

"Well make sure you hit him for me too. Could you believe that? The nerve of him. Always implying that we like each other. Ridiculous and he's suppose to be so smart."

"Yeah," Achilles added softly. "Ridiculous."

Silence grew between them and though neither showed it, both boy and girl were pained by their words.

"Hmm," Andra sighed glancing at her watch. "I better get going."

"Yeah, my aunt and uncle should be back at any moment."

"I hope you feel better Achilles."

"I'm getting there," he answered with a weak wave. "Andra!"

"Yes."

"Thanks for coming by."

The girl smiled before walking out and closing the door gently behind her.

Damien Parker had given up looking for Madame Fi La Reye, but her riddle still left his mind baffled. Hoping to relax his mind and gain a little more perspective, he headed into nearby Louis Armstrong Park. *Cursed woman,* he had asked for some answers to clarify some things, and she responds by giving him a riddle. *What is this golden seal? True heart's desire?* The heart is a fragile and fickle thing – a heart's desire could be anything, but what had him confused the most was the first line to the riddle. *Hmm… a paladin was another name for a knight or champion. A knight who longs for the walking dead? What a Knight of the Order? Another of the Seven perhaps?*

Just when he was beginning to develop a path of thinking, his mind changed directions. *What if the Paladin is me? Longing could mean anything – could mean to pursue, fight, love? No, that couldn't be it. And who guards the land and who guards fire?*

He was so lost in his thoughts that he barely heard his name being called. His eyes surveyed his surrounding before his eyes met the angular face of a Native American.

"Damien Parker right?" the Indian replied extending his hand. "Ah, I see you don't recognize me."

"No, I remember the face. We met at Boys State," the other responded sensing a vague familiarity. "I remember your face. It's names I have a problem remembering."

"Yeah. We were in the same city. I was the sheriff."

"Sheriff? Of course Seneca Maza. How you been man?"

"No different than the last time you saw me. How has life been treating you, Mr. Speaker Pro Tempore?"

Damien winced just slightly. How the devil he managed to end up as the second in command of the Mock House of Representatives, he didn't have a clue. All he had wanted was to be a representative of his city – a nice simple, quiet position. Then again, his life seemed to always end up with some bizarre twist. "My life? Bizarre as always and as usual a woman is the cause of it."

Seneca glanced behind him, pointing to where an elderly woman was sitting Indian style on a blanket beneath an oak tree. "Tell me about it."

"Who is she?"

"My paternal grandmother. Come I'll introduce you. Gives me a reason to stop meditating." Damien followed him. "Grandmother, this is Damien Parker, we went to Boys State at LSU this past summer. Damien Parker, this is my grandmother, Jadzia Maza."

"Pleased to meet you ma'am," Damien replied.

Jadzia Maza's bowed head did not move, and her eyes remained closed.

"Grandmother has been trying to instruct me in the art of reaching the spiritual plane," Seneca whispered. "Magic mumbo jumbo."

"I wouldn't take her so lightly. Magic isn't something you should fool around with like a hot potato," Damien answered. "Besides, I thought all you Indians were into that mystical stuff."

"Something I'm sure you have great knowledge of."

Damien shifted his gaze to Jadzia Maza. The old woman's eyes were opened and staring straight at him.

"Magic is what makes our world what it is," the woman continued. "Something you children must today comprehend."

"Now see what you've done!" Seneca interjected with a sigh. "Watch, she'll be telling you the story of the Guardians next."

"Who are the Guardians?"

"The Guardians according to Indian legend are members of the races of man who protect the elements of the earth. You know the old alchemy elements – earth, fire, wind, water."

"No heart," Damien chimed.

Seneca gave a humph. "This is Indian folklore, not some cheesy environmental cartoon. According to the stories, each race was given a particular element to protect, kind of the Creator's way of balancing things out."

"And you don't believe it."

"It's a story Damien – folklore! No different than Greek mythology or American tall tales."

"Truth is often thought to be a tale until it's too late," the old woman scoffed.

"See. I've been dealing with this all day today," Seneca whispered.

"To be honest. I agree with her." Damien stepped past the bewildered Indian boy and sat on the blanket in front of the old woman. "Mrs. Maza. Can you tell me about the Guardians?"

Chapter 8

Andra Alexander was an emotional hurricane and the music on the radio was not helping to ease the troubling winds. What was I thinking; telling him all of that? Granted, it was a known fact that Andra's mother had raised her alone, but few knew of the effect the whole situation had on her. Usually it was something she kept locked inside – at least until today. She completely vented all her sadness and frustration in front of him. Why? Why did I do it? You were trying to make him feel better. No, that's not it, there's something else, but that couldn't be it – I despise Achilles Harmon. *Ha! Admit it girlfriend you like him.* It would never work. He's a *sweet* ...total jerk. I'm classy. I'm with the in crowd, *whom you have no respect for,* he's one of the outcasts. All we do is argue, *he's not afraid to challenge me.* I **hate** him. *You're falling in love with him.* Could you imagine us as a couple? *I'd be with someone who likes me for me not because I did a triple double last night.* Damn.

"You look stressed girlfriend."

Andra turned in surprise to see a young woman, about 21, sitting beside her in the passenger seat. Even more shaking was the fact that Andra didn't panic instead she trusted her. For no apparent reason she trusted a complete stranger, yet something told Andra that this was no ordinary stranger.

"Guy problems," the woman declared.

Not a question – a declaration how could she know? "You wouldn't understand."

"Let me guess. He's sweet, caring, strong, but vulnerable and you're scared of killing him?"

Andra's eyebrows raised. "Something like that."

"Hey a woman's life is all about risk."

"Huh?"

"Sometimes being vulnerable is the only way we acknowledge the fact that we're human. You shouldn't look at it as being a weakness or an excuse not to take on an opportunity. Besides girl he's kind of cute."

"Wait! How do you know ..."

"Girlfriend. You're a warrior and so am I. People like us would like to be human, but we rarely get the chance. You better take the opportunity while it's knocking. Oh yeah, they're honking at you!"

"What?" It was then she noticed that every car behind her was honking. She glanced up to see a green light and accelerated the car forward. "Okay who are you and... "

The mysterious young women had disappeared. Andra stared at the empty seat unsurprised that the woman had vanished. After all, she had appeared into her car out of nowhere so it was no surprise that she popped out the same way. She sighed and returned her focus on driving.

"Why is Enrica always late?" Serena asked as she and Sara sat in the food court waiting. "I said specifically 1:00. It's now going on 2!"

"Enrica barely comes to class on time. What makes you think this would be any different?"

"Because it's shopping and Enrica loves to shop! Let me see if I can reach her on her cell phone."

"Not necessary, there she is."

"Took you long enough," Serena scolded as soon as Enrica was in earshot.

"Serena what is up with your man?" Enrica inquired completely ignoring the fact that she was late.

"What do you mean?"

"Why is your man going to a speech tournament rather than prom?"

"Enrica it's the biggest tournament of the year. For them it's like the football team going to the Superdome."

"But to skip prom Serena?"

"Lake Charles isn't that far from New Orleans. He could go to the last half of the tournament, if he advances that far, in the morning and be back by 6. Besides Damien hasn't even decided if he's going."

"According to Jimmy and Scooter, he's going."

"Enrica, have you been eavesdropping again?"

"Hey, I'm just looking out for my girl."

"You were helping when you almost caused Damien to confront Will about buying me a candy gram last year."

"Well how was I supposed to know? Serena and Serlena sound almost alike."

Serena could only roll her eyes toward the ceiling as she shook her head. "I'll talk to him about it later. Can we please get back to the business at hand? Should I go to Champs or to Footlocker?"

"Champs? Footlocker?" Enrica retorted in confusion. "Why we going there?"

"She's buying Damien a football jersey," Sara answered. "Isn't that sweet."

"A jersey?"

"He's always surprising me with gifts," Serena explained, "and I want to do the same for him."

"Oh yeah, heck the teachers are still talking about what your man did for Valentine's Day. That was pretty romantic I have to admit. I'm gonna be tagging along with you Friday just to see if he pulls off an encore. But knowing Damien he'll probably top that."

Serena had almost forgotten that Valentines Day was around the corner. "I know, but it's not just Valentine's Day. He does little things like that all the time and if he's not doing something, he's saying something. He does it all without my asking, and I hardly do a thing for him."

"So let me get this straight? Your man romances you to the point of being the most envied girl at John

Ehret High, and you're buying him a football jersey. How sweet."

"Not just any jersey – it has to be a Tennessee Oilers or a Tampa Bay Buccaneers jersey," Serena countered, not failing to notice the sarcasm in Enrica's voice.

"What? Your man doesn't like the Saints?"

"Damien can't stand the Saints."

"Let me get this straight. Damien hates the Saints but like the Tampa Bay Buccaneers? How's that?"

"I don't know something about a black kicker and scoring and nearly advancing to the Super Bowl the year of his birth."

"Never mind. I don't wanna know. Let's just go shopping."

"Can I at least finish this last fry?" Sara exclaimed.

"Hurry up," the two girls replied.

Damien Parker had just finished listening to Jadzia Maza's words. Apparently, humanity was divided into four races: the Caucasians or Europeans, the Africans, the Orientals, and the Natives of the Central Continent – the Americas. Each group received a special charge over a particular element. The Europeans were charged with fire, which accounts for their ability to manufacture firearms and explosives. The Africans received water which accounts for their knowledge of irrigation and naval navigation. The Orientals received wind which resulted in a mastery of balancing mind, body, and soul – to which wind and breath are essential – the martial arts. And the Natives of the Americas became the guardians of the land.

Seek those who guard the land. Could it be he is supposed to find Jadzia Maza and Seneca. No, most likely Seneca. She wouldn't be training him if she didn't believe he had the ability to harness and use magic.

The soul who guards fire. Definitely a white person, but without a name he was looking for a needle in a haystack. Curse Madame Fi La Reye and her riddles. Well Mrs. Maza had given him this much information. Might as well see if riding her coattails could lead to a little bit more.

"Ms. Maza, you said the time of the Guardians was near right."

"Yes."

Could her time of the Guardians be Madame Fi La Reye's Eve of Penance?

"And do you know who I am?"

"Damien, what are you talking about? Seneca inquired. "You've been listening to her for so long your …"

"Hush Seneca! This child knows his destiny. Relax Damien Parker, Chosen Child of Water, let the spirits talk to you."

Damien closed his eyes.

"Feel the spirits move within you. Enhance it, consume it. Flow with it."

Damien relaxed, focused, and found himself in the Dreamtime.

He could see the house.

He saw the candle burning in its wall.

He knew it burned for him. The door opened as he approached it.

He saw them, but he couldn't believe it. It couldn't be, they had been destroyed; consumed by the fire that nearly destroyed him. Not only were they alive, but they were older.

"Hello, we've been waiting for you," one of the children said. She was beautiful, an angel above all other angels. She wore a silver gown that sparkled and as she moved it seemed as if the earth itself moved to avoid her stepping upon it. Her face was tanned like copper, and her brown hair was fixed in a ponytail that slid a little past her shoulders.

"Who are you?"

"We are the ones you seek," another girl replied. Her blue silk dress flowed down her body. Her eyes displayed an innocence he never seen before and knew he would never see again. Her pale face shone as her laughter rang like bells.

"Do you not know who we are?" a tall Indian boy chimed. He was dressed in yellow robes.

"Do you not know who we are?" He turned to see a tall, dark boy, dressed in black, his face showed relief one minute then pain and regret the next.

"We are the reason you are here," the girl in the green tunic and cloak replied.

"You are the reason we are here," another replied. Tall, regal and handsome, he wore a gold sword on his side. His princely robes were gold as well but at times seemed to change colors from gold to white to green to purple and back to gold.

"You know who we are?" This time the voice came from a tall, handsome female clad in red armor, a blue cloak flowing down her back. A large sword stained with blood and dirt was in her left hand in a warrior's salute. An inscription was on the sword, but because of the dirt and grime, all he could read was FOR THE KING I BE UNDRA.

"Yes he knows who we are," the silver gowned angel replied.

"Speak our names," the Indian boy commanded.

"Speak your name," the Prince requested.

Damien Parker awoke. "Did you see what I saw?"

"No!" Jadzia Maza answered. "The spirit's message is for you and you alone. But the spirits did tell me that for you to succeed you must go beneath the water."

Beneath the water? What could it mean? She had been in the Dreamtime just like he had been. Then again, in the Dreamtime nothing is what it appears to be. Words can never be taken literally. One has to look beyond the obvious, and you never have the same experience twice. Which wouldn't be so bad, if the very next experience wasn't related to the previous.

"Anything else?" the boy asked.

"No."

He stood up. Part of him wanted to ask about the Maderan, but if the Dreamtime didn't show it to her then. No, he needed to take the pieces he had and try to put them together – before he asked.

"Thank you Mrs. Maza." He started to leave when she reached up and grabbed his hand.

"You are one of the Chosen, Child of Magic. You may call me Mother Maza and indeed that would be of great honor to me if you did so."

"Yes ma'am. I mean Mother Maza." He turned and walked past a confused Seneca.

"What was all that about?" Seneca asked.

"That child, Seneca, is as beyond human as we are beyond animals."

"Grandmother, I don't understand."

"You will in time, but right now the Spirits await you."

Why am I not surprised? He watched Damien Parker walked out of the park before shaking his head and settled back down on the blanket.

Erthur Eugene straightened his tie just as the creek of the door caught his ears. "Is everything ready?"

The nod answered the question and the minister gave himself one last look-over. "Then let's get to work." He led the procession into the conference room where faces greeted him. His heart lifted as the applause filled his ears and the despair on their faces changed to smiles.

A full house, Eugene thought. We had only planned for fifty but look at this, there must be over 200 people here. Many of who are among the most influential circles of New Orleans. The first move has been made; all he could do now was wait for the counter. But that would have to wait, right now ... "Friends, Brothers, Sisters, Christians. We find ourselves in a time of great distress."

The mayor of New Orleans had been looking forward to the long weekend. He needed the break. The public was already screaming for Fischer's head – and now damn Grant Pershing was adding fuel to an already burning furnace. It wasn't that he liked Fischer – he hated the man and at any other time he would be enjoying this for all that it was worth, but the election was right around the corner and things like this had a way putting people under.

So far, three protests, over 150 arrests; 25 people currently in the hospital. A completely unacceptable casualty list and more fighting laid over the horizon. He cursed Grant Pershing, the Times Picayune, Andrew Fischer, Darnell Coleman, the NAACP, and fate.

He smiled as he noticed the soft touch on his shoulder; married life was new to him but he loved it and her.

"Penny for your thoughts?" she asked, hugging him closer. Her perfume was intoxicating.

"Trying to find a loophole that allows more moments like this."

"Well you keep looking and ..."

Damnit! What happened now? "Hello?"

"We have a problem boss."

"Tell me about it," the mayor thought. "I know Karl; I've read the article. What choice did I have? It was on the front page. And knowing Pershing he left just enough ammo to roll into Sunday."

"It's not that sir. It's something worse."

The mayor remained silent. With any other person he would have dismissed it as exaggerating the issue, but this was Maynard Karl, the prodigy who years ago had propelled him to the top of the New Orleans oligarchy, a mixture of youthful energy and stamina with a craftiness and ruthlessness that was beyond some who had been in the game for decades. That had been nearly eight years ago, and even though Karl was 35 years old now, he had not lost a single step in either area. If Maynard Karl worried, every sensible politician between Baton Rouge and New Orleans worried.

On the other hand, the beautiful figure in his sight stilled any urgency Karl's voice may have stirred. "Come on Karl we both know Pershing has some more trouble to spread tomorrow, and I agree we should troubleshoot this ASAP, but this can wait until Monday."

"Erthur Eugene is here."

The mayor wondered if his wife heard him curse. Quickly he calmed himself. "Are you sure?"

"Apparently, he arrived today sir. He's already spoken to one mass audience today, and I'm sure the press was there."

Perfect. So far the Fischer situation had been confined within the state, at worst Mississippi, Alabama, and maybe parts of Texas. Erthur Eugene would turn the situation into a national sideshow, which would only cause the situation to linger longer than it should. That could spell trouble.

"I've already called Langley, he's cooperating fully."

Silence. He and Langley didn't see eye to eye on most things, but he could see the common view on this one. The last thing either the mayor or the chief of police wanted during this weekend was riots and Erthur Eugene was a walking riot factory.

"I've already set up a meeting."

"Good, we need to get on this ASAP." "Damn," he sighed as he hung up the phone.

Serena Martin was beaming as she stepped into the house. Her smile quickly vanished as her eyes noticed Victor Morris sitting on a barstool near the kitchen.

"Hey Serena," he replied with that sly smile of his.

"Hey Honeybun," another voice greeted.

"Hello Daddy," Serena answered. Her eyes though were still glaring at Victor. *Wipe that smile off your face, player. Anything involving you and me goes through me, not my father.*

"Vic and I were talking about the gala on Tuesday."

Vic! She could hardly believe it. Damien was lucky if he was actually called by a name that started with a D. *Vic!* "Really? So I'm not engaged yet or anything like that?"

"No, no," her father replied with a laugh. "We were just talking about the plans you two made."

For a man who had been alive for nearly fifty years, her father could be oblivious to the obvious. Maybe confusion will work where sarcasm didn't. "What plans?"

"The plans you two arranged to go to the gala on Mardi Gras."

"Yeah Serena," Victor added, his voice showing confusion. "I thought we were going together. At least that's what I remember."

You lying ... Serena calmed herself. "Since when? Besides, I have this major test in physical science when we go back to school Thursday that I really need to study for."

"Dear, you have all weekend to study as well as Monday and Wednesday."

"Dad, tomorrow is Sunday. Maybe Monday and Wednesday but that would be ..."

"Since when did you start shopping at Champs?" Victor inquired, noticing the bag in her hand.

"I'm kind of curious myself," her father chimed.

Serena sighed as she pulled out the jersey. "It's a present."

"For me? Thank you Serena, but I don't usually like the Buccaneers but ..."

"It's not for you nitwit."

"Who is it for?" her father asked.

Serena sighed again. "I bought it for Damien Parker."

"Damien Parker!" both men exclaimed in unison.

"Good God! Now he has you buying clothes for him. Sheesh Serena."

"He doesn't have me doing anything. He's been nothing but kind and considerate of me, and you know it lame brain. I just wanted to show him the same kind of appreciation." Her eyes drifted back to her father. "He doesn't even know I bought it."

"I'll bet," Victor sneered. "I don't understand it sir. Damien Parker is a nobody and a trouble maker. It's obvious he's a bad influence on Serena."

"Bad influence? What's bad about a guy who's smart, cares about the community, is a natural leader, works for his money..."

"Serena," her father retorted gently.

"Remembers birthdays, Valentine's Day, is a published writer, no criminal record..."

"Serena!" His reprimand was louder this time.

"Did I mention that he listens and has every girl at John Ehret High wishing that their boyfriends were the same way. Oh yeah, he has a 3.8 and a 30 on his ACT! What's your average and ACT score, Victor?"

"SERENA!"

"Then again, almost all people who want to make the world better are bad influences, right Daddy." She didn't wait for an answer; she quickly walked up the stairs into her room and closed the door.

Chapter 9

"Oracle."

"Yes Damien."

"I need to know everything you can tell me about a Maderan."

Silence.

"Now Oracle."

"Maderans, usually mistaken for demons are really a natural anomaly of magical energy that resulted from the Rapture."

"Anomaly? What do you mean?"

"The banishment of the Daemonites caused a fluxuation in the magical flow of energy. That fluxuation lead to the creation of the creatures known as Maderans. Being that this occurred within the "physical" plane as you call the current surroundings around you, Maderans are – 'creatures of nature.'"

"You mean this thing is like a vampire?"

"In a sense. Maderans are walking famines. No matter how much it consumes, its hunger is never satisfied. Its diet of fear and madness only fuels its craving for more. May I add Damien Parker that Maderans are among the most powerful creatures of magic and will be a formidable foe – even for you at your best."

"You make it sound like it's unbeatable. Kind of extreme even for your pessimistic self, Oracle."

"Few of the Order or the Abyss have survived an encounter with a Maderan, Damien Parker."

"How few?"

"Next to none. The fact that Marie Laveau was able to contain her cemented her reputation as the Queen of the Voodoos"

Man, next to none! That made it real likely that more people drank from the Holy Grail than survived Maderan encounters. *Few of the Order or the Abyss.* Obviously, this thing isn't something that is easily controlled, and from Oracle's description, a killing machine that kept going like the Energizer Bunny on Mountain Dew. Someone had to be either really desperate, stupid, insane – or really powerful. All of which bothered him. Damn.

Jonathan Parker could only groan as he heard the details of the meeting from his fellow Masons.

Erthur Eugene, here in New Orleans. The Erthur Eugene who was responsible for a new Black movement that was slowly forming in the South and West Coast. Eugene claimed to be promoting Civil Rights awareness, but Jonathan had his doubts and he wasn't the only one.

He eyed the newspaper sitting on the floor next to the sofa. Yep things were going to get ugly here in the Big Easy. He heard the door open and seconds later his son popped through. "Hi Pop. Hi Mr. Mac."

The man next to his father smiled and hailed a
greeting before giving his initial tease. Damien couldn't
help but feel cheerful. His Uncle Mac had always been
playful; his only major flaw was that he was a Dallas
Cowboy fan and he flaunted it. He noticed the newspaper
on the floor and reached for it. His smile faded as he read
the front page.

"Erthur Eugene is here."

The boy's eyebrows raised at the mention of the
name. A slight wince showed in the right side of his face.
"Great." He didn't attempt to hide his contempt.

"Damien isn't too big a fan of Erthur Eugene
either," Jonathan explained to the surprised man sitting
next to Mr. Mac.

That was a mild way of putting it, Damien
thought. Erthur Eugene to him was a personification of
how far in the wrong direction the country was heading.
Any country with at least half its populace possessing
common sense would heave at the thought of such a man
being able to command any audience much less a large
one. As far as Damien was concerned, Erthur Eugene was
a fusion of Stalin and Hitler at their worst with a much
darker tan. Heck, it wouldn't surprise him if the man from
his dream was Erthur Eugene.

"What the problem with Brother Eugene?" the
man asked.

"We don't see eye to eye on a couple of things,"
Damien replied. He could already see where this would
lead to, and he didn't really have the time or the stomach
for trading bards with a fool over Black history. He

excused himself and started toward the kitchen where his mother was sitting at the breakfast table playing her keyboard.

"Tell me if you know what this is Damien?" she inquired as he fixed himself a glass of grape juice. Her playing was at first awkward and clumsy, but soon the piano lessons of her youth surfaced.

"Beethoven right? The Fur Elisa right?"

"Fur Elise."

"Close enough."

"Was not. If this had been a quiz bowl match that answer would have been considered wrong."

"Which is why I thank God for Loni every time we have a match. She's the music and arts expert."

"So is the Harmon boy ok?" his mother asked.

"Huh?" Damien replied. "Did someone call here again?"

"No it's just that I figured you would go see how he was."

Damien sheepishly placed his hand behind his head caressing his palm over the back of his head. "Am I that predictable? But Achilles? He's fine. They should be letting him out of the hospital today or tomorrow. That clock is fast right?"

"You know that clock isn't fast."

He yelled in panic before drowning down the rest of the grape juice and rushing off to his room with his mother closely behind.

"I'm suppose to meet Serena at the movies."

"You and Serena have a date."

"Yes ma'am." He grabbed a dark blue Reebok polo shirt out of the closet and a pair of blue jeans.

"What are you going to see?"

"Don't know," her son replied as he flew past her into the bathroom. "It's her turn to pick the movie."

"Does her father know she's going?"

Damien winced. His mother knew all too well the ongoing dramatic triangle involving Serena, her father, and himself. "I hope so. Although I don't think I can lose anymore brownie points." *You can't lose something you never had.*

Exhaustion filled Erthur Eugene as he stepped into his hotel room and closed the door. Being that it was Mardi Gras weekend, it was a blessing that this had been available. He collapsed onto the chair and slumped his head into his hands.

"Lord, give me strength," the minister prayed. This was going to be tough. Already the devil was at work here. God help us.

A knock interrupted his meditation.

"Come."

A crack formed in the door, revealing a flustered face.

"Come in Charlie."

"I'm sorry to interrupt sir, but the mayor just called. He wants to meet with you – tonight."

"Tonight?"

"Yes sir, at 8pm to be exact."

The minister lifted his tired eyes to Charlie before staring at the ceiling. Time ... never enough of it. He sighed before leaning forward preparing to rise from the chair. "Page Reverend Stiles. Tell the mayor we maybe 10 minutes late ... and Charlie has our Good Samaritan called?"

"No sir."

Eugene sighed. "Have Abdullah and Lewis work on finding him."

"Right away sir."

The door closed leaving Erthur Eugene alone.

Two doors down, Rioley Boullard never noticed as the demon entered; its mind filled with hatred and disgust as it observed him. So pathetic, so worthless and weak. Why the Creator valued such beings it couldn't fathom. So easily could this human be killed, but humans did have value – at times, and now was one of those times.

Creeping like a shadow, the demon invaded Rioley's mind. It could sense the rage and confusion burning within, but it wasn't enough to taint the magical balance – to provide it with the nourishment it craved. But the human could do something about that. "You want justice," it hissed in the man's head.

"Yes," Rioley thought believing the demon's words to be his own.

"Justice must be served. It must be shown that this injustice will not be tolerated. Would he had been paroled if his victims had been white?"

"No," Rioley answered.

"What he has done deserves death! Does not the Bible demand one to defend the honor of his sister. Did not Dinah's brothers avenge their sister's rape?"

"Yes."

"LeBeau and all like him must be killed. They defiled our women ... use them to DESTROY US. KILL THEM! ALL OF THEM!"

"But LeBeau is a man. Can I ... Do I have the right to ..."

"You must kill him. Kill him before it is too late. Is he different from Seachem? He is evil ... EVIL!"

"Evil," Rioley wheezed softly.

The door to his room opened. "Hey, are you going to the meeting with the mayor?"

Rioley snapped out of his stupor. "A meeting with the mayor? Tonight?"

"In about an hour. You don't have to if you don't want to. Well?"

"Well what?"

"Are you going or what?"

Nah, I'll stay here. Hey Charlie, is Lewis going?"

"No, he and Abdullah are working on something else."

"I'll stay here and help them then."

"Okay then." The door closed behind him with a click.

Rioley fell back onto the bed. *Thomas LeBeau is a man, but he's an evil man. Justice will be served and LeBeau will die.*

Outside Magnus laughed as he watched Rioley Boullard's room. The fool had been so easy to manipulate. He will serve his purpose for him well. Again he laughed, everything was falling into place. Soon he would have the keys to the seals, and the Guardian would be destroyed. The Day of Reckoning was drawing near. His laughter continued as he disappeared around the corner.

"Listen Mr. Eugene, we understand you're trying to help the Coleman boy. A great wrong has been committed. Even now an investigation is being arranged to look into the matter."

"Mr. Mayor while I appreciate that the matter is being looked into, but in all sincerity to turn back now would convey that the system is infallible when indeed it is not."

"Mr. Eugene."

"Reverend."

"Reverend Eugene, has it crossed your mind that first, the actions of the court system are out of the reach of City Hall and second, the effects that your acts could have? Instead of helping Coleman and the city of New Orleans, you are becoming a disturbance to justice being done for him and the preservation of order for the city's citizens. Already riots are threatening to break out."

"Mr. Mayor I assure you, I want to avoid any kind of chaos and disorder as much as you do."

"Then stop this."

"Stop what?"

"This false fever that you are advocating. You have these people thinking that the system doesn't work; that they cannot rely on their own judgments in the choices they made in the voting booth."

"Mr. Mayor, we do not mean you or the city any harm. We only wish for a wrong to be made right. Right now four girls are defiled and dead, and a reformed young man is still imprisoned. A young man reformed by the legal system. Yet he stays in prison while a monster is loosed? This wrong has been repeated time and time again. That is why people lost faith in their elected officials, Mr. Mayor and that happened long before I got here."

"We understand that. We're trying to remedy that."

"Are you Mr. Karl? Or are you merely concerned with re-election damage?"

Karl remained silent.

"Reverend," the mayor explained. "I understand the wrong that has been done, but Andrew Fischer has been in service of the city of New Orleans for many years. Over 30 years to be exact. There are many who feel that such service deserves at least the benefit of a doubt."

"And what has that doubt done but brought the snowball that you are now facing?"

"True, but that is the risk we take when we trust. For all of Fischer's mistakes, there have been those who have been given a second chance and used that chance wisely. Nothing is perfect, sometimes there are knicks that we must bang out, but at least allow us the chance to bang them out. I assure you an investigation is being done. We will get to the heart of this matter."

"And what assurances do Mr. Coleman and his family have; or the families of those girls?"

"Do you think they want riots occurring in their name? Jesus Christ man, no one benefits from that."

Erthur Eugene rose from the table, his face a collage of disgust and sadness. "Gentlemen, when you are ready to address the matter at hand, we will talk. Until then, I will not shrink in neither my commitment nor resolve." The words seem to echo as he and his party walked out the conference room.

"My God!" the mayor exclaimed. "Is there any way you can arrest him?"

"For what!" Langley, a huge black man replied. "Talking in a church? Granted, I could throw grounds of disturbing the peace, but I'm telling you either two things will happen: the city will be burned to the ground or I'll

have to let him go, but not before you'll have to add the
ACLU to your list of worries."

More unnecessary publicity. "You're right,' the
mayor agreed.

"Maybe this will all go over easy," an aide
suggested.

"Are you crazy?" the mayor responded. "This is
Los Angeles 1992 to the hilt. Only instead of the police
department it's the court system."

"We could try to convince Fischer to retire – or
take a holiday." Karl suggested.

"Hah! Fischer would entrench himself in his
courtroom just to spite me."

"What if it came from someone else?"

"Like who? Andrew Fischer isn't exactly known
for listening to reason. Who would he listen to?"

Karl's eyebrows raised. "I think I may know of
someone."

"Who?"

Karl leaned over and whispered a name in his ear.

"Would he do it though?"

"He will."

The mayor breathed a sigh of hope.

Damien Parker was all smiles as he and Serena walked out the theater, his face beaming as he admired the jersey he was wearing turning as if he was a model at the end of a walkway.

Serena laughed. "I'm glad you like it."

"Like it?" He displayed his trademark grin before quickly appearing in front of her and pulled her close for a kiss. "What do you think?" he whispered gently poking her nose with a finger.

The girl responded with a kiss of her own.

"Does your father know you bought this?"

"Yes," she replied, wrapping both her arms around his arm as they walked. "He actually likes it."

"What!?"

Serena smiled. She would tell him about it, but not now. Now she was enjoying the moment. "You're glowing you know."

"Am I?"

"Yep and the aura is unusually bright." That made her very happy. She probably could have given him a Dallas Cowboy jersey, and he would have been ecstatic about it.

"Wait up. Did he know it was for me?"

"Yes."

Damien eyed her suspiciously. "Before or after he said he liked it?"

"Hmm."

"I knew it!" Damien replied as they reached their vehicles. The rest of his comment died in his throat as a sensation came over him.

No! Not here, not now! He reached for his staff hidden on the side of his bike. "Serena."

She saw it land in front of her. She held her emotions in check as she summoned her magic. A demon, a large demon with a large power surge. Long ago Morgoth had explained demonic hierarchy to her, which surprised her being that demons existed to cause chaos and yet there was an established chain of command. At the bottom of the hierarchy were the lower class demons, not too powerful and easily vanquished. Then came the Archdemons, the first class of daemonites, usually classified as B and A class. And then there were the S class, the Raizarons. Morgoth had once told her that any human who willingly took on an S class demon were at least one of three things: very experienced with their magic, a Knight of the Order, or very stupid. *From the amount of power I feel emanating, he's definitely an archdemon. Well Morgoth said they would get more powerful.*

The demon merely stood there, eying them both, crouched and ready for a confrontation.

They could run, maybe draw it away but what then. No she couldn't endanger Damien and if it wanted, it could rip him apart like a rag doll.

"Damien," she ordered, "Step back! I can deal with this."

Damien's shock at her words almost made him drop the cane he now gripped in his hands. "Wait a minute. You can see it?"

"Look, I know this might seem crazy but something is... Wait a minute what did you say?"

"I asked if you can see it, which obviously you can. As for stepping back, I'm afraid I can't do that. Part of the job and all. Stay behind me." He paused and gave a quick glance. *Why do I keep getting this feeling? Like there's some kind of force tugging at me. Is there another creature of magic nearby?*

The hiss of the demon brought his mind back to focus.

"Damien, this isn't the time for bravado."

"Oh I know. Step back." He stepped forward, his staff glowing with a white light that flowed into him. Both demon and girl stood in awe as they watched black armor materialize around his body along with a long purple cape that billowed behind him.

Serena gasped as she recalled her dream and the warning it foretold. She had ignored it; dismissed it as an illusion in her mind. Now for the first time she was afraid of the possibility that it could be more because now the Knight of her dreams was standing before her, and his face was that of Damien Parker.

Chapter 10

The armor, the cape, and the hat – all exactly the same as it had been in her dream. However in place of the sword was a glowing white staff. For a moment, Serena stood in awe – he was magnificent. He was still Damien Parker in every way, the height, hair, weight, skin tone and yet he was so much more. This is Damien Parker? My Damien Parker? Her awe then turned to fear, for what once had been her greatest wish could be her worst nightmare.

She watched as her Guardian and the demon advanced toward each other; the two circling each other, each searching for an opening. The Guardian, however, was having trouble keeping his focus on the demon. His thoughts kept drifting to Serena. How would she take all this? No, can't think on that now. He recalled the first battle with this demon, hoping to remember something that would make this battle short.

"Guardian."

"Malagant. Round two isn't it."

Malagant snarled, his hairs bristling.

The Guardian eyed the blade in place of what should have been a left hand *or paw*. "Shall we dance." He braced himself and prepared to strike as the demon flew toward him. But the demon seemed to slow in midair.

The Guardian glanced at Serena, her eyes confirming his guess. *She's doing this. I thought it was because she was terrified that she could see the demon, but I was wrong. She can see it because ... she possesses magic. That's what I was feeling, and why I felt something similar last Friday at school — it was her. Later Parker, right now your attention is needed somewhere else.*

The demon was knocked back as the Guardian unleashed his magic out of his staff. Howling, it picked itself up before charging toward him, but the Knight of the Order simply sidestepped and swung his staff. Fire ignited as the wood hit the demon's back causing it to stumble forward — straight toward Serena Martin.

Malagant gave a gleeful smile as he catapulted toward her, his blade ready to deliver the decapitating blow.

No time to duck. In desperation she willed forth all her magic, praying it would be enough, knowing that if it wasn't this would be her last breath. She heard her name being called — a cry of desperation and concern. Relief took hold as she saw the vicious creature fly wide to her right as purple lightning hammered against its side and back.

The Guardian closed in, lightning and energy slamming into the demon as it twisted to avoid the punishing blows.

In a move of desperation, Malagant managed to put himself between the two. Trying to avoid hitting Serena, the Guardian toned down his assault. Malagant with surprising quickness managed to knock the Guardian back. The demon swung around to finish off Serena, but the girl ducked and managed to keep away. She attacked again with her magic, but Malagant was not hindered. Terror and surprise filled her as she watched the ill effect of her magic, but she regained her composure and rechanneled her effort.

Malagant suddenly hunched over in pain. His insides were killing him. It was as if they were on fire. He bellowed as another of the Guardian's attacks sent him sprawling on his back. As he struggled to his feet, he noticed the Guardian standing between him and the girl, cane in hand. He struck the ground with it, energy and force rippled from him like a wave. Malagant could only roll with the punch as the effect knocked him back about a good 20 feet.

Malagant glared at them, his red eyes flashing with rage. He wanted to taunt them, dare them, force them to make a mistake of confidence, but Malagant knew to stay would invite death. "You have not seen the last of Malagant, Guardian! We will meet again … you and your friend." With that he launched into the night sky.

The Guardian only watched as the demon flew away. Twice now that demon had managed to escape him, but he couldn't dwell on that now. He could feel her eyes staring at him, and he knew that they were both contemplating the same question and the effect their answers would have on their relationship.

She was wondering what she was doing here. She didn't belong here – she belonged at school with her friends amidst band practice and student council meetings. Those were the light of her world. This place with its dark, dreary; sinister vibe wasn't.

She could feel it in the air, hear it calling her; attempting to seduce her. What to do? She proceeds ahead, caution guiding her steps. A click startled her before a throne appeared illuminated in blue light.

"Hello Sara."

"Who are you? And ... and where am I?"

"Who I am is unimportant – for now. As for where you are – that you already know. Can't you tell, can't you **feel** where you are?"

Someplace evil. "Wha What do you want?"

"What do I want." The man laughed.

Sinister. Dark. Evil.

"Right now I have everything I want." He pointed his hand toward the dark void and another blue light appeared – this time illuminating a column, chained to which was ...

Sara gasped. *Serena. No!* At least it appeared to be Serena Martin, but instead of the vibrant Serena she was accustomed to seeing, this one was pitiful. Her shoulder length hair was tussled and tangled. A once beautiful gown now clung to her in rags, but it was her face that distressed her as the pitiful being turned her head to see Sara. A haunted face filled with a fear and hatred that she could not comprehend.

"Sara! Sara, please help me ... help me." Her voice was filled with desperation.

"What have you done to her?"

"Why punishing her of course.   Her and you."
Joy was laced in his words as he gestured his finger, and a
door opened behind him from which entered a tall, well
built female carrying in her hands a whip. She made her
way toward Serena.

"Why are you so shocked Sara? You knew this
would happen after that day in the park. You both had
your chance and you both choose foolishly, but there's
leniency in your punishment Sara. We believe you to be
manipulated but that was all we could do."

"What do you mean leniency?"

"I mean you have no fear of being chastised.
Unlike your friend here." As the words were spoken, the
female pulled the whip taunt before moving her arm back.
"Observe."

The female threw her arm forward, causing the
whip to strike Serena's back.

"Ahh, I love it when she makes it fun."

"Stop it!" Sara yelled.

"Stop. But we're not even half way done yet."

The female flung another blow on Serena's back.
Her screams filled the room as the flogging continued.

"Stop!" She tried to run to her friend's aid, but
her legs wouldn't move.

"Oh Sara, I thought I had told you. All you can
and will do is watch."

Serena screamed again.

"Please for God's sake stop!"

"Why? This is becoming enjoyable." A laugh escaped his lips.

Sara winced, she could feel Serena's pain as if it were her own.

"Don't you just love the way she resists trying to scream."

"No I don't! What kind of monster are you?"

Serena screamed again.

"Thank you so much."

Another scream.

"Stop it! You'll kill her!"

"If she was only that lucky."

"Punish me instead."

"But I am punishing you Sara. You don't think I can see how painful it is – you watching as your friend endures lash after lash." He laughed again. "Quite amusing isn't it."

Sara closed her eyes hoping to shut the sight away, but her friend's screams resounded in her ears as tears ran down her face. *Please stop it. Stop it please! God make it stop!*

Magnus smiled, he could sense the pain of her helplessness, her hatred, and her guilt. Yes Sara Winters, dream. Immense yourself in your fears. She was not the first whose dreams he had tainted with suffering, and she wouldn't be the last. But he had to admit there was something about her – an intoxication that he never felt from others.

"Magnus."

"So you have returned."

"You said the Guardian would not have help from the girl! Both nearly destroyed me!"

"But they didn't."

Malagant merely growled. "More to my own devices than yours. I have little reason to trust in this plan of yours."

Magnus stepped up to the demon. "Then you are a fool! Do not misjudge genius due to a lack of patience!"

"Delay only aids the Guardian."

Magnus sneered. "Fool! I am two steps ahead of Damien Parker! He moves solely at my will!"

"Then why haven't you destroyed him?"

Geryon Magnus gazed at the night sky as he stepped into St. Louis Cemetery. He could feel this fear, the terror as a scream shrilled in the night. A smile formed on his face as he inhaled the dark taint in the magical energy around him. This is the way it should be. He continued on, navigating the catacombs of tombs and monuments until he reached the desired one.

Foolish humans. Did they believe these trinkets have any effect? He placed his hand upon the cement box; smiling as the eerie green glow luminated around it. He could feel it stirring; feeding off the imbalance of magic. Foolish humans, so weak and gullible. He reflected on the events he had set into motion. Already Sara Winters and Serena Martin were acting upon their nightmares – his nightmares. Erthur Eugene was conducting his religious crusade as if he was playing an instrument to his conduction. Soon all of New Orleans would be divided – providing the hatred and fear needed to free the Maderan. It had taken time to weaken the Voodoo Queen's spell, but it had been time well spent. Soon New Orleans would fall, the Seals would be his. The Pattern would be undone and nothing, not even the Guardian would be able to stop him.

The Guardian of the Seals.

Malagant as usual worried too much. Granted, the boy did possess more power than any of his predecessors and had proven himself resourceful, but still he was young and inexperienced. The mechanics of the demon's plans were already in motion – most of which he was sure Damien Parker had no awareness of. By the time he did find out, it would be too late.

Besides Parker was human and humans were weak – they deserved to be destroyed. Magnus despised the humanity he once possessed; like a plague it kept coming back to haunt him over and over again. But that will soon change. Soon all humans would be destroyed – a mere memory if even that. The Guardian couldn't change that – he would soon be abandoned by Serena Martin. He would be alone – and vulnerable.

Do not underestimate the Guardian, Magnus.

Fool. You give the Guardian too much credit.
He may have defeated Malagant twice, but would he be
able to defeat the banes of humanity itself. We will see,
won't we. We will see.

Sunday
February 9th

Chapter 11

He awoke with a start, scrambling off the
ground. He was in a forest from the look of things.
But how? He recalled something, a dream. No
stronger than a dream – a premonition.

Where was he?

Where were the others? At least he
remembered there being others. He noticed the road
and slowly moved toward it, kneeling in search of
tracks. A noise quickly brought him to his feet.
Someone's coming. His eyes stayed on the road as a
procession slowly made its way towards him.

It was them – all six of them, all on horseback.
Now I remember, the Prince. Of course!

They stopped, all except the black steed of the
warrior woman which reared violently on its hind legs
before being gentled by its master.

"Well, well the shaman has decided to stay
with us after all," the warrior replied. She wore red
armor with a broadsword across her back. A short
sword hung at her waist and a shield hid her lower left
arm.

He remembered the rumors he had heard about her. It was said that she was ageless and had fought in countless battles and have never met defeat. She was imperious to any known magic or weapon. Her helmet was off now, allowing her handsome face to be seen. Black hair flowed down her shoulders and her eyes flashed with confidence. Behind her sat Death, robed and hunched over, his image more pitiful than fearful.

There had been scorn in her voice and the shaman didn't like it. "Judgment coming from one who leisurely rides with death."

The warrior scoffed. "A coward and a fool! He cannot even tell life from death or vice versa. He is a waste of time! We should continue on without him."

All eyes drifted to the tall figure on the white horse. His purple robes and gold cloak only enhanced his natural display of royalty. "You seem to forget it is I who determines who shall and shall not accompany us."

"Your Lordship!"

"Enough." It had been a mere statement but it thundered through the trees. A shadow seems to envelope him and the entire forest came still. "Please," he added softly as the darkness faded.

The warrior merely gave the prince a different look but said nothing.

"You've been with us a long way now," the prince replied. "We'd appreciate it if you'd remain with us."

There was something familiar about him. The shaman knew him from somewhere, from some other place and time. There was something about this forest, something not right and real about it.

Where am I? Why am I here? Answers, I need answers. "Who are you?"

Was that a smile? Why is the prince smiling?

"We are the answers to the questions at hand."

What does that mean? "I'm sorry your Highness, I don't understand."

"Join us and you will understand everything."

What's happening? Something is wrong. Colors and shapes spun around him. Everything started to become hazy and yet everything was also becoming clear. How? Ohmigod! The amazement of the revelation was still upon him when everything went black.

His eyes opened. *Where am I? Who was he?* He sat up. *Seneca Maza. Slidell, Louisiana.* He took a deep breath before rising to his feet and then he remembered. *Why am I not surprised.* He rushed to the dresser and pulled out a shirt.

Join us and you will understand everything.

The spirits will instruct you child.

His grandmother was right, the spirits had instructed him. He tied his hair back before walking over to his desk and pulled open a drawer. Seconds later he pulled out a stapled batch of papers and headed out the door. Now it all became perfectly clear. The person he had to find, the central piece in the oncoming battle was Damien Parker.

Why is this taking so long? It's 12:45! We should be out by now. Why can't our services be more like Catholics – 55 minutes tops – done.

Damien Parker let his head fall into the bowl of his right hand, eyes drifting around the church sanctuary until a painted window caught his attention. *Parker you know full well your bad mood has little to do with time or church service. You're still worked up over last night.*

Last night:

They stood there facing each other.

"Ohmigod! Ohmigod!"

He's still silent. The look on her face said confusion but he knew she was angry, he could feel it scorching the back of his mind like a concentrated sunbeam.

"Damien?"

"We need to talk."

Silence

"Serena."

"Stay away from me! Stay back! I can't deal with this right now, it's too much."

He didn't follow after her or try to call her when he got home. He understood her confusion. It was one thing coming to terms with your own possession of magic, but learning that your boyfriend or girlfriend of nearly two years possessed it as well was definitely a stunning development.

What he didn't understand was her anger. From the way she handled herself she was definitely familiar with the magic so she had to understand why he never told her. He wasn't angry with her for keeping her magical abilities secret, to him it all made perfect sense.

The only thing that really baffled him was why he had never realized it until now. *That's simple Parker. She would still give you that feeling even if she didn't have magic.*

He sighed. Maybe she just needs to calm down, allow rational thought to sink in. However that burning sensation was still in the back of his mind. *Maybe not. I'll never understand women.*

His eyes drifted back to the pulpit, revealing to him a sight that almost caused Damien to yell. "They can't be serious! Are they crazy? How could they allow him to come in here?"

Erthur Eugene in his mind was a disgrace to all servants of the Creator – he was a fanatic opportunist who took advantage of people's fears. He didn't tell people what they needed to hear only what they wanted to hear. No that wasn't the entire truth – his dislike for Erthur

Eugene really came from his hatred of human weakness —
only weak beings found solace in hearing that all of their
problems are someone else's fault; that everything is
entitled to them merely because of some aspect of the
past.

What they're letting him speak! I can't believe this!

"I can't believe this."

Serena Martin paced her bedroom like a trapped
animal while Morgoth sat on the bed listening to her
ramble.

"I can't believe this — all this time he's been able
to do magic and he never told me! Never told me,
Morgoth!"

Morgoth lifted his head from the bed and gave
Serena a bizarre look. "If I recall didn't you keep your
magic hidden from him?"

"I didn't know he possessed magic. If I knew I
would have told him."

"And did it ever occur to you that he may have
had the same train of thought?"

"You don't understand Morgoth, he could be one
of the Nesteas you kept telling me about!"

"Nestari!" Morgoth growled.

"He could be one of the most powerful beings in
the magical world.

"Wait, you knew there was a Nestari in the city
didn't you?"

"Almost every magical creature knows of the Guardian's presence."

"You knew! You knew that one of the Nestari was here and yet you never told me!"

"Serena don't be foolish. Did you ever think as to why in a place that is a focal point of magical energy like New Orleans is, that you hardly ever faced a demon more powerful than a B class. And contrary to what you'd like to think the city had defenders long before you arrived here."

"But you could have told me Morgoth!" the girl hissed.

"Is it my place to tell you? You have senses Serena; their not the most attuned but you could have noticed that there was something to him that made him special other than the fact that he loves you." The golden wolf paused momentarily. " Or maybe you didn't want to see it."

"What do you mean!"

"Look deep down Serena, your anger stems not from the fact that Damien Parker has magic, but that his magic is more powerful than your own

Serena stared at him in disgust. "Morgoth! How can you say such a thing! I've known for years that my magic isn't as powerful as others," she hissed.

"Yes, but you are not as close to them as you are to him. You have great pride in your magic Serena as you should, but pride is becoming something else" The golden wolf jumped from the bed to the floor. "In fact you do seem to be what is the term? A green-eyed monster."

Fury filled her as the words faded across the recess of her mind and for the first time she contemplated using her magic on him, but before she could reflect or act on the matter, the door opened and Morgoth leaped through the window just as her mother entered.

"Serena?"

"Yes ma'am."

"Well sweetie – you've been kind of on the temperamental side lately." She leaned over her daughter's shoulder. "It's not that time of the month is it?" she whispered.

"Mom!"

The older woman grinned. "So how did the movies go last night? You and Damien have a good time?"

"I went to the movies with Sara, Mother."

"Serena. Woman to woman I understand. I know your father doesn't see Damien Parker as you and I do, but eventually he will come to see him for the nice boy that we know him to be. It's just going to take a little time."

Serena sighed. "Yes ma'am I understand."

"Good." The mother gave her daughter a hug. "Remember Serena you don't have to keep secrets from me. I understand the difficulties involved in being a woman, no matter what it is you can always talk to me about it."

"I know now Mother."

There it was again, that word – secrets. She held secrets from her parents, from her friends. Her boyfriend held secrets he kept from his parents. Ha! As close as Damien and his parents it wouldn't surprise her if his parents knew about his magic. None of his friends knew and if he had his way she wouldn't know either. *Am I any better? Here my mother opens the door for me to tell her everything.* Yet she knew she would never be able to tell her mother everything.

"You know you still haven't answered the question sister girl."

Serena eyed her mother suspiciously before giving a faint smile. "The movie was fine. It was after the movies that the problem occurred. I saw a – different side of him."

"What kind of side?" her mother inquired, her voice laced with concern.

"Nothing really bad Mother." *At least I hope it's not bad.* "It's just I thought I knew everything about Damien and yesterday I …" she paused before looking her mother dead in the eye. "Mom did you ever want someone to be something only when you find out they are what you desired, you find yourself wishing he wasn't."

"Ah so that's what it is. Yes I have."

"What did you do?"

"I tried to live with it, but some things are just not meant to be."

"So you ended up regretting it?"

"No, no. While it didn't work out between us for a time we did have something special and nothing will ever change that. Damien is a very promising young man and I have a feeling that you two will have something special no matter what happens."

Serena smiled. "I'll remember that Momma."

"Okay dear." She walked out the door and gently closed it behind her.

Serena's smile faded as the door closed. Yesterday she had to admit she was awestruck by the magical arms that appeared around him. His moves were graceful and magnificent even though she knew he had yet to fully tap into his potential.

Beware the Guardian.

Could she trust him?

Beware the Guardian ...Yes beware of me.

She sighed again. Dream or no dream one thing was certain, the relationship between her and Damien Parker would never be the same.

Chapter 12

Glynn Turner's house was a two story house in the central area of Metairie. As Cole followed Turner's wife Alanna upstairs towards his study, he couldn't help but give an air of approval. While it wasn't as lavished as Cole's house on the Westbank, there was a feeling of homeliness that Cole couldn't help but appreciate.

Glynn Turner could be argued as the focal point in Andrew Fischer's legacy. It was his case that set into motion the events that would lead to the current situation that had Cole here now.

A troubled kid seemingly on the road to nowhere, Turner found himself in Fischer's courtroom facing charges of theft and drug possession. It was his third time committing a felony and any mercy the police or DA might possess had long been spent.

However Turner was given leniency by Andrew Fischer. Instead of 5 to 10 years Turner received a 2 year jail sentence and two years probation after serving his time. In addition he was forced to attend mandatory education programs and from that point on Turner's life complete turned around. By the end of his jail sentence he had earned his G.E.D and started attending classes at nearby Dillard University. Four years later he traveled to nearby Southern University in Baton Rouge to pursue his law degree. Papa Fischer as Turner playfully nicknamed the judge watched with pride as his child climbed the ladder of achievement and like any good father would do; he made sure his ward had a job waiting for him when he graduated 2 years later. At age 27, the boy who had been dismissed as a lost cause was now a judge's clerk in the largest city in Louisiana.

"Ah Mr. Cole. What brings you to my door this nice Sunday afternoon?" He did not look at Cole instead his eyes stayed on a brief he was reading.

"Did you see today's front page?"

"Yes I gave it a glance."

"And what do you think of it?"

"Like the hymn says 'this too shall pass.' Andrew Fischer is a good man and like all of us he does the best he can."

Cole had coolly been admiring the wood panel walls. An eyebrow raised as he heard the statement. He said nothing; instead he casually walked to the desk before quickly slamming his hands down upon it. *That got his attention.* "I don't think you're fully seeing the entire picture. Good God man! Washington and the NAACP are asking for his head! Heck this is unprecedented – the NAACP calling a scalp hunt on a **Black** judge!"

Turner stared Cole dead in the eye. "Come on Cole, he was drunk at a party! He doesn't even remember being in that office, much less what they were talking about!"

"Come on Turner don't tell me you went to Dillard and Southern and didn't get a course in Race and Perception 101. Let me give you a refresher though. Black judge is in White man's office taking money then 2 weeks later White boy is let loose who is related to guy who handed Black judge the money! No matter how you add it up it all equals B.A.D Bad!"

"So what do you want me to do?"

Cole leaned closer. "Convince Fischer to resign."

"What's wrong? Last I recall the mayor didn't mind seeing the judge under fire. What, the fire is spreading to City Hall?"

"You don't see the amplitude of this situation. This has us on the verge of something this city has not seen for a long time. This could light this whole city up! We can't have this during the largest tourist attraction of the year, and with Erthur Eugene being here you know that is a real possibility. So tell me what you want Glynn – order or chaos?"

Damien Parker growled as he started at the computer screen searching frantically for an answer but for the umpteenth time his efforts returned nothing. *God this riddle is crazy! Let's try this again. Two times I've seen seven people in the Dreamtime. Madame Fi La Reye's riddle has me seeking six. No seven, it has to be seven, but who? Could it be the seven are the one who suppose to gather? If that is the case where are they?*

"Damien?"

Damien almost snapped, but stopped when he looked into the face of Seneca Maza.

Seek those who guard the land. Maybe he's sought me. Luck? Whatever it is I'll take it. "Seneca? What brings you here? Kind of far from the 'Dell isn't it?"

"Lookin' for you to be honest."

He must be one of them. "Me? Why?"

Seneca's face flushed with embarrassment. "I had a vision this morning and you were in it."

"Your dream didn't happen to include six other people did it?"

"Counting myself yeah seven in all."

Coincidence? Right. He looked around before grabbing Seneca and dragged him toward the nearest table. "Okay, tell me everything."

Part of Seneca wondered why he was doing this. It had been a dream nothing more – a fantasy conjured by all the gibberish of his grandmother and Damien Parker. The rest of him knew better.

"It came early this morning. I awoke to find smoke figures surrounding me, calling me. Then there's this mist and the next thing I know I was in a forest dressed in the garbs of a shaman. Six others appeared on horseback – a female knight who addressed me as a shaman. Riding with her was a cross between the hunchback of Notre Dame and the grim reaper – and I called him Death."

Could the paladin be a woman?

"I remember the Knight scoffing me, saying I don't know the difference between death and life. Also there's the lady – a radiant figure in a silver gown that glowed like the full moon at night. She was accompanied by two other women apparently by their appearances – her wards.

Then there was the prince – you."

Damien gave him a confused look. "Me?"

"Yes. It took a few minutes for me to recognize you, but nevertheless it was you. You were wearing a purple and gold robe and you were authoritive and powerful in ways that permeate the common definition. Don't ask me how or why, but somehow I knew that he was the key to everything. The one who could answer my questions."

"Did I? I mean he?"

"Actually you gave me more questions than answers. But you did say that this group was the key to all the answers and that if I joined you I would eventually have them." He laughed. "Next thing I know I awoke to find myself back in my room. So Damien I accept your offer – the spirits instructed me to join you, so here I am."

Damien Parker had been listening in earnest as Seneca Maza described his dream and the similarities between their two dreams gave him a newfound hope. *So seven is the magic number and that seven includes me. That leaves 5 others.*

"Did you recognize any of the others?"

"No."

"Would you recognize them if you saw them in person?"

"Of course."

"Funny your Dreamtime experience seemed a lot clearer than mine."

"Speaking of which, what did happen when you meditated with my grandmother?"

"I had a vision – almost exactly like yours. To be honest the third such vision in as many nights."

"Wait a minute! You trying to tell me we had the same dream!"

"Similar," Damien replied with a strong emphasis. "Similar, very similar but not the same. My dream had seven individuals, but at first they were children. However yesterday in the park with your grandmother, they were older – four girls and three boys. Among them a girl in a silver gown, a Native American shaman, a tall female warrior and a prince just like in your dream. They were talking to me."

"What did they say?"

"They commanded me to say my name."

"Sounds simple to me. Did you?"

"I couldn't. I was pulled from the Dreamtime before I could. What was real confusing was they asked me to say their names as well." He frowned for a second. "What race was everyone in your dream?"

Seneca hesitated for a moment, wondering what relevance did that have. "Hmm myself – Indian, one White person, and including you four Blacks."

"What about the Grim Reaper?"

"That monstrosity! I don't know I couldn't see its face, but I guarantee you that thing is a what, not a who!"

"Then who represents the wind?"

"Oh now I see. You really think this has to do with that legend?"

"So far it makes sense. Both our visions had us searching for seven people. Three of which are of the four designated races."

"Note three. Why only tell us of three Guardians when we need four and what about the other three."

Damien shrugged his shoulders and sighed, but he did have a point and there was little room for error when dealing with these things. Even reasonable assumptions could put them on the path to ruin. "We still haven't accounted for the skeleton."

"The Grim Reaper? That's death! What else is there to account for?"

"But didn't you say the knight scolded you about not knowing life and death. Wind according to the legend was the vessel for knowledge. Isn't life and death often assailed in religion and philosophy as an understanding of the world around us?"

"Yeah I guess."

"So maybe the Grim Reaper is really a representative of wind."

"The Grim Reaper is an Asian! One question why?"

"You are asking the wrong individual."

"Come on Damien that's crazy."

"Is it? Did you see the Grim Reaper's face?"

"No, but no Oriental can look that short and deformed even if he was face to face with Fat Man at Nagasaki!"

"I'll admit it does sound crazy, but trust me things will be even crazier by the end of this. Come on."

"Wait up!", Seneca interjected while chasing after him. "What do you mean? How do you know its gonna get crazier?"

"I've done this before." He gave him a look. "I'm curious, how did you know I was here?"

"Your father told me when I went by your house."

A look of disappointment flashed across his face. "Oh. I thought the spirits had told you."

"Nope. Sorry to disappoint."

"Don't worry about it." He smiled as a familiar sensation flooded through him causing his smile to fade. *Something is here. And it's not good. But from where?* He focused, searching as far as his abilities would allow him. *Come on. Come on. There in the park.* "Seneca I need a favor."

"What is it?"

"I need you to find your grandmother, I need some information from her."

"About the Guardians? Bu…"

"No. About something else. Ask her what she knows about a Maderan."

"A Maderan? What the heck is a Maderan?"

"I'll explain later."

"What do you mean you'll explain later! Damien where are you going?"

"No time to explain. I'm assuming you still have my number right?"

"Yeah."

"Good."

"Damien!" The Indian sighed before letting loose a growl, "Why do I even try?"

"Yeah I'll be there in a little bit Ma," Enrica finished before flicking off her cell phone and tucking it into her purse. She was strolling through City Park where there was suppose to be this fly concert. Only thing that was flying though were the birds. A sound in a nearby bush caused her to pause, a second later her eye caught sight of the culprit.

Smiling, Enrica crept around the bush before dropping to her knees. "Look how cute." She reached out and grabbed. To her surprise it didn't try to get away. "Look at the cute little bunny," she cooed. "Such a cute little bunny. Give me kissy." She gently stroked its soft fur as she continued through the park. She had never been much of an animal lover – she hated dogs, detests cats, but there was something about rabbits that did something to her. She didn't know what it was, all she knew was that whenever she saw anything in the rabbit family she turned into some kind of maternal monster.

The rabbit, which from its size was barely beyond its baby days, seemed to take well with its human stepmother. The animal merely sat in the girl's arms, its head occasionally moving around. One could have accused the animal of mumbling from the way its mouth moved. However the animal didn't make a sound, that was until a man's German Shepherd saw the bunny and snapped at it. Panicking the rabbit tired to hop out of Enrica's arms, but at the last possible moment the girl tucked the rabbit in her arms like a running back receiving a football and what happened next scared Enrica to death.

Andra Alexander just couldn't get herself into the game. Part of her wondered if she wanted to. It was the third Tulane game she had been to this year. She recalled last December when a recruiter flew her to Duke University to watch a game there. Oh she could feel the pressure, most definitely there was the pressure to win, but it was not as terrifying as what she felt at LSU, Tulane or Auburn. Even John Ehret seemed wanting compared to what she felt at Cameron Indoor Stadium.

At Duke it seemed as if the audience really appreciated the game and understood the stakes involved and strived to relieve the player's burden as much as possible.

She recalled Achilles Harmon, how they shared a common degree of loneliness. It was lonesome being her, beneath all the recruitment, news coverage, and magazines there was a core of pressure and loneliness. She considered herself lucky – at least she had one parent and there existed the possibility of getting her father back in her life. Achilles didn't have that option, both of his parents were gone – taken. *In a sense I don't blame him. If I lost Mom I'd probably consider ending it all.*

A shot by a Tulane player caused the center to explode jolting Andra from her train of thought.

The demon could not help but feel disgust as he silently slipped into the room where Victor Morris sat watching a basketball game with a few of his friends. His mind was as simple as a child's textbook. Look at them, he thought, weak and pathetic. How such cretins were left with free will he would never understand. The creator was foolish to place such faith in these creatures. There could be only one justice for men – slavery or destruction.

He crept upon the foolish boy before softly grabbing his shoulders. Victor didn't move, rather he continued conversing with his friends while Magnus entered his mind and began sowing his seeds of manipulation.

Remember how she humiliated you yesterday. Threw Damien Parker all in your face. Why? She's challenging you, she wants to see if you are a real man. To see if you can master her.

Yes, Victor agreed, she's testing my authority, my manhood. I'll show her. I'll prove myself worthy of her. I will show her that I am the master she seeks.

Magnus smiles. It had been too easy. To Victor Morris those were his own words, his own deductions.

Why should he not believe them? Yes the fool was thoroughly convinced that Serena Martin wanted him and in his lust he would do anything to get her. Anything. Now that the pieces were set, it was now time to spring his trap. Magnus once again laughed as he slipped out the room.

    Sara knew something was bothering Serena, but she couldn't figure out exactly what. Yesterday she had been so excited and now ... probably something her father said. Serena had recounted to her time and time again about her father's disapproval of Damien Parker. What Sara couldn't understand was why.   "I take it your dad wasn't thrilled to find out you went to the movies with Damien."

    "No actually he still doesn't know."

    Sara's eyes widened. "What Damien didn't like his jersey?"

    "No he loved it. Sara?"

    "Yes."

    "Have you ever thought something of somebody, only to learn that they were somebody totally different?"

    The girl's face avidly displayed her bewilderment. "Yeah."

    "I mean someone you were really close to. Someone you thought would tell you everything about them yet kept a tantalizing secret."

    "Well, don't we all keep things from people – nightmares, bad experiences, crushes? I mean come on

Serena I'm sure you haven't told me every single aspect of your life."

Serena eyed her in shock.

"And you shouldn't," Sara finished.

Serena turned toward the mirror, staring at the image that stared back at her, wondering if she could see her soul in the glass. What kind of soul would I have, she wondered.

She wasn't entirely sure if she could say that Sara Winters was her best friend, but out of the people she knew in New Orleans there no one else closer except Damien Parker. It was Sara who befriended her when she first transferred to John Ehret, who showed her where everything was, who gave her that friendly smile whenever she needed it. It was Sara in whom she confided her feelings for Damien Parker. There was nothing she kept from Sara, nothing except her magic. She feared her finding out, dreading the effect it would have on their friendship, or was it something else. *Is Morgoth right?*

"Something happened last night."

Sara almost stopped breathing, her recent nightmares came to mind. "Did something happen to Damien?"

"No Damien's fine. What makes you think something happened to him?'

Should I tell her about the dreams? No it was just a dream Sara, nothing more. "So what happened?"

"We … we had an argument."

"That's not unusual," Sara chimed. "I mean couples argue all the time. I mean it's your first argument right?"

"Yeah. I mean it's not a big deal, it's just that it kind of bothers me a little that we actually had an argument." *Liar. It bothers you a lot.*

"I could see why it would bother you."

"Sara I'm fine. I just need to get out. Come on, let's go to the Riverwalk."

"Yeah it is such a nice day and maybe the fresh air will get your mind off Damien."

Serena turned and gave her a look Sara had never seen before. "Here's the deal. No bringing up that name OK."

"All right," Sara responded as they left the room.

The door closed with a thud as the sound of footsteps on wood echoed through the house.

"Enrica, is that you?"

"Yes Ma," she hurried into her room and softly closed the door before collapsing onto the floor, hugging herself.

Ohmigod, Ohmigod It happened again! Just like the last time.

She couldn't recall how they made their way up to her, but they seemed so innocent, so pitiful she couldn't help but give them a hug, just to let them know someone cared. Then it happened, she couldn't explain how but she could feel their hunger, an emptiness that she couldn't fathom. She could feel the invisible bands connecting them and then the hunger pains seem to diminish as another feeling grew stronger, a feeling of nourishment, of fulfillment. Scared she pulled away, her face frozen with fear and confusion.

Those children thought I was an angel. Even now she could see them smiling, running around the hall with the usual vigor of four years. Two children whose faces showed pain and fatigue only moments before. *And I had done it ... I had done it. But how? Why? And then it happened again today. I felt everything, its fear, its pain, its memories. What's wrong with me? Am I a saint or some kind of freak?* She pulled her legs further in, extending her arms further around herself. *Why is this happening to me?*

Sara was grinning from ear to ear as she and Serena Martin walked along the Riverwalk near downtown New Orleans. They had spent about two hours browsing through the shops and Sara honestly believed it had served its purpose. Serena seemed to be herself again.

"Feeling better?"

"About what?"

"About your argument with Damien."

"Oh that. I had almost forgotten all about it." Which was a complete lie. For the last hour and a half all she had done was think about that night and about earlier today. *Was Morgoth right?* She had believed that she was angry with him because he had kept his magical abilities secret even though his intentions were solely to protect her from those would hurt her to get to him. *The truth is …* The truth of the matter was that Morgoth was right, part of her was jealous – for the first time she was no longer the great hope protecting her peers. She was second to a being greater than her in power and knowledge – a being who was her peer.

She had convinced herself that she detested the uniqueness that her magic brought when the truth was she cherished it. She took great pride in knowing that among her peers she alone could naturally use magic. No, that couldn't be the complete reason. While she will admit to being envious of the Guardian she was not that shallow.

Beware the Guardian … Yes Serena, beware of me!

Her dream. Despite all that she and Damien had shared, despite watching him fight against Malagant, she … she didn't trust him, not like before. Where did that leave her?

"Sorry," Sara apologized softly. She gave her a book and started smiling again, but her smile suddenly faded as her eyes caught the glimpse of a man. *No it can't be! That was a dream! No! He can't be real, but he is and if he's real then …* She glanced back at Serena in horror. *No, no that can't happen.*

"Sara, you ok?"

No I'm not ok! Calm yourself Sara. Calm down.
"Serena."

"Yeah. You sure you ok? You look like you just saw a ghost."

Sara glanced back before stopping Serena. "Serena."

"Yes."

"Yesterday ... I had a dream about you."

"Okay."

"You had been kidnapped and imprisoned by a man who tortured you while I helplessly watched. I dismissed it as nothing but a dream, but then I just saw him."

"Saw who?"

"The man from my dream. Oh God Serena there he was in plain sight. God what if that dream was a premonition of some kind?"

"Sara, Sara calm down. Now where is he?"

Sara turned and pointed. "He was right over there!" she exclaimed.

Serena followed the finger's lead. A man was standing there, but what grabbed her attention was the tall immense figure that stood behind him. He was partly hidden in the shadows, but she saw enough to recall his name.

Malagant.

She reached into her purse. God I pick a perfect time to leave my cell phone in the car. "Look Sara, here are the keys. I want you to go back to the car grab my cell phone and call Damien Parker. Just hit any of the arrow keys when you turn it on and it should show a list of names. Tell him Malagant is on the Riverwalk."

"What? Why call Damien? Why not the police?"

"Sara trust me, Damien is better suited for this."

"What if he's not there?"

"Pray that he is. Go! There's no time to loose."

"Serena, let me go with you."

"Sara go I won't do anything dumb or dangerous. Go!"

A sigh of reluctance came from Sara Winters before she started back toward the car. Serena waited until she was out of sight before returning her attention to Malagant. Where did he go? There. She hurried at a brisk pace as she pursued him into the parking lot of the Convention Center. She kept a safe distance, creeping from car to car when the demon abruptly stopped. From the shadows emerged a male figure. *Was this Sara's mysterious man.*

"Hello Serena," a voice hissed.

Serena quickly turned. "Victor! What are you doing here?"

"I've been waiting for you."

"Waiting for me? Victor I don't have time for your ..." she paused, a strange feeling filled her as a shadow loomed over her. Seconds later a blow knocked her to the ground and hands fell upon her. She struggled trying to summon her magic, but before she could unleash it a flash filled her eyes and an explosion filled her head. The last thing she heard as she slipped into unconsciousness was horrible laughter and a voice inquiring something about being her master.

Chapter 13

Damien Parker froze as a strange sensation slammed into his awareness. His reflexes slowed as the sensation flooded through him leaving a slight migraine, but also an empty feeling of concern that tingled every one of his senses with alarm.

He was familiar with being flooded by sensations, every time there was a ripple in the magical balance the wave of that disturbance crashed into him like the tide at the beach. However there was something different about this – it seemed more distinctive, almost personal. Only one voice crying in the dark and even more bizarre the voice seemed to be calling for him specifically. But from who?

Who ever it was unfortunately they would have to wait. There was still the matter of this demon apparition that he was following. It was evil, yet the presence it sent was not the same as any creature he had faced before in his battles against the Abyss. *Whatever it is it must be fearless to be prowling about in open daylight.* He made his way out of the park, pausing for a moment before continuing down Loyola Avenue away from the French Quarter.

To be honest he was surprised by the move, usually most demons tried to draw him into the French Quarter, which was always filled with people and with its short streets and numerous alleys the perfect place to either lose or ambush someone.

His pace quickened as he smoothly turned the corner of Loyola and Poydras expecting to run dead into the apparition. To his surprise though, nothing happened.

What? No way it could have known that I would take Loyola?
He turned, searching frantically for the vile creature. *Come
on. Come on, where are you?* His concentration waned as the
sound of a car honk filled his ears and the image of Andra
Alexander caught his eye.

She was in her red Ford Mustang and Damien
found himself wishing he had been born a girl. Girls just
had to give a look and bat an eye and they got whatever
they wanted. Let him ask his father for a Mustang and see
what happens.

Sure son as soon as you give me some Mustang money.

Who was he kidding? He could have been the
reincarnation of Jesus Christ he would still have to "earn"
whatever he wanted.

"You look lost. Need a ride?" Andra chimed as
she pulled the car over to the curb.

"Nah just lost my walking partner that's all."

"Would that be Serena?"

"Nah I'd never lose her. Besides she's mad at me
right now."

"Damien Parker in the doghouse! Now that's a
sign of the Apocalypse."

"Ha, ha!" Damien laughed back sarcastically.

"Well you two better make up. I'd hate to see
such a cute couple break up."

Damien now stared at her dumbfounded. *Boy for
two nobodies we sure have a lot of observers.* "I can only try
Andra."

"Damien Parker, the model Stoic of John Ehret High. Don't try to front, you know you would be devastated if you two broke up so you better do more than try you better …"

Damien noticed that she seem to be looking behind him and from the look on her face. He turned and sure enough there it was – the apparition he had seen at the library, but he was more amazed at the realization that just dawned on him.

Andra can see it

"Andra stay here." He turned to pursue, his hands gripping tightly the cane he had pulled from his tote bag. Already he could feel the warmth of the magic coursing through him. *Where are you? Typical. Do these creeps have any idea how predictable --* He ducked anticipating the attack as the sword sliced through the space his head had previously occupied a second ago. The Guardian backed away so he could eye his attacker and he didn't like what he saw – a Shaq sized behemoth covered with azul armor laced with spikes and spines. On its belt was an assortment of arms: a mace, a battle ax, and a small sword. In its hand was a broadsword whose blade was almost as tall as Damien.

I guess the Abyss decided to take off the gloves. He ducked again as the broadsword came flying toward his head. *Let's see if this metallic Wilt Chamberlain wannabe can take as much as it dishes.* He could feel the magic lancing from him, a fury of power that generated sparks the size of soccer balls as it collided with the armored being.

The creature stumbled back, but only slightly. The Guardian again took the offensive – white bolts of magic pounded on the giant warrior knocking it back. Leaving nothing to chance the Knight of the Order moved in for the kill.

Suddenly an uneasiness fell upon him. His head was throbbing and his insides churned furiously. Worse, everything started spinning. He tried to focus, but for some reason he had difficulty concentrating. *Why are my legs feeling like jello? I feel like I've been running a marathon for two days straight.* It was then he noticed the hands around his waist. *What the ...* He twisted and maneuvered himself into a Tai Chi throw.

He found himself gasping for air and the only thing that kept him from collapsing onto the ground was his cane. He edged closer, curious as to who or what had the ability to do this.

The answer sickened him. It looked human, but it was deformed and thin. The catlike eyes seemed on the verge of popping out of their sockets. Chunks of the yellowish skin seem to flow down the creature's body the way real glass flowed in windows.

God it looks like it went through the Bataan Death March, the Holocaust and 25 to life in a Russian Gulag all in succession. He spun around, quickly unleashing his magic. The attack sent the giant monster backpedaling. "Like I was saying earlier. Do you creeps understand how predictable y'all are?" He yelled as purple bolts lashed out from the cane wrapping around the azul knight. The Knight of the Order closed in and slowly the azul knight was forced to its knees.

Oh no you don't. He turned his waist and adjusted the magic so that the bolts flowed from his free hand, sending the second apparition crashing back into the wall. *I barely felt him coming. But how? It must have to do with the close proximity of the two. For some reason my senses seem to think of them as being one... No way.* The world suddenly became a blur and when it cleared the Guardian was seeing the sky before the image of a descending mace caused him to roll out the way.

He flung his cape over his body and summoned a cloak of shadows. He trudged towards the wall, carefully trying to avoid the deformed apparition as it came near. Its bulging eyes searching wildly before moving toward the giant specter.

The Guardian gave a sigh of relief, but knew he wasn't out of the woods yet. He could barely stand and was probably in serious need of the Resurrect Sleep. He crept slowly and cautiously along the wall, managing to place himself behind the armored colossus.

Now's my chance. He took a breath and prepared to attack when with amazing quickness and immense power the armored monster elbowed him in the stomach.

The assault knocked the breath from his lungs and he collapsed on one knee. Worse his cloak of invisibility vanished revealing the vulnerable Guardian. *How did it know I was there?* He struggled to breathe as a scream filled his ears. *Andra! Didn't I tell her to ...* He caught sight of the girl who was hiding behind a waste bin. *She'll be killed. I have to do something.* He snatched off his cape and flung it toward the girl with all his might. The cloak seemed to sail on the air itself as it magically expanded and enveloped Andra Alexander in a human sized metallic cocoon.

That should keep her safe and out the way. He brought up his staff to deflect the blow of the mace. The staff held off the blow, but the force of the effort knocked Damien flat on his back as the armored nightmare stood over him, preparing to bring down its mace again.

Why is it hesitating? He rolled his eyes back and to his surprise in front of Andra was a knight sitting upon a horse. Its breastplate and helmet were a fiery red and the armor protecting its arms and legs were gold. In its hand was a long silver sword. The horse raised its hind legs before charging toward the behemoth. The Guardian rolled out the way and watched as the charger galloped past him and collided with the armored giant creating an explosion of light that forced him to shield his eyes. When he finally opened them the charger and the apparition were gone. He fell onto his back in exhaustion.

"Andra? Wake up. Can you hear me Andra?"

Her eyes opened to see Damien Parker. A moment passed before she quickly sat upright. "Why did you throw that thing over me? I almost suffocated!"

Damien gave her a perplexed look. "Andra, what are you talking about?"

"What am I talking about? I'm talking about you stuffing me in some kind of opaque giant saran wrap while facing some kind of metallic monster!"

Damien gave her a glance before sighing. "You could have hit your head pretty hard. Relax."

"How can I relax? There's a giant monster on the loose?"

"I'll admit he was a pretty big guy, but I wouldn't call him a monster."

"He was wearing dark armor like some Middle Age knight and you was in a bodysuit of some kind."

"A bodysuit? Me?"

"And what happened to your hat?"

"What hat? Look Andra I don't know what happened, but ..."

"No someone, something was really here!"

"Someone was here. We heard a scream and you saw someone and I chased him to this alley, but he managed to slip by me. Next thing I know I hear you scream and I found you lying on the ground."

"What?"

"You sure you ok? If you want we can go to the hospital?"

"No," Andra interrupted. "I'm fine." *Could I have been dreaming?*

"Here let me help you up."

"Thanks." *But it seemed so real.* "Damien you ok?"

"I'll be fine."

"You sure? You're holding your side."

"Just a knock on the side. Like I said the guy managed to get the jump on me."

"You're all right! You're sure you can ..."

"I'm fine. I'm not parked too far from here."

Andra gave him a suspicious glance. "Okay." She backed away slowly and paused before turning and disappearing around the corner.

"Grandma! Grandma! Open up."

A minute before a click sounded and the door opened revealing the face of Jadzia Maza. "Yes child what is it?"

Seneca quickly walked in and bend over to catch his breath. "I ... I need your help Grandmother."

"What for child?" the elderly woman responded.

"I need to know about a Maderan."

Jadzia Maza's bronze face nearly turned white. "Dark things you seek knowledge of child," she replied harshly. "Dark things!"

"So you do know what this thing is that Damien is talking about?"

"Know of yes. Only darkness this path leads to. What brings you to seek such a path?"

"The spirits instructed me to, Grandmother."

"The spirits! Explain child."

"I talked to the spirits. I concentrated. I let go and they came to me. The spirits came to me!"

"Of course child. The spirits seek to enlighten us all. Continue."

"Well they told me to find Damien Parker, so I did and now we were talking about these people we are suppose to find and then at the last minute something spooks him and he runs off, but not before ordering me to ask you about a Maderan."

"A grave development this is." The woman shook her head.

"Will somebody tell me what a Maderan is? And what does it have to do with me and Damien Parker?"

"Come child, all will soon be revealed."

Chapter 14

Damien Parker groaned as he collapsed onto the patio chair in the backyard. His head was still spinning and his side was aching as he leaned back into the chair. In the west he could see the purple and orange sky surrounding the setting sun.

Another day and I'm still no where closer to finding out what all this means.

He closed his eyes briefly as he tried to will away the pain. For the most part he had come out that battle fairly intact. *Yeah who are you trying to fool Parker, you probably have a cracked rib, maybe two ... but it could be a lot worse.*

He fought to keep his eyes open, but they closed and he drifted into unconsciousness.

Damien ... Damien Parker

He awoke with a start in the darkness. He was on a bus. *A bus? How? Am I in the Dreamtime?* No, he couldn't be --- there was something different about this place, something unusual that he normally didn't feel in the Dreamtime – a void of some kind.

Is this reality and he just awoke from the Dreamtime? "What?"

Guardian ...

That voice. It's coming from somewhere on this bus. Someone knows I'm a Guardian of the Cross, but who? Is it a friend ... or a foe.

Come to me Guardian.

He dragged himself from his seat, glancing around, searching for whoever this person could be.

Guardian.

The back. Damien slowly made his way up the aisle, his eyes still looking, still searching and then he saw him – the face from his dream, the face in the fire and sitting next to him was …

"Yes it's really her.   Surprising how easy it was to capture her."

Damien started to advance, but the motion of the two disguised demons in the adjacent seats stopped him. That and the realization that his staff was missing.

"What do you want?"

"Ah the direct type. I like that. I want the seals." He stroked Serena's cheek. Damien fought back the impulse to attack him.

"What are you talking about?"

"Oh don't play coy Parker."

"This is between you and me. Leave Serena out of this."

"But she is involved. She is a servant of the Order as are you, but if you want her you'll have to come get her."

"Get her? From where?"

"No where too far. The old Westwego Airport."

"Hun? Wait!"

He only laughed and the last thing Damien sees is Serena's face and the plea in her eyes.

I'll be waiting Guardian.

His eyes opened slowly as the cool wind caressed his face. The patio. Then the bus, the demon, Serena. The Dreamtime. *But what does it mean? The seals?*

I'm afraid it is exactly what was said.

"Oracle I thought you couldn't enter the Dreamtime with me?"

"I can't, but that wasn't the Dreamtime. It was a message."

"What? It couldn't be."

"It is."

"How do you know? For all I know it could be a trick to interrupt me from stopping the demon."

"I assure you Damien, the message is real."

No! Oracle had warned him about this and now … No it couldn't be happening.

I don't believe it. I don't.

The squeak of the back door caught his attention. "I thought I heard you back here," his mother said.

"Yes ma'am just watching the sunset that's all. Isn't that right Snowy." The dog licked his hand as it gently stroked the dog's nose. The animal noticed the mistress of the house and advanced toward her, only to have Marie Parker yell and bat her hands in the poor animal's face.

Dejected the animal slowly returned to Damien and settled next to his chair, head rising in ecstasy as his master scratched behind his ears.

"Oh yeah there was a call for you from a Sara Winters," his mother said. "Something about meeting Serena downtown and Malagant being on the Riverwalk."

Damien jumped out of his chair. "When was this?"

"She called while you were at the library. Who is Malagant?"

"An annoying pest," he answered as he ran toward the phone. "Did Sara leave a number to call back?" He tapped the caller id. *Serena's cell phone.* He dialed the number hoping and praying that Serena answered. A hope that receded with each ring and faded when another voice answered.

"Who is this?"

"This is Sara? Damien is that you?"

"Yeah Sara it's me. Is Serena with you?"

"No! I haven't seen her since she send me to call you and that was about an hour ago."

Damien Parker's body froze, his mind completely oblivious to the world around him as the realization settled in.

"Concentrate. Feel."

I'm concentrating! I'm concentrating! His nostrils flared resulting in a cough. "Where are we?" he sputtered. His annoyance grew with each echo of his question. It ignited when he realized he was alone. "Where am I?"

"At the Eternal Temple."

"What temple? I thought **we** were going to see the spirits to answer my questions!"

"If I recall child I said that all would be revealed to you."

"I hate to be the bringer of bad news Grandmother, but nothing is being revealed to me right now!" Eternal Temple. There was nothing here but fog. Why is it so cold? His eyes noticed the reminisce of a trail. "Am I suppose to follow this? Grandmother!"

Silence.

"Grandmother!" He sighed and started up along the trail. He had not been walking long when he stopped, surprised by the strange fog that now surrounded him. *Jesus Christ What's next?*

He continued walking, only this time at a slower pace, hoping that he was still on the path. The fog by now was so thick he could barely see around himself. "Okay Grandma a little help would be nice!" He continued on and noticed a lift in the fog. His eyes made out the outline of a wooden hut.

Okay now what? Am I suppose to enter the hut? He contemplated a decision when he noticed the fog had made it for him. The fog had once again thickened in every direction – except one.

The spirits will guide you child.

The spirits will guide me. Well let's see where they want me to go. He approached the door to the hut. Slowly lifted up and veil and stepped in.

"Okay something's up," Seneca thought as he surveyed his surroundings. He was seeing it, but he couldn't believe it. He had entered a hut barely big enough for six people and now he was seeing this. It was incredible. It reminded him of those pictures he had seen of Mayan temples in his classes and on the Discovery channel, but nothing in class had prepared him for this. The walls seemed to climb forever and as far as he could see there was no roof. "This is incredible!"

"We are glad you appreciate the beauty of the Eternal Temple."

Seneca wheeled around. "Who said that?" he barked.

"We did."

"Do not be afraid."

He followed the voices, but he couldn't believe the source they were coming from. They were hovering above a pulpit, one far longer than any he had seen before. There were four of them – neither possessed a human shape, rather they were columns of light and gas. Miniature stars for lack of a better word.

"Welcome Seneca Maza." A masculine voice came from the red star on the left end. "As you may know you are entitled to four questions."

Four questions. Already he had thousands of questions, none of which pertained to the objective which had sent him. *Is it really them? Him? It? How do you address the spirits?* He nearly blurted out a question when a voice in his head reminded him of purpose. Four questions.

"Where in the city known as New Orleans is the creature known as a Maderan imprisoned?"

"Sealed beneath the tomb of the water child – she who is known as the Voodoo Queen." It was the yellow specter that answered. Its feminine voice caressed him like a lullaby sung by a loving mother.

"How could it be freed?"

"One would merely have to disrupt the balance enough for the Maderan to receive enough hatred and fear to feed upon and free itself from the seal of the Voodoo Queen." This time the blue one answered with a deep masculine voice laced with a booming authoritive bass that reminded him of Barry White.

Two questions left. *Better make them good.*

"Is there currently anyone in New Orleans who can destroy the Maderan?"

"Yes." Again the feminine voice filled him with comfort.

Last question. "How can one of the Chosen kill the Maderan?"

"The Maderan is a powerful creature," the blue spirit replied, "but it can be killed by any of the Nestari – but only if they have faith in themselves and their purpose."

"We have answered your questions."

Seneca's eyes moved over to the green specter shimmering in the center. It was the first time he had heard it speak. He found himself in awe by the gentle voice, but it was not done yet. It moved slowly, levitating on air until it was directly in front of him. "And now Seneca Maza, we have a question for you."

"Serena."

The haziness disappeared as her eyes slowly opened and a moan oozed from her lips. She tried to move but found the effort difficult.

"She's awake. Are you all right?"

"Who are you?" She sat up but the world began spinning and fell back against the wall.

"A friend. What were you doing in that parking garage?"

Parking garage. She remembered now, she had followed Malagant to the parking garage when someone snuck up behind her.

"Did you see who attacked me."

"Ms. Martin, that doesn't answer my question."

She shook her head before trying to survey her surroundings. The man in front of her was slightly taller than Damien Parker, his blue eyes blazed with a light of urgency. "Who are you? And how do you know who I am?"

"As for who you are I took the liberty of checking your id." A short figure emerged from the shadows carrying her purse. "As for who I am you could say I am in the balancing business."

"The balancing business? What kind of explanation is that?"

"Clarification can come later. Right now I want to know why you were following that man in the parking garage."

"I can explain that later, but right now I need to know who attacked me."

"Kind of strange really. He looked like an ordinary high schooler but ..."

"But what?"

He possessed some kind of staff. He looked like a Knight of the Order if he hadn't ..."

"If he hadn't what?"

"If he hadn't changed, I would have believed he was one of the Nestari."

Serena fought the wooziness, eager to find out whatever or whoever attacked her. "What did he change into?"

"He became this kind of beast. The next thing I knew I saw you turn around and the instant after you were on the ground."

Serena merely sat there stupidified.

Yes the seeds of mistrust germinates. "The creature dragged you over to where the man was standing, another being stepped out of the shadows."

"Malagant."

"What? How do you know of …"

"I was following him. I had sent Sara to get … and I followed him." Her voice was a series of mumbles. Her eyes were blank. It was as if her soul had been sucked right out of her.

"Wait you mean you can see? Then you can use magic."

"Yes," she stammered.

"I'm sorry. My name is Magnus. I was pursuing Malagant and another demon which lead me to New Orleans."

"Are you one of the Chosen?"

"No I was here to warn one of them – a Knight of the Order who was suppose to be residing here, a Guardian of the Cross."

"Damien Parker."

"Who?"

"Damien Parker, he's the Guardian of the Cross?"

"Are you sure?" His eyes noticed a small set of eyes in the shadows. He knew who it was; he had been waiting for him because it meant that Damien Parker had arrived to rescue Serena Martin.

Now the bait has attracted the game. Now all I need to do now is wait to spring the trap.

Chapter 15

Damien Parker really couldn't remember how long he stood there lost in his own fantasy world of pity and anxiety, however he eventually managed to will himself to action and instinct took over from there. First he had ordered Sara to take Serena's car to her home and wait for his instructions. It took some convincing, but eventually he got the girl to agree.

That left only one other thing for him to do. The orange pinkish sky was now dark purple as he rode into the abandoned airport outside the suburb of Westwego, waiting for Magnus to make the next move.

Time and time again Oracle had warned him about this very situation. He already had an idea as to what Magnus' strategy would be.. With Serena came the possibility of forcing him to a mistake. The Guardian would act with his heart and not his head; and that would enable the demon to destroy him. The sad thing was his plan may work. *Would you sacrifice yourself for her knowing what that would mean for the city, for the world?*

He didn't have to answer because he already knew he would.

His train of thought was disturbed as a strong sensation came over him. *Okay you want me to play follow the leader hun. Okay I'll play along.* He edged the motorcycle ahead toward the impending encounter.

"Wait someone is here."

"Who?" Serena inquired.

"I'm not sure." He walked over to the railing and managed a sly smile as the door to the warehouse slid open and a tall teenager stepped through. Immediately his eyes glanced up and locked upon Magnus' face. His eyes displayed a confidence that Magnus found annoying. He wanted to turn away and yet he couldn't.

Damien wasn't surprised by the face, he had encountered it twice in the Dreamtime. "You looked younger in the Dreamtime you know."

Insolent youth. Magnus fought to stay calm. He needed to play the role a little longer for his aim to be accomplished.

"What's wrong?" Damien continued. "You went to a lot of trouble to get me here and now when I arrive all you can do is give me the silent treatment?"

More silence.

"Well answer this. Where is Serena?"

"Who is that?" Serena asked as she again tried to get up on her feet.

Magnus turned to eye her, his face full of shock and surprise. "It's ... It's him."

"Who!"

"Him! The one who attacked you, then drugged you."

"Drugged me?"

"Yes."

"Hey! Who are you talking to up there?" Damien yelled.

Serena gasped. *No it couldn't be.*

"Serena stay down. You have to rest," Magnus replied feigning concern.

"No I have to see if it is who I think it is."

"Well let me help you." He allowed her to place her arm around his shoulder and slowly edged her toward the railing.

"Where is Serena!" Damien yelled.

"Right here," Magnus responded. "Safe from you!"

As the words reached his ears Damien caught sight of Serena Martin's face. *What's going on? Her face. She's terrified – and not of him, but of me! I smell foul play.* "Serena, are you all right? What did you do to her? Who are you?" His anger flared as the girl collapsed and fell limp into the demon's arms.

"Who I am is unimportant. What is important is who you claim to be."

"Who I claim to be?" *What is he talking about?* "I claimed to be nothing less than what I am – a Guardian of the Cross." With that he focused and with a soothing ease, that still managed to surprise him, the magic flowed within him, transforming him, strengthening him. He felt his cape wrap around him accompanied by an aroma of lavender mixed with rosemary. He inhaled it, relished it before with a sweep of his arm the cape billowed back and settled behind him.

Magic exploded from his hands, colliding with a dark shadow followed by a wail of pain.

"Hello Malagant." The Guardian turned but couldn't believe the abomination he found himself facing. It was standing straight but there was a deformity to it, much more than the hunched figure he had encountered earlier in the alley. A strange smell accompanied it, but the creepiest thing was the lumps that moved up and down within the creature's skin. Its face was deformed, full of scars, lumps, and gaps where the skin had rotted away. A lump rolled into one of those gaps revealing the lumps to be cockroaches, maggots, and worms.

Gross.

The creature cocked his head back and belched out a swarm of hornets. The Guardian ducked and the swarm flew over his head, but then the swarm turned and came right back at him. The Guardian draped his cape around him, summoning his magic to create an armored shell around him. The hornets attacked viciously but the shell held.

Moments later the Guardian rose from his protective cocoon unleashing a whirlwind of white fire that consumed the hornets. *What?* The sensation barely registered in his brain when he felt something hard collide with his midsection. Seconds later his back ached as it collided with the wall.

The stars cleared from his eyes as the being responsible hurled a giant mace toward his head. He rolled out the way and unleashed his magic into the demon knight. The magic stunned the armored juggernaut, but did little else. Back on his feet again, the Guardian prepared for a second attack when fatigue and dizziness flowed through him. *I don't believe this – I fall for the same move twice!*

He grabbed the arm and executed a throw, hurling the apparition into a head-on collision with the armored knight, knocking both to the ground. *I don't have time for this. I have to go get Serena.* He started for the stairs when a glimpse in the corner of his eye advised him to dodge. His eyes noticed the weapon that dug into the floor – a scythe. Even more incredible was the creature to which it belonged – a short, hunched figure dressed in robes covered with a hood. Bony hands wrapped around the weapon and instantly he knew who the apparition was – or at least what it was suppose to be an image of. Death. *Wait a second … war, pestilence, famine. Oh god the four horsemen! How could this be happening?*

Death primed itself for another attack. Guardian sidestepped before sending magic into the creature sending it sprawling, but he couldn't relish the moment. His side was still aching from War's attack and he still hadn't fully recovered from his previous tangle with War and Famine. *And it wouldn't be long before Malagant would recover from that attack.*

There was no way he would defeat all five of them. He scrambled to the stairs, racing up with all the effort he could muster. "Serena." She was still unconscious. "Serena, wake up! Serena wake up it's me Damien!" *She's out cold.* From the corner of his eye he could see Death climbing up the stairs and a cloud of gnats gathered at the top step and condensed into the form of Pestilence. He gathered Serena in his arms and ran as fast as he could until he reached the stairs at the other end. He glided down the stairs, landing with a roll on the hard floor. *No way I'm going to be able to carry her out before they catch up.* Summoning the last of his strength he dragged Serena underneath the staircase before draping his cape over the both of them and called upon its magic.

The Time Picayune front page was the main story of the 10'o clock news as Charlie flicked off the television. "Well looks like we've been given an opportunity here. If tomorrow goes unhitched then victory will be imminent. So does everyone know what they have to do tomorrow? Obama."

"Everything ready on my end," the tall dark man replied.

"Why are you here anyway?," yelled another man sitting on the bed. "You're not African-American!"

"What do you mean?" Obama replied, his voice filled with shock. "I'm African by heritage and I am American!"

"Don't use that P.C. crap on me! I know who you are. Your parents are immigrants. Neither of them can trace their roots back to slavery. They didn't build this country like my ancestors did. They didn't toil day in and day out in cotton fields or had to endure being called boy or gang raped!" He turned to Charlie. "We don't need him, he's as bad as they are."

Obama looked at the man in disgust. "Are you that stupid? Do you truly believe that the only people who

have suffered in the world are the American Negroes?
Are you that naïve?   Do you think we are living the high
life in Africa? You really think we are all just sitting on the
coast eating caviar?"

"If we're all so stupid, then why don't you go back
where you came from."

"Shut up both of you!" Charlie yelled. "We're not
here to fight each other. If you act like this tomorrow we
might as well go back home now in defeat!"

"Who died and made you God?" the man replied.

Louis grabbed him by the neck and slammed him
into the wall. "You know I'm getting tired of your
foolishness."

"Oh and you're the model of Black citizenry aren't
you," the man shot back.

"Enough both of you!" a voice commanded.

All eyes turned to the doorway where Erthur
Eugene stood. "Louis let him go."

"I just come from comforting three families over
injustice done to them and their loved ones and I return to
find you all at each other's throats! Those three women
lost something that they can never get back and they are
currently a greater exhibition of brotherhood and strength
than you who claim to be men! Right now there is a man
rotting unjustly in prison and you are out here free fighting
over a label!"

No one dared moved as Eugene continued. "In
here there is only one enemy and that is injustice and if
you can't grasp that then we don't need you on this team.

One army, one crusade! Now I'm going to ask this just once – who wants to back out? Did you hear me? Who wants to back out?"

"Sir begging your pardon, but I think I speak for everyone when I say no one wants to back out. Sir."

"Is that so?" Eugene shouted.

Silence.

Eugene gave them a look over. "I said is that so!"

"Yes sir," one person answered.

"Yes sir," another exclaimed.

"Yes sir."

Soon the room was filled by yells of "Yes sir."

"One army! One crusade!" Eugene yelled.

The room shook to the response. "One army! One crusade!"

"All right then." Eugene glanced at Charlie. "I think you were in the middle of something when you were interrupted."

"Yes sir," Charlie answered and continued while Erther Eugene watched from the corner. *God help us as we head into the Valley of the Shadow of Death.*

"Serena. Serena, wake up."

She gently squirmed as she heard the voice, a warmth of safety oozed through her causing her to smile as her eyes opened. The nightmare was over, she was safe. The haze cleared to reveal the loving face of ---

Her breathing abruptly stopped as the figure
before her came to view. She quickly sat up noticing the
dark cape covering her. Memories and events flooded her
mind. "Where am I?"

Damien Parker, the Guardian, instinctively
reached out to soothe her. A strange soft pain stung him
as she moved back. "Serena, it's me Damien. Relax." He
allowed the magic to reside from him. "See it's me."

"Where are we?"

Damien sighed. "We're in the park back in
Woodmere. Your car's parked over there."

"Woodmere? But how?"

"I managed to hide us from the demons back at
the airport until it was safe. Then I had Sara meet us.
You've been out the whole time."

"Where is Sara?"

"Shh. She's home."

"What happened?"

"I was hoping you could tell me. Sara thinks you
were drugged. Thankfully though it was only meant to
keep you sedated. What happened? You sent Sara to
summon me. Something about Malagant."

"I had followed Malagant when I ..."

"What? What happened?"

"I ... I saw." *Beware the Guardian ... Who did attack
me? There was something familiar about him. I knew him but I
can't remember from where ... Beware the Guardian ... He looked
like one of the Nestari but then he changed, he became this hideous*

beast ... Beware the Guardian ... It's him, the one who attacked you, then drugged you! Beware the Guardian ... Yes beware of me."
"What did you say?"

"I didn't say anything. You were saying something about Malagant and then you just stopped. Are you okay?"

Serena slowly rose to her feet. "No I'm all right." *Beware of me. I love you Serena.* "I gotta go."

"Wait! I'll walk you to your car."

"No! Stay away from me Damien, Guardian if that's what you really are! Stay away!"

"Serena calm down. I know you've been through a lot today but ..."

"Stay back," she hissed. She continued to step back from him, eying him with every step until she started down the path into the woods towards her house.

Damien Parker could only watch as she disappeared into the shadows of the night. For the second time he saw an expression on her face he hoped never to see. His heart ached as he watched the path, hoping that she would come back, hoping that her face wouldn't display the emotion he last saw upon it. An emotion that bothered him as no demon he had face or would ever face could. An emotion called terror.

Monday
February 10th

Chapter 16

Geryon Magnus watched from the window as the rays of the dawning sun scaled back the darkness of the night. The horsemen had failed to destroy the Guardian and that left him with a feeling of unease.

Magnus you fool, you been listening too much to Malagant's whining, so the Guardian still lives. His presence had yet to effect his overall plan. The Guardian still was not aware of his plans for releasing the Maderan. Even if he was aware, Erther Eugene was preparing a protest that at its conclusion would incite a race war that would leave New Orleans in ashes and that was only the beginning. By the end of it all, those hypocritical humans and their country would be the first to fall in the coming reckoning. No one could stop the events he had flung into motion – not even the most powerful of the Nestari.

Yes, the Guardian is irrelevant. He turned to the assembled host before him, Malagant and his created manifestations of the Four Horsemen. True Damien Parker had held his own against the five of them, but he had not defeated them. The next time he and Damien Parker meet, the Guardian would be facing seven, perhaps eight. Yes there was still Serena Martin, the girl was so afraid of the Knight of the Order she might use her own magic against him.

Yes victory is mine. It's just a matter of time. I just need to be patient.

Fire, pain, hatred. Extreme burning hatred. God he could feel it coursing through him like a poison burning the very blood in his veins. In his delirium he started to see faces.

You will die Damien Parker. The man who kidnapped Serena.

You must go beneath the water. Jadzia Maza.

Damien, wake up. Serena?

We've been waiting for you Damien Parker.

You mustn't die Child of Water.

That voice?

The sleeper must awaken... Who are you? Whom do you seek?

Die Guardian die. Die ... Die.

His eyes opened. Where am I? His mind navigated a maze of confusion and grogginess as he struggled to sit up. Pain racked through his entire body but he completely ignored it as the face looming over him came to view.

That's impossible! It can't be! "How? How can ... can you ... can I ..."

"Faith."

"Faith?"

"Yes. Nothing else is needed."

"Could you be a little more clearer?"

"Not a necessity.   The answers you seek are in front of your face."

"Oh if it so crystal clear how come everybody but me seem to know! And who are you?"

"Funny I was just about to ask you the same thing."

"Enough with the games!" He lunged forward to grab but missed completely.

"Who are you?"

He wheels around. How did he get there? *"Me? I am Damien Parker!"*

"That is our name, but who is Damien Parker ? What makes Damien Parker unique?"

"I'm … I'm the Guardian."

"Yes we are the Guardian. But that is only part of the answer."

"We? Are you trying to say that you … are me!"

"He's not the only one."

That voice! My God it's her. He smiles as she approaches and takes his hand. The softness of her touch soothes him, relaxes him. He closes his eyes letting the comfort of her touch ooze through him. *"Who are you?"* His question was one of bewilderment.

"Damien Parker! You know good and well who I am! Just as the Guardian is a part of who you are I am a part of you as well!"

"What part is that?" His voice a psalm of confusion.

She leaned her forehead onto his with a softness he never knew before. "I am your heart. You belong with me Damien, to the world of magic. It's your destiny, our destiny."

His eyes opened to partial darkness. How long had he been in the Resurrect Sleep? He sat up and eyed his alarm clock. 6:00 AM. Six and a half hours. He fell back onto the bed, his mind drifting back to the previous night – six and a half hours ago to be exact.

He had just returned from Woodmere and had barely showered and eaten when his mother showed up to the door of his room with the phone in her hand. "It's for you."

From her voice he knew it wasn't Serena. "Hello?"

"Damien it's me Seneca."

"So did you find anything from your grandmother?"

"She went ballistic when I mentioned the name."

"How bad?"

"She was terrified! I've never seen my grandmother like that before."

"So what did you find out?"

"Apparently this is some kind of Freddy Krueger type creature that gets its kicks out of killing people after feeding off their fears. It was trapped by Marie Laveau in some cemetery."

"Yeah St. Louis Cemetery. Anything else?"

"Only that to free it would require a lot of unstability to the magic whatever the heck that means. Oh something else along the lines of fear leads to hate hate leads to feasting and feasting leading to killing. She was on a Yoda moment that for certain."

"Nothing about killing it!"

"Oh yeah it can be killed, but that's where things get kinda crazy.   Apparently someone in New Orleans, one of the Nestari they …"

"I know who they are, I'm one of them remember and I have a feeling you are too."

"Well that's good because the Nestari can kill the creature but." He hesitated.

"But what?"

"Only if they have faith in themselves and their purpose."

Faith.

"Anything else?"

"No that's it for now. I'm sorry I couldn't be of any more help."

"On the contrary you've been a big help." He yawned. It had been a long day, he was amazed he wasn't bawling in pain. His body was battered, bruised, he was sure he had a broken rib or two. He was functioning on fumes right now and tomorrow would be even harder. He would need all the rest he could get. "I'll talk to you tomorrow."

"Okay see you then."

"Bye."

He had barely been able to trudge to the front room to put the phone back. When he finally made it back to his room his body collapsed onto the bed and surrendered to sleep.

There was still pain in his side, but other than that he felt refreshed.

"Good morning son. I thought you would be sleeping in today."

He was so into his own thoughts that he overlooked his mother completely.

"Habit," he replied in a gruff voice as he trudged into the kitchen and opened the freezer.

"I'll be happy when he's locked up! They should have never released him in the first place!"

"Let who loose?", her son replied as he placed a plate on the island cabinet and returned to his mother's side. *LeBeau! He's being moved today! I had almost forgotten.* "Oh that. Oh well I'm sure there's going to be someone from the NAACP yelling and screaming about it."

"And him. I wonder why your daddy doesn't like him?"

"Because he's an egomanic opportunist who seems to believe that the Final Solution should be implemented on white people!"

"Oh how do you know Jonathan?"

"Just listen to the man Marie. Every word out of his mouth is the White man did this, the White man did that! Granted Louisiana does have its share of Caucasian loons, but not everyone White goes out of their way to stifle Black people. Never mind the fact that the mayor – in fact that last three mayors as well as the police chief as well as almost ¾ of the parish is Black! But all of New Orleans' problems are the fault of White people! Now if you want to look at the Saints I think he would have a point. I don't think they can get any worse!"

His mother gave her 'I give up' sigh but Damien remained silent, his eyes fixed on the television watching clips of past events when a disturbing feeling came over him.

⚜ ⚜ ⚜

"I thought you would be sleeping in," Shadrea Martin chided gently as she noticed her daughter sitting in the breakfast nook.

"I had trouble sleeping," Serena responded.

Her mother paused her usual breakfast prep to eye her daughter. "Boy trouble still."

Serena often marveled at how her mother always seem to read her like a book. Indeed so intuned was Shadrea Martin with her only child that she sat down beside her.

"I've been having these dreams. And in them Damien was my Knight and I was his charge. And I was happy. Perfectly content. But the truth is I wasn't. I hated her, hated myself because I was content in letting him protect me. And now…now I'm not sure about anything about myself about Damien."

Shadrea hugged her daughter and pulled her close. "Serena, oh baby you're missing the point. When you have someone that's special, that you can trust them to protect you and be there for you through the best and the worst, you embrace that honey because that's special.

I've always told you that deep down you know what is right and what is wrong based on what you feel. So the question you need to ask yourself is --- what do your feelings tell you about Damien Parker."

Chapter 17

For the umpteenth time he tugged at his shirt
and scratched under his arm. The morning was
humid and muggy, worse it was smothering him.
The horrible thing was that it was only 9:00. Thank
God he didn't think he could handle the noon day
heat.

His eyes glanced down the street, waiting for
the inevitable moment of truth. Nine o' clock – a
parade was starting. No that's tomorrow, the famous
Zulu parade. He could see it all before him: the large
floats crawling down the street, the colorful collage of
ribbons and confetti, balloons billowing in the
morning wind. The thunder of the crowd filled his
ears as images of people crowding together appeared
before him.

It had been ages since he had been to a parade
but he recalled the thrill he felt watching them and
that childish aspiration resurfaced. According to his
father only actors and heroes received parades.
Heroes received them because they deserved it, but
that rarely happened because the former was so great
at appearing to be heroes that people often cast aside
the true heroes and enhance the false ones. A
teacher had told him that most people wouldn't
recognize a real hero if their soul depended on it.

A sigh of regret drifted from him; true heroes did what was necessary but he couldn't deny that once, just once he would like to be recognized, praised and acknowledged. Especially after all the trouble he had put himself through. Today he would protect countless number of lives from terror and danger.

A smirk snapped from him as he kicked himself for having such thoughts. He would never receive a parade – heroes like him, were never praised. Only hatred repaid their vigilance. Hatred. The Almighty was indeed a unique entity; to allow one to be hated for destroying hate. Hmph. A storm of hisses and yells erupted and he realized that his moment of truth was at hand as the squad of police cars pulled up. Two officers made their way from the front car and stood between the crowd and the street. Another pair of officers got out and opened the back door to the middle car. The crowd's jeers grew louder and then he saw him.

The look on LeBeau's face was one of mockery and defiance. The jeers and curses of the crowd didn't seem to phase him , in fact a smile shinned from his face as his escorts assembled themselves around him. *He's smiling! I can't believe it! The guy had a lot of nerve.* For a brief moment he wished he was here for LeBeau, but someone else was more important, more dangerous.

He knew he was around here somewhere
looking all smug and superior. Just who did he think
he was? What made him think that he was so holy, so
special, so deserving of respect? He scratched an itch
as the noise of the crowd grew louder.

Disgust filled him as he watched them but he
wasn't sure who he was more disgusted with: the
crowd or the man who had assembled them. As far
as he was concerned they were all fools, blind sheep
following the first voice that told them what they
wanted to hear. Didn't they know that they were a
danger to everything that true patriots like him sought
to protect. He scoffed. These weren't people, they
were animals, fanatics blind to the dangers that they
actually represented.

Father forgive them for they know not what they do.
Indeed it was people like them that doomed people
like him to a life of eternal vigilance. *Father take this
cup from me.* No, now was not the time to be weak.
Those in whom my will is done shall be strengthened.
It was then that an image came before him – an image
of darkness, of evil. Behold I stand at the valley of
the shadow of death, but I shall fear no evil for thou
art with me thy rod and the staff. With that he picked
up his rod and patiently adjusted his aim.

I am that is. My wrath shall yield through
thee. And then he saw him.

For the longest time he had been telling himself that patience was a virtue, but he was reaching a point where even that long held belief was losing validity. LeBeau had arrived and was surrounded by a mob of cops. Had he been wrong? Granted the revelation had not been sent through the Dreamtime but still every instinct within him said that something was going to happen. Neither LeBeau nor Eugene were aware of the roles they were playing.

Where is it gonna come from? Where? The real tragedy of the whole situation was not the chance of him failing to stop the spark of a potential racial firestorm but rather he could be completely wrong and wasted two hours that have been better spent resting or reconciling with Serena.   Nah she'd still be sleep right now. Something had to happen or it would be at least a week before that little voice of regret in his head would let him live it down.

He paused, he didn't need to see the handle on the pistol to know his objective – the look on his face was a dead giveaway of his intent. Immediately he sprang into action, his motion fluid, his thoughts focused and his wall of magic formed.

The Guardian could hear Erthur Eugene's screams, begging, pleading the assassin to put down the gun. However the gunman's face displayed one of twisted anger as his arm lifted up the gun and two flashes preceeded two small booms. The bullets stopped in mid air inches short of the intended victim before dropping to the ground.

The man screamed a curse as he prepared to squeeze the trigger again, but the Guardian loosed a bolt of magic knocking the assassin senseless to the ground. He surveyed the crowd before releasing his magic as he merged into the crowd and slowly made his way back toward the end of the block where his motorcycle was parked. He glanced around to make sure no one was watching before casually starting down the street relieved that he been able to stop a major part of the demon's plan. Then he heard the gunshots.

Damien Parker cursed himself. *How could I have been so off? How could I have not thought that there would be a backup plan. Damnit.* It all repeated in his mind over and over again. His hearing the gunshots. Him returning to find Eugene sprawled on the ground bleeding. Damn.

The 35th repetition had just finished as he pulled up into the driveway and froze as a sight caught his eye. Part of him rejoiced but he knew also that he would be lying if he didn't admit that he was also frightened. He closed his eyes wondering if it was real or merely an illusion, but as his eyes opened and he saw the figure sitting on the porch swing he knew it was real that he was really her – Serena Martin had come to see him.

For the longest time the two merely stood there watching each other from afar. Neither wanted to make the first move – or rather the first mistake. It was easier and safer to react rather than act.

Finally Damien slowly proceeded toward her, his steps slow, his body language awkward. He had never been this nervous about approaching Serena since … since … Heck even that night at Homecoming had been easier. His eyes never left her though, never blinking as the distance closed between them. She stood and fidgeted her arms along the chain of the swing.

Suddenly they were face to face, but neither spoke. If acting was possibly more dangerous than reacting; saying the first word presented an even greater peril.

"Hey." The first move.

"Hey yourself."

"Funny I was thinking about passing by your place on the way back here. I guess it's a good thing I didn't."

"I didn't want to disturb your father so I just decided to."

"Wait for me out here."

"Yeah." They both turned away from each other briefly.

"I've been thinking about you a lot lately," Serena said.

Damien's eyebrows raised. "I was under the impression that that was a usual thing."

"Not like this."

"Serena before you go any further, I've wanted to tell you for the longest about my magic, about being the Guardian. So," he reached out and took her hand. She didn't pull away. "So I'm going to tell you everything about me. Everything." He motioned for her to sit and then he sat down beside her. He sighed, he knew that telling her wasn't going to be easy, mainly because he was still coming to terms with it himself. It had all been over a year ago, but he would never forget that day in May.

Chapter 18

Like many life altering events, Damien Parker's transformation from ordinary teenager to Guardian of the Cross began with a phone call. It was May, that time of year when graduates walk the aisles and threw up their hats, when textbooks and tablets were set aside for enjoyment and recreation – and when young men and women made their debuts in the social world.

One of those making their debut was the daughter of Victoria Zachery better known as Mrs. Zack, one of his mother's cohorts at work. However her daughter's big day had one small problem. A debutant had to have an escort, something her daughter was currently lacking and Mrs. Zack had called Damien's mother wondering if her son would mind resolving the dilemma.

Needless to say Marie Parker gladly volunteered her son, however she was surprised to find her son not sharing his mother's joy. It wasn't that LaToya Zachery was ugly, in fact she was quite lovely, however her ideal conversation consisted of gossip and shopping and her idea of fine reading was Cosmopolitan, Soap Opera's Digest and Vibe magazine. She hated sports, sci fi, and politics – no way he would be able to deal with her for three hours.

The main problem was the fact that he would be escorting her to a debutant ball which to him was a long dreary bore filled with endless oohing and ahhing that amounted to nothing. As far as he was concerned debutant balls belonged on a United Nations list of cruel and extreme punishment.

Mother's though have a strange way of compelling things from their children especially their sons and in the end he agreed to endure the torture of debutant escort, which led to a sunny Saturday afternoon and a trip to the tuxedo store.

How or why he choose that particular tuxedo shop baffles him to this day. One of the great mysteries of the Order he supposed. Regardless he stepped into that shop and looked around. Style was everything – even if one was going to a torture chamber, but in the end he decided that sometimes simplicity was best and went with a simple black tux and vest.

He had to admit he took a delight in seeing himself dressed up. It was while he was standing there admiring himself that he slipped in, Amanesh Kadesh, the Emissary, whose sole task was to ensure the ascension of the next Guardian from the previous.

There he was, amonished with the image he saw in the mirror, never noticing the tall dark Emissary until he spoke those fateful words: "Would you like a cane or top hat with that sir?"

"How much extra is it?"

"For today sir they are free."

"Well … *I guess it couldn't hurt* … Yeah."

There are times when the moment between those words and what followed seemed to be an eternity and other times a mere instant. Regardless though his life changed forever when Amaneh Kadesh returned with a cane. "Your cane Lord Guardian."

Damien looked at him in surprise. "Lord Guardian? Please! I don't look that good, but thank you for the cane." He reached for the cane and when his fingers wrapped around the wooden rod, pain raced through his body. It was as if he had touched a lightning rod just as it had been struck. He tried to let go but his fingers wouldn't relax their grip instead they squeezed tighter till he could feel his fingers embedding themselves into the wood.

Pain flooded through every nerve of his body. His eyes burned in his head. The pain was indescribable; it was as if every fiber of his body was being sliced simultaneously with razor sharp blades. His entire body shook, the cane glowed with a fierce white light.

In his heart and mind he could feel something unlocking, something freeing itself. *What … What is this?* Suddenly he felt nothing, no that wasn't accurate he did feel something. He felt relaxed, calm as if everything else had melted away leaving this … this enlightenment, this ascendance. His eyes seem to see everything and anything. His mind aware of everything including someone else. No what he felt here with him was beyond him, her, it – to use pronouns to describe his companion would be an insult – the English language in fact every human language was too limited to describe this force that he was surrounded by.

Suddenly he found himself encountering images and several forms of men appeared before him one by one, even more surprising was the sense of familiarity that struck him as he saw each one. One of the specters stepped forward and touched his forehead – and awakened his understanding.

Wait ... these people are all – my ancestors. But what does this mean?

The images and the specters twisted and churned around him like a whirlwind and

he heard a voice.

Damien Parker, Child of the Nestari

We offer this gift to you

A power unequalled we bestow upon thee

But with our gift comes a price

As with all great power, comes greater sacrifice ...

Fear gripped him. *What sacrifice? Why me? I didn't ask for this?* No he had seen other things in addition to the images of his ancestors. He had seen a great need – a need that only he could fulfill as had his ancestors before him. *So be it.*

The maelstrom of images accelerated faster, slowly condensing itself until it converged into its eye, an eye of the storm that consisted of Damien Parker, or what was left of him. He could feel the energy shifting, molding itself and him until finally he opened his eyes to see himself floating in a sea of radiant blue and white light. His tuxedo was gone, replaced by a dark body armor that felt like a second skin. A long royal purple cape floated billowed behind him. Inside he could feel a power churning, awaiting to be unleashed.

I understand. In the name of the Order so shall I be – a Guardian of the Cross.

"So what happened next?"

"Nothing. I blinked and found myself back in the dressing room. The Emissary had gone, but I still had the cane." A chuckle erupted as he tapped the butt of the cane on the concrete. "Next thing you know I started seeing demons and other things. Then I started fighting them. Took a while to get use to it all, heck I was just coming to terms with the whole thing when I met you."

He stared straight ahead, his eyes never blinking. "That day the world became clearer – and scarier."

Serena was glad he wasn't facing her so that he couldn't see the embarrassment on her face. A year. He had been shackled with the burden of being one of the Nestari. One of the Chosen. *Compared to him my life is merely a case of a pimples. I had 11 years to come to terms with the burden of possessing magic. All he's had is a year.*

"Scary the things that are asked of us."

Damien Parker sighed as he heard the sad taint in her voice. "Yeah," he agreed. "I certainly don't remember being asked to be the one who prevents apocalypse from coming a day or two early." He sighed again, only this time the sigh was heavier, sadder. "Or maybe I did."

"Come on don't be so hard on yourself," Serena chuckled. "Nobody could ask for this."

"Didn't I? I always wanted to be a leader, to be someone who would change the world." He found himself laughing softly. "Be careful what you wish for …"

he paused and flung off his fingertips an imaginary pebble. "You just might get it," he finished.

They found themselves staring at each other, face to face. Each locked on the eyes of the other.

"I'm sorry," Damien replied.

"For what?"

"For not telling you sooner."

"You couldn't have known." For the first time in a long time she smiled at him and slowly she started toward his face.

"Well from now on, we fight together."

She paused, her lips now so close to his she could feel his breath. "Always." *Should I kiss him or keep talking?*

He saved her the decision by kissing her, but he cut it short. "Good, cause I'm going to need your help."

"What do you need?"

He leaned in closer. "I need you to keep your pager on you tomorrow and answer if I call."

"Tomorrow? Why not today?"

"Oh today too, but there's something you need to know."

"Okay then explain it to me."

"Okay." He started to pull away from her.

"Oh no! After you kiss me."

He stroked her long brown hair, smiled and kissed her passionately.

True he had told her about how he became the Guardian and everything regarding the Maderon and Madame Fi La Reye's riddle, however … how do you explain an entity that you couldn't see and that only you could hear to someone else? The answer was simple – you don't.

Heck there were times when he barely understood it.

It was the third night in a row, three nights he had been plagued by the same nightmare. Him floating in a city of fire, from a distance a vibrant voice implored him to find her – at least from the sound of the voice the being was a she.

"Where are you?" His question always yielding the same response from the endless sky. "Damien Parker … find me."

"I can't find you if you don't show yourself."

Find me …

For three nights and three mornings he woke with that command in his ears. He stared at the corner of his room where the white cane laid against the wall at the foot of his bed.

Three days that cane had been sitting there … three days of hearing voices and having nightmares. Three days of questioning his sanity. All because of that cane. Touching it that afternoon in the tuxedo shop had done something to him. As he would walk he would see eyes staring at him and if he was careful he could see small to medium size bodies scampering in the shadows, yet he seem to be the only one who could see them.

Then came the voices. At first he had thought it to be his mother, but after thrice approaching her and thrice her denying any such thing he dismissed it as him working too hard. Then came the dreams.

Three days.

Three days the same thing. Three days he pondered on taking that cane and throwing it into the river. Three days he decided against it … and now.

Am I truly on the wrong side of the River Sanity? He was beginning to doubt the benefit of a doubt he had given himself. He found himself tormented by it, obsessed until finally sleep overcame him and his eyes closed. Indeed Damien Parker had reached an edge, but it was the edge of his patience.

As he drifted through the blue green sky, a fury of determination burned within him, fueling him as he focused and dug into his heart and soul as he had never done before. Then he felt it, a sensation that pulsed through him and an inate familiarity accompanied it – a familiarity that made him trust where this sensation directed him to go. He followed it, swimming through the sky till his instincts told him to stop and he just floated there waiting. It was there he could feel it. Something else was here with him. Of that he was certain.

"You can talk you know, I know you're here."

Silence.

"Who are you?"

"A figment of your imagination," a feminine voice answered.

"I don't believe you."

"Why? We are in a dream."

Part of what she said was true. Part but not all. "This plane may be dream but you are not. Now who are you?" He felt a slight shift. *She's it. Whatever is moving, it's her.*

"I hope you know I am quite aware that you are behind me. Now can you please answer the question. Pretty please."

"What do your instincts say I am?"

"Would I be asking if I knew?"

"Maybe."

Damien relaxed, again annoyance fuelled him. He looked directly at her, but he noticed he wasn't looking with his eyes. *What the …* Even more bizarre was the shape that appeared before him. *Good God!*

Suddenly laughter echoed around him. "Congratulations Damien Parker. I am Oracle and you have passed my test."

"Test? What test?"

"**The** test and now … wake up."

Wake up. He sat up in his bed. *Was it all a dream? No it wasn't.* "You can come out Oracle."

"But I am out Damien Parker."

"What are you talking about? I can't see you."

A chuckle chirped beside him and slowly drifted in front of him. "Humans. So insistent on seeing everything. Sight is just the cover of the book of perception. There are so many other wonderful ways of perceiving the world that your five measly senses do not begin to cover. Sight is so … limited. No wonder you humans have so many problems."

"So why might I ask are you here? Besides to drive me insane."

"Why I am here to train you of course."

"What?"

Training – more like on the job training with the emphasis on the job than on training. He was glad not all his teachers believed in Oracles training methods. Typical woman. He always referred to Oracle as a she and Oracle more oft than not launched into a tirade of how limited he/she identification was. However one couldn't help but think of her as a woman. She was always putting her two cents in and was never satisfied with anything. He could count on one hand all the compliments he received from Oracle in their year time together. Though he had to admit he had learned a lot under Oracle's tutelage. He had learned about the power of harmony, the Order, which surprisingly turned out to be quite similar to many aspects of the martial arts --- discipline and unity of mind, body, and soul. Most importantly, he learned about the power of hate, the power of the Abyss.

Driven by their desire to control, the Daemonites exist only to taint the natural order of the world. Deviance being their discipline and purpose. Hated, lust, greed & selfishness the tools of their trade, the Daemonites manipulate the sentient races of the world, creating the tainted magical energy on which they feed.

Like the Order, the Daemonites were spawned of the rhythmic forces that had spawned reality. Lacking the understanding of the Order and seeking to dominate that which even the Order itself understood should and could not be dominated, the Daemonites nearly destroyed existence itself and thereafter were imprisoned in the Abyss. But as with all things, the prison holding the Daemonites wasn't absolute, even from the Abyss the Daemonites found ways to circumvent the natural order, weakening their prison in the Abyss. The Order though foresaw all this and sent the Nestari, champions sent to protect the races of the earth from the trials of the Abyss.

Just surviving Oracle's training equaled achieving three purple hearts, but he had to admit her efforts had paid off. He understood the necessity of it; although he wished she understood his dating Serena. He had never seen Oracle so livid, but for all her mayhem he ignored her counsel. Serena gave him hope – a hope that he could be a normal teenager, just one with a little more knowledge and responsibilities.

Truth was though he could never be normal – he wasn't even human anymore if he ever was. That afternoon his whole body had been made over – everything that defined him was pure magic. He was a result of two schools of magic, an inheritance of both his maternal and paternal sides of his family. From his paternal side came Voodoo and Shaman magic and of course the dominant Cyrenian magic that he inherited from his maternal side.

His mother was a descendant of Simon Cyrene, the man who carried the cross and as a result became the first Guardian of the Cross.

There was no getting around it, the staff once received implanted within the Guardian all the memories and lives of the previous who bore the burden, or at least that was suppose to happen, but for some reason with him something had gone wrong. The memories and experiences of the previous Guardians instead of being a smooth, cohesive download had instead been a jumbled arrangement of noise. He wasn't even sure if all their memories had transferred to him. Tried as he could to remember things of the past he could never get beyond his own --- and the few times that he did it was always in bits and pieces, never a clear picture.

As far as Oracle or any magical creature knew, no previous Guardian ever had a problem with the transition of memory. Maybe it was a blessing in disguise, the whole process was supposedly a baptism of grief and sorrow that only the most vigilant could endure. Once you were a Guardian you were more super than man and Damien often wondered if he really wanted to lose that much of his own individuality. Without their memories, while he still possessed the power he was still Damien Parker and only Damien Parker.

Right Parker. Keep telling yourself that, but you know the truth. Truth was that to a degree the man was taken out of the equation, from the water he had emerged a new creature – a suriana uchawi, a child of magic.

And yet I don't feel different, but how would I really know? As far as I know I could have always been different and all this been is just a wake up call to make me aware of it. He had kept all that from Serena, partly because he was afraid of how she would take it and secondly because he himself was afraid of what it would confirm. The previous Guardians at least had the certainty of whom or what they had been to hang on to, to give them an identity, a purpose they could at least call their own. He didn't have that because no one was sure what he had become and seemingly no one knew what he had been when he was originally born.

Maybe Oracle was right. Darn it.

To say that the mayor was pissed would have been an understatement. Sitting in his office with Cole & others advisors, breaths heavy, face purple, eyes flaring while he talked to Langley on the phone for the third time in six hours.

It wasn't that he was concerned for Erther Eugene. On the contrary he couldn't be happier with that particular result. A hospitalized Eugene couldn't stir up trouble in his city.

What he did mind was the means in which Eugene was hospitalized – or at least how exposed the cause was. It was one thing to be shot on a street or a park by some hoodrat. Things like that just happened and were left as circumstance. To be shot in the city plaza while leading a protest and stopping another assassination was inexplicable. One didn't even need to throw in the nice detail that Eugene's assassin was white to understand how thin the ice was.

Fischer's scalp hunt already had the city riveting at the seams, but he had hoped the rave and reveille of Mardi Gras would have distracted attention from the ordeal enough for the situation to be handled quietly.

Eugene's presence had all but destroyed that plan. His assassination had buried it. What had been a minor annoyance had become a horrific setback. Only the fact that Eugene survived the ordeal kept the powder keg from exploding.

All this was in his mind as he cussed Langley, who of course cussed back. And so they cussed back and forth for about 40 minutes. Just when it appeared the mayor was calming down and gaining control of the conversation, one of the two must have said the wrong thing because again the mayor started cussing and the tirade continued for another twenty minutes. Finally apparently both men gained their composure as the mayor launched into a short sermon on the good of the city and the obligation of government.

He hung up the phone gently and collapsed into his chair, eyes closed in contemplation till finally he spoke.

"Well how is he?"

Cole was the first to speak. "The doctor reports that he's in stable condition."

Thank God

"Unfortunately there are bigger problems."

The mayor gave Cole a look.

"There's a crowd slowly gathering at the hospital. And ... LeBeau is dead."

The mayor's face was one of mixed reaction. On one hand LeBeau was going to die anyway. Four dead black girls in the prime of their childhood, previous record too. Yeah if he didn't get the death penalty, one could easily justify him deserving it. Unfortunately now was not a good time for anyone involved in this matter to pop up dead.

"How?"

"Shot on the way back to jail. One arrest was made. We think it might have been arranged. One of the girls killed was a sister of Alfred Carvin, a known member of the Crypts. The suspect is a member of that same gang."

"Jesus Christ!"

"There's more sir. Bufford just called in. Seems the wife of the man who shot Eugene has reported receiving phone threats."

"Of all the days for this crap to happen," the mayor muttered.

"In regards to that sir..."

"Dang it, I'm not even suppose to be here! I'm suppose to be spending quality time with my wife." Quality time with the Mrs. must have definitely been a worthwhile thing for he spat another spew of curses in which he cursed Langley, LeBeau, Fischer, the Times

Picayune even the office of mayor itself. The other
staffers exchanged looks; two slowly back towards the
door. Cole simply waited calmly for the tantrum to stop,
which in five minutes did.

"Like I was saying sir, we may have to cancel the
parades tomorrow."

"No."

"Sir!"

"No! Mardi Gras hasn't been cancelled since,
since ever! That trend isn't gonna be broken today, not on
my watch!"

"Sir!"

"No Maynard!"

"What cha doing son?" God how long had she
been there? Had he been thinking out loud? He noticed
his notebook. "Oh nothing Mama, just trying to figure out
this silly riddle. I heard you had a special guest today."

Marie Parker gave her son a kiss on the cheek.
"Oh yes that Eugene fellow. Well despite what you and
your daddy say about him – the man had angels watching
over him. We had to perform surgery but he's expected to
make a full recovery. The bullets were all in the area of his
heart and lungs and amazingly neither organ were hit."

She noticed the look on his face. "What's wrong
son? You look sad. You wanted him to bite the big one?"

"No Mama!" her son quickly hissed. "I was just
thinking about this silly riddle. God I wish I could give

stuff like this up for Lent!" He paused. *Lent ... Repent. Oh God Mardi Gras!* "Mardi Gras!"

"Well yes son Mardi Gras, the last day before Lent or the last day you can sin before you have to repent as we learned it – to the dismay of my teachers."

Oh God Mardi Gras is the Eve of Pennance! That leaves only a day. One day to stop the Maderan. One day to find the other five. Junk!

Chapter 19

Heihachi Mishima grabbed Jin Kazuma and executed a vicious slam. Achilles silently swore twice as the K.O. confirmation flashed on the screen. His first swear came because the old man had beaten him for the fourth straight time against his third different character and second one was due to the fact that he had already invested $2.00 in the silly machine.

His temper was still flaring as he watched the continue countdown. By the time 'Game Over' flashed on the screen he had not only cursed Heihachi, Law, Paul and Jin Kazuma but he also vowed never to play another Tekken arcade game as long as he lived. A glance at his watch did little to improve his mood, the movie started in 15 minutes and his boys still hadn't showed up yet.

He sighed, pondering on his lot in life when a sight came before his eyes and he found himself wondering on the workings of God and yet for a strange reason this encounter seemed – divine.

"Achilles?"

Immediately he was petrified. Andra had never spoken his name with such – warmth before. From the look of her friends he wasn't the only observer of her deviant behavior. "Hey." It was all he could say, he was too shocked by the warmth of her voice to go into battle mode. If the warmth of her voice had shocked him, he didn't know what he was feeling when he felt the warmth of her embrace. No he took it back he knew exactly what he was feeling: fear, surprise, but also a disturbing sense of content that oozed all through him.

This can't be right, not coming from Andra Alexander and the day I desire to hold Andra Alexander is the day Superman has an obsession for kryptonite.

She pulled away, but still held him at arm's length. "What's wrong? You okay?"

This was ether a nightmare or a prank. "Nothing." God he was whispering. "Who are you?"

A sly smile crept on her face. "I'm Andra silly."

"You can't be Andra Alexander. Andra doesn't hug anyone; especially me." He leaned in close to her ear. "Are you feeling okay?" he whispered.

"I'm fine," she whispered back. "Why?"

"You're not spewing venom," he hissed. "You're usually poisoning my ears with insults."

He had hoped that she would cuss him out and restore their relationship to its proper scope, but instead she put her hand on his chest. It wasn't that that terrified him though, the smile on her face was the culprit for that. A smile of genuine, frightening warmth.

"There's a first time for everything," she whispered. She slowly slid her hand down before moving it back to his hand.   She started to pull away but before he could let go she pulled him to her.

Achilles almost smiled. *Ah here it comes, the knife to the heart.*

"Call me tonight okay."

"You sure you're feeling all right?" His voice was now more of a plea than anything else mainly because he wasn't sure what he would do if she wasn't joking.

"I'm serious."

He glanced down at the paper in his hand. A hand she clinched into a fist. She was nuts, she had to be. It was the only possible explanation.   "Andra … you sure you okay?"

"Just call me," she hissed, sounding a little more like the Andra he knew.

"If you don't call me Achilles Harmon I'll be on your doorstep tomorrow morning!"

"What the hell is going on around here?" Achilles thought to himself as he watched her walk away. "The world is about to end. That has to be it."

A sigh of annoyance oozed from Serena Martin as she walked out of the Rite Aid store. Her day might have been over at work, but her night was just beginning.   She had noticed the darklings through out the day, an usual number of them which wasn't good at all. *Damien's right. There's something evil and powerful at work here. I only hope we can* …

She froze as she saw him sitting on his motorcycle. *Only Damien Parker would do something like this.* "What are you doing here?"

"Something I want to show you."

"Can't it wait till later. My parent barely let me take the car to work today. I have to get home. If I'm too late they'll never let me do it again."

"No. It can't wait."

"Why? Is it the demon?"

"Yes and no."

"Tonight is the calm before the storm. Tomorrow is the endgame, either the good guys win or the good guys die; if not both."

"What are you talking about? You're one of the Nestari! You can defeat any demon!"

"See that's more a theory than a law."

Serena started at him. "No!" she exclaimed strongly. "I'm not going on no last ride and then lose you!"

"Damnit Serena!" Only a woman could make a man who refused to curse, curse. He grabbed her and pulled her within arm's length. "I'm not asking for one last ride, I'm asking you to let me show you what we're going up against."

"Who cares what we're going up against!"

"Being that I'm a Guardian of the Cross, it matters to me! I can't go into battle with the stakes this high and not have you know everything!"

"It doesn't matter to me that you are one of the Nestari!" She calmed herself. "I realize that now."

Damien stepped up to her. "It matters to me. No more secrets."

"Okay where are we going?"

"You'll see."

Although Damien's helmet protected her face, the rest of her body could feel the lash of the wind as they cruised down the Westbank expressway. Her hands tightened around his body as he leaned, steering the cycle into the adjacent lane.

She wondered if her hold on him was too tight for he glanced back at her for brief moment. That thought disappeared as she saw the mischievous grin that was upon it.

He's about to do something crazy. Something he's never done with me on this thing. Probably why he insisted I wear my helmet. If it's that crazy he should have his on too.

"Hang on Serena. I'm about to try something."

"Try what?"

"Well try is an inaccurate word. I've done this lots of times, just never with another person on board."

"What are you going to do?"

He laughed. "Watch."

A mesh of purple material billowed from his back above and around Serena. She recognized it as the cape he wore when he was the Guardian. In awe she watched as the cape stretched and arranged itself around her and the rest of the bike, merging with the metal frame of the vehicle; encasing the vehicle in a kind of armor without sacrificing the streamline form that made the vehicle so mobile. In fact Serena noticed that arrangement seemed to enhance the mobility of the bike, for as they entered the Harvey tunnel the bike seemed to be moving faster, easing in and out of traffic like the wind.

She closed her eyes and tightened her grip around Damien's waist, but not out of fear, but out of excitement. She opened her eyes and found herself yelling so the thrill wouldn't cause her to explode. The world seemed a beautiful blur, her soul and body felt light and she believed that they were riding on air and not on the road. A fear did come to her though, a fear that this would eventually end forever, but as they passed the New Orleans skyline she promised herself that she and Damien would have many more moments like this.

The moon beamed across the clear night sky and he watched it with a startling calm that frightened him one minute and comforted him the next. Morning would soon come and with it would come a battle.

He had never been one for gazing at the moon but then again he wasn't the same person he had been before.

All because of one question.

"And now Seneca Maza we have a question for you?"

"Yes."

"Are you willing to sacrifice everything for your fellow man?"

He had never expected them to ask that of him. Neither did he expect the answer he gave: *Yes.*

Why did I say that? I'm no hero, no warrior and yet I accepted the call of one.

"Then Seneca Maza, step into the light."

It was his last chance, his last chance to avoid the destiny he had so valiantly avoided. One chance to leave the tradition and burden of his family behind … and he let it go. Instead he stepped into the light.

To say they changed him was false. Instead they awakened something. What he had no idea. He hadn't even bothered to tell Damien Parker when he called him, it wasn't time yet. It wasn't a cope out, he didn't know how but he knew the coming day would be a testing one and that scared him. He was scared of what that day would do to him and what he would be upon its completion. Tomorrow the world would end or it would continue, but he knew regardless of the outcome he would never be the same Seneca Maza ever again.

"Where are we?" Serena inquired, glancing around at the complex that obviously was a housing project.

"Storyville."

"Storyville?"the girl exclaimed, "Where the heck is that?"

Damien suppressed giving her a strange look. "4th Ward, not far from Treme."

"4th ward!" Serena exclaimed. "Why in the world didn't you say that in the first place?" she finished before punching him in the shoulder.

"Because," he laughed, "Storyville is in the 4th ward, or at least was."

"Well how am I suppose to know that? You know I'm not from here!"

"Ow!" Damien yipped as he tried to stymie his laughing knowing that laughing would only make things worse. "Why you keep hitting me?"

"That's for trying to make me feel dumb?" she answered before landing another blow.

Damien laughed. "Jesus Christ! You mean you've been here for 2 years and haven't heard about Storyville?"

"Well I haven't."

"Sheesh! I thought you took Louisiana History last summer at UNO?"

"I did. We didn't cover anything on Storyville."

"Jesus Christ! No wonder we're dead last in everything! We can't even teach our history right!" He shook his head, then continued. "See back in the day either in 1897 or 1898, this alderman by the name of Sydney Story thought he'd cleanse New Orleans of its sins, i.e. prostitution, gambling, etc, etc by legalizing them and placing them in a back alley enclave. The hope was that with the sins of the city being confined in a visible jar --- the ones who did know how to get there would be shamed away by public exposure. Thus the sins of New Orleans would slowly wither and die."

"Let me guess --- it backfired."

"Did it! The fool forgot he was in New Orleans, the original Sin City! Before there was Vegas, there was New Orleans and when Vegas is long gone, New Orleans will still be setting the standards on sinning. Only difference between Vegas and New Orleans is style. Vegas believes in flashy lights, New Orleans, we like our sinning down home. Anyways by the 1920's Storyville wasn't just a bane on the Story family, but upon the nation itself. So ... they tore down the area and built the Iberville Projects. And whala!"

Serena only gave him a look. "You still haven't answered the important question Damien, why are we here?"

"You can't feel it?"

"I see darkings and surprisingly they don't seem to care too much about the presence of a Guardian."

Damien sighed. "Forget about the darklings," he scolded. "Look, let yourself go. Just momentarily."

"Are you crazy? Do you know what can happen ..."

"It won't happen. I won't let it get you. I promise. I'll pull you back."

Serena complied and immersed herself into the magic, relaxing herself as ribbons of magical energy rippled through her. It was then she noticed what he was talking about, for there was a taint, a savage terrible darkness that tried to infest her. Her throat felt congested, as if someone had forced her to swallow a bag of marbles --- hot, rough marbles. Finding herself slowly suffocating in hatred and despair, she pulled herself together and managed to turn herself away, rising out of the taint back onto the gentle surface of the magic force.

"What was that?" she inquired, surprised to find herself whispering.

"That," Damien answered, "is the Maderan."

Tuesday
February 11th
Mardi Gras

Chapter 20

Confidence hymned from him as he walked down
the dark street, cloaked in the darkness of the night.
Events had transpired accordingly, all that remained was
the En Prise. Before the endgame could begin though
there was one last thing that needed to be done.   One
final piece to set on the stage.   The drama was nearing its
tragic end and its tragic hero was on the eve of his
downfall despite all his efforts to prevent it. But that was
what makes it tragic.

His smile widened as he cut through the yard,
every step placing him closer and closer to the second
story window where she slept.   He was wondering on
whether he would kill the girl now or merely cause her
pain.   To be honest he had thought of many pleasures he
could have with her.   All of them delightful – and painful.

Estacy filled him he wasn't sure what it was, her
magic wasn't that strong especially in comparisons with
others he had faced.   Was it her youth?   Her innocence?
It certainly wasn't that she was someone's beloved, he had
done that before. No, not a beloved of a Guardian. Yes
that was it.

He stretched out his hand and reached for her
mind. If only she had more power, then at least it would
be a challenge. Suddenly he pulled back and fought an
urge to scream.

What was this? Some kind of barrier! But how?

"I had a feeling you would show up here."

Of course! The Guardian! He turned to face the Knight of the Order. "Damien Parker!" he hissed. "So the dashing knight has come to save his princess."

"That's twice you have said my name, yet I still don't know yours. Come now I'd at least like to know the name of my prey before I kill it. Come on, you know names only work to ill effect on dragons."

"The name is Magnus."

Oh yeah I definitely struck a cord. "See now was that so bad?" He paused briefly. "Look I know all about Mardi Gras and your plans to release the Maderan. Nice plan I must admit; too bad I have to kill you now to end it."

"Sorry," the demon hissed, "but I can't allow that. See I plan on killing **you**." In a single fluid motion Magnus backed a step before catapulting himself high over the roof of the house before the Guardian could muster an attempt to stop him.

No matter, you have to go to St. Louis Cemetery to resurrect the Maderan and I'll be waiting. He allowed himself a sigh of relief before he turned and walked out to the park where his motorcycle was waiting.

What time is it?

He could tell from the illumination of his room, the fluttering of birds as they wake to endure a new day and then there was the percussion of his mother and her fumbled pots.

The urge to sleep rumbled through him like the growl of an empty stomach. No that was his empty stomach, but he could also feel sleep close behind him murmuring, enticing him to turn and enhance her gentle peace.

Yeah right. Sleep often proved more tumulus than peaceful. He couldn't really recall when sleep was gentle or serene. Sleep had become a tool, nothing else.

He fought the urge to turn around; instead he trudged into the kitchen where his mother was sitting at the breakfast table in her scrubs sipping milk from a mug. He had expected his mother to have today off like his father but then again while the mail might stop on holidays, illness, stupidity, and carelessness did not and if they were going strong then so would the need for a hospital.

"Cheer up Momma; at least you get to rest this year instead of being out half the night."

It was a tradition between the two of them to attend the carnival activities downtown Marrero or New Orleans. When the tradition started his father was finishing up at nearby Dillard University and by the time his father had graduated from college his disdain for Mardi Gras had reached its zenith so he never accompanied them despite the fact that he was usually free Mardi Gras evenings.

Damien chuckled. There were three holidays that always turned Jonathan Parker into a gruff goat. Mardi Gras, Kwanzaa, and Halloween. His problem with Kwanzaa was that the seven principles of the holiday were

suppose to be exemplified daily and besides the whole
Christmas season allowed one to celebrate those same
principles anyway.

The problem with the other two was summarized
in his father's infamous Holiday of Evil theorem.
"Halloween," he would always scoff, "admits straight up
that it's a devil's holiday. Mardi Gras on the other hand is
twice as bad – a Christian holiday that's been taken over by
the devil."

His arguments never stopped the mother and her
son from attending parades or trick or treating. However
those traditions were all but laid to rest by puberty. Trick
or treat lost its appeal in middle school and by his junior
year his mother had been replaced by more acceptable
company – his fellow peers.

Marie Parker only sighed and her son understood
it. His father had explained it to him countless times
before. Women especially mothers have difficulty dealing
with change.

Yes no matter how tall I grow or how much hair I
get on my face my mother will never see me beyond the
age of twelve. He stood there wondering if his children
would have to deal with such foolhardiness from him;
when his mother spoke.

"I suppose you're going to spend all day with
Serena."

Damien couldn't help but give a slight wince. His
father had also explained that spicy tone that often
accompanied any talk of Serena. The knowledge never

made dealing with the tone any easier nor the look on his mother's face when she used it.

"Serena wants me to accompany her to a gala tonight so there's a chance I might be home late tonight."

"Late?"

There she goes again. "Yes maam the gala doesn't start until after dark."

"How late?"

"About 1 AM."

"1 AM! What times does it start?"

Damien sighed mentally. He knew his father was in the next room listening, waiting for the right moment.

"My question is where is the gala?"

Great now his father had jumped in.

"It starts at 8 in one of those old halls where the krewes throw their silly annual balls."

"Who else is going to be there?" his mother inquired.

"Her parents, some other bigwigs and unfortunately us."

"Well nice knowing you son," his father added patting his son on the shoulder.

"I know; I hate those things."

"So why are you going?"

Damien gave both his parents a look that brought a sly smile from his father and nothing from his mother, both wisely dropped the subject.

"So you're not going to the parades?", his mother inquired.

"Oh I'm going with some of the guys," the boy lied.

"Is that Harmon boy going with you?"

"Who? Achilles?"

"Ahh that's his name. That poor child I hope he is feeling better."

"Wait up," Damien stammered, "how do you know about that?"

"Come on son you did bring him to the hospital where I work, where your picture is splattered all across my locker. That and his grandparents called Sunday."

"I don't remember them calling here."

"That's because you wasn't here when they called."

"And you both forgot to tell me they called." He opened the cabinet and reached for a bowl.

His mother merely shrugged and returned to reading her paper. "That poor boy, your daddy has no understanding; calling him a walking corpse."

Jonathan Parker's voice bellowed from across the other side of the house. "Dag gone it Marie there you go mixing up my words again."

"Jonathan! You didn't call that boy a walking corpse Sunday?"

"I said the suicidal are the walking dead."

"Same thing."

"No it's not. You said I called the boy a walking corpse when I didn't."

"You said the suicidal are the walking dead."

"Yup said dead, not corpse." His voice lowered slightly as he entered the kitchen.

"Jonathan they're the same thing. If you're dead you're a corpse. If you're a corpse, you're dead."

Jonathan Parker merely swiped the rest of the newspaper before prancing back into the sunroom as it was called, but not before poking his head back in the kitchen for one final word. "How do you know and besides the point is I said dead not corpse."

Marie Parker's face was one of annoyance as Damien heard her muttering on the similarities between dead and corpse. Each cycle becoming fainter and fainter; his pop tarts were just popping out the toaster when her yell rumbled throughout the house.

"GIVE ME BACK MY PAPER JONATHAN!"

However his mind was focused on something more important.

The walking dead …

The paladin who longs for the walking dead.

A paladin – a knight, a champion.

If Achilles is the walking dead .. then ... then it could be that.

Seneca, Achilles, Andra – all people I know. Yes it makes sense now why Andra could see the demon.

He ate quickly before scrolling back down the caller id and hoped.

Chapter 21

The morning was cool yet humid as Seneca Maza stood at the edge of City Park.

When standing at the abyss looking down and seeing apocalypse staring back. How does one not think of all this as a heartless, godless, universe; how does one not doubt.

He knew he would be lying if he said he never had doubts – he was human after all. Regardless of all the spirits had done to him he was still human.

And yet you still keep going. Why? Because for every doubt there is also a possibility for hope.

He exhaled. He was ready for whatever it was that fate had in store for him. He proceeded into the park but not before sending a magical summon.

The scent of the river flared in the morning breeze caressing his face as he shifted the motorcycle down the street and around the corner. He didn't care that he was riding at least 40 miles above the speed limit, he had on his helmet.

Whew. He shifted his body, putting the vehicle into a turn. It wasn't until he was about a block from Achilles' grandparents' home that he eased off the accelerator. Within a minute or two the vehicle had been slowed to a crawl. *Ahh here we are.* He pulled to a stop, but not before noticing a red Mustang pulling up to the house. An instant later, the figure of Andra Alexander emerged and started toward the front door.

Damien kicked up the acceleration whirling past house. *No doubt about it, she's definitely going to the house where Achilles lives. What's Andra doing here? Relax Parker this might actually save you some trouble if I really have this figured out.*

He sped around the corner and made a u turn before parking the bike at a safe distance where he could observe the house.

Achilles had answered the door and went back in only to show up a second later with a jacket. The pair walked back to the Mustang and got into the car. The purr of the engine sounded and the Mustang pulled off. Damien waited until they had turned the corner before following them.

They were currently on Interstate 10 heading downtown. *Where the heck are they going? And why are they going together?* The wheels of his mind were attempting to churn out a possible reason when the sight of the Superdome caught the corner of his eye. *Andra and Achilles … in the same car, heading to the same destination. Heck this would be the day for it to happen too. Well whatever the reason I'll just follow them and pretend to surprisingly run into them. Then I can explain.* He just hoped they would believe him.

What the … There was no denying it he felt a presence in his mind. Someone was calling him and not just anyone. *Seneca? But how? I definitely didn't sense any such ability before? Why does he want to go there?*

Damien growled. There was only one way to find out, but first things first. He accelerated the bike, keeping himself a safe distance from Andra's car.

"I hope you have a good reason for diverting me out here?"

Seneca Maza opened his eyes. He had already known who it was before he had come within 30 feet of him. "I don't know. Seemed like a good enough spot."

"All the way to City Park?," Damien exclaimed. "Do you know I'm missing a chance to catch a coconut?" He gave a mock sigh before continuing.

He hasn't asked yet. Why?

"I know who the people are in our dreams. Well most of them." *He's wondering why I haven't asked about his powers yet.* Damien had known by looking beyond that he had been changed. *It wasn't just his new abilities --- his whole outlook on the world has changed. Just like me.* "You can relax Seneca I already know. It was the spirits wasn't it"

Seneca relaxed; the burden he carried seemed lighter – no that wasn't the right word. Shared, yes shared seemed more appropriate. He didn't answer him directly, but he knew he didn't have to. "So who are they?"

"Surprisingly I go to school with them."

"Do they know?"

"No. I was in the process of explaining when someone summoned me here." The tone changed as Damien gave a sly wink. "Sounds like anyone you know."

"Sorry."

"Don't worry about it," Damien replied with the same smile he had shown Sunday at the library. A smile that waned through a slight grimace.

"You feel it too hun?"

He felt it all right. Hatred, fear. They seemed to wrap around his throat and choke him. "Damn fools they don't know what they are doing. Come on we don't have much time."

Seneca followed behind him. Neither saw a sinister figure step out from behind the trees watching the pair until they disappeared from view. Then with the same stealth he had displayed while watching them, he turned and walked off in the opposite direction.

The Guardian was not surprised to see an abundance of law officials at the parade. He had been surprised that the parade wasn't cancelled. The events at the courthouse Monday had triggered rioting in the city. Most of which had taken place not too far from here. Then again it wasn't too far from here that one went from relative splendor to slumming poverty.

To be honest that was the story of many of America's larger cities, but few seemed to be surrounded by it like New Orleans. Many cities were able to hide such aspects of their reality – either it was swept away under a fantasy carpet of success and achievement or covered like a horrible scar with layers of clothing. For New Orleans though, there were just too many scars and they were too deep. No amount of clothes could ever hide them from being exposed and thanks to Erther Eugene – and in part to himself, what little clothing there was had been eaten away, leaving the scabs and burns for all to see and cringe upon.

As he and Seneca moved along the crowd, looking for any sign of Achilles and Andra, he couldn't help but notice the looks of uncertainty and deception on people's faces. Try as they might to disguise the ugliness of their city in celebration, they couldn't. The illusion was gone – and he in part shared the blame for that.

He heeded everything as the pair continued their search. His face hardened as he glanced upon his watch. The parade was already half way over and there was still so much ground to cover, so much at stake.

His court of thought was adjourned by Seneca's voice. "Any sign of them."

The Guardian snarled. He had sent someone to watch over them but in keeping track of them the possibility of that person finding him to tell where they were was almost hopeless.

Time to get lucky. "There."

Seneca followed his arm across the street where a boy and a tall girl stood.

"We have to get across the street." It was easier said than done considering the trailer size floats following each other down the street.

"Okay Stan, what's the plan?"

"We either wait for the parade to end or we wait for a gap."

"So which option?"

"Which ever comes first."

The gap had come first, but after watching what had happened to a spectator who ran into the street to get a souvenir, the Guardian decided to wait. The spectator had gone to grab a Zulu head that had landed in the street. He managed to grab the Zulu head, but not before the police were reaching for him. The man put up a resistance, but all he got for the effort was a slam to the ground and a recital of Miranda. Had there not been a good number of officers to provide backup, a few of the man's friends might have acted on their hostility instead of just voicing it.

No, the city was on edge enough as it was, it didn't need anything to stir up the cinders into a full flame so he decided to wait. That was when Andra and Achilles decided to come closer to him.

"Follow me," the Guardian commanded. Seneca was surprised at the trouble he had keeping up as the Guardian snaked through the eerie crowd, his cape waving behind him like a green flag in the wind. *If not for the cape I probably would have lost him immediately.*

Damien's stomach held a hollow feeling as he watched Andra Alexander and Achilles Harmon. *Look at them. I always knew those two had a thing for each other. How can I ask them to do this, to lay what could be their lives on the line especially Achilles. For once he's not brooding.*

"Andra! Achilles!"

The pair stared in amazement as they turned to see Damien Parker. Both recognized him but they also noticed that there was something about him – an awe that neither had seen in him before.

"Damien," Achilles answered, his normally almond hewed face was a light beige.

The Guardian conveyed a sly smile. His friend would receive his due from him, that he promised, but not now. He would do that tomorrow when all this was over with, if any of them survived to see tomorrow. "I need the both of you to come with me."

"Come with you?" Achilles chimed dumbfoundedly.

Andra merely eyed him curiously. It wasn't uncommon for people to come to Mardi Gras parades costumed, but there was something familiar about the garb he was in. *That cape!*

Achilles however still commanded his faculty of speech. "Where? Why? This can't wait?"

"No!" the Guardian sighed. "Look I'll explain everything, but not now, not here."

Achilles stared at Damien before the Guardian realized that he was actually staring behind him.

"He's with me," the Knight of the Order replied. He had almost forgotten about Seneca. *What. No!* The Guardian turned as Andra and Achilles gave a side glance as screams and a series of crashes came to their ears. Andra bullied her way to where Damien Parker and the Indian stood and followed their eyes toward the end of the street. That's when she saw them.

A low curse came from behind Andra as she eyed the four monstrous beings. Horror gripped her as she recognized them. God it couldn't be, but there they were in plain sight exactly as they had appeared in the painting in the cathedral: Pestilence, Famine, War, and Death – the four horsemen of the Apocalypse.

She prayed that this was all a dream but she knew this was real. Their steeds were as daunting as the horrors that rode them. Clouds of teal vapor exhumed from Famine's dark steed, its eyes burned with madness and when it neighed one only heard a song of frenzy and confusion. Pestilence's white steed was an image out of a nightmare. It's strong, sturdy legs seemed more appropriate on a lion than a horse. Then again a horse normally didn't breathe fire or have tails that caused sparks to flash in the air with its wag. And then there was Death. Its pale horse was everything that one feared from its rider's embrace. Its mane was ragged; its figure small and brittle and with every motion a creek of pain and sorrow hissed through the air.

Her terror was equaled with amazement as she noticed Damien Parker stepping from them, heading straight toward the four behemoths. "Andra," he replied. "Keep Achilles safe. Seneca let's see if the makeover the spirits gave you is worth anything."

Achilles and Andra both stared at each other, their faces full of confusion – and embarrassment.

She's suppose to protect me?

I'm suppose to protect him? Even more startling to Andra was the calm in his voice. *God this is too much.* She noticed her hands gripping tightly the arm next to her. "Achilles?"

"I don't know," he responded. "Just do as he says."

Andra gave him a look. *What? How am I suppose to protect you, you're calmer than I am!* Her eyes returned to Damien Parker. The way he walked displayed calm and collected focus. *Here he is about to face the heralds of the Apocalypse and he's treating it like we're reading Hamlet back in English class.*

Why now. They couldn't have waited an hour. Oh well. This time it's going to be different. The Guardian paused, Seneca stopped right next to him. Two of the Nestari versus the personifications of man's worst fears. So who's first?

As if hearing the question, Death charged toward him, his scythe ready to cut the Guardian in half. The Guardian drifted back and whirled around causing the scythe to miss completely. Magic flared from the white staff and lanced into the side of the steed. A pitiful moan filled the air as the steed jumped back. The Guardian loosed his magic again, consuming the specter of death in white fire.

A yell had come from the crowd, but the Guardian was already aware of the danger as he moved aside to his right causing War's mace to hit nothing but concrete. A quick turn placed him in front of the horseman's vile steed and magic flared again from the staff, sending lightning down the beast throat causing it to bellow in pain.

You again. He turned and brought up his staff deflecting Death's scythe away long enough to deliver another assault of magic that send the horseman sprawling.

Andra watched the dance with amazement. The boy alternated between his foes as if he was at prom or homecoming dancing with two admirers at once. Even now he deflected the armored knight's mace just as the grim reaper raised his scythe. Before she could even yell a warning, Damien was already in motion and the scythe only hit what appeared to be his shadow.

How can he move that fast? It was as if he had left his shadow behind. Her eyes filled with even greater amazement as Damien suddenly appeared along side the grim reaper and stuck his staff into the calf of his steed before unleashing a bolt of lightning. Then with a smoothness and grace she had never seen before he spun as if in a whirlwind back to War, his staff colliding with the behemoth's mace producing a loud crack that left everyone watching dazed.

If she was amazed, the crowd was bedazzled. Each move Damien made released a chorus of oohs and ahhs. "Achilles, do you …"

"I see it. I just don't believe it."

The Indian wasn't doing too bad himself, however compared to Damien Parker, the difference was large and obvious. Parker's motions seemed to be an art in and of itself while the Indian was barely holding his own. Even now Damien was executing a 360 degree flip spin between his opponents that only a gymnast could fully appreciate. As his toes barely touched the concrete, a sweep of his left arm sent his cape billowing above and behind him enough to avoid causing an accidental trip. As the green cape settled gently over his shoulders and back Andra could have sworn she heard chimes.

As the Guardian slowly straightened, a growl of frustration snarled from him. No body had moved, rather the fools were standing and cheering like this was some kind of performance.

I can't chance using my full force, I might accidentally injure someone – or worse. At the same time I can't keep this game of tag going for much longer either. Something's gotta give.

He turned and gave a sweep of his staff. I hope this works. His eyes turned to the right where he saw Seneca scrambling to his feet after dodging one of Pestilence's claws.

"You all right?" he inquired.

The Indian gave him a glance. "A little winded, but for the most part I'm okay."

His exhaustion showed. His chest heaved and compressed as his lungs swallowed gulps of air. So much sweat had poured down his forehead that trails could be seen and spots littered his shirt where perspiration had collected.

This has to end now. "Seneca. Take Andra and Achilles and head toward the motorcycle. I'll be right behind you."

The Indian hesitated.

"Go! I'll be fine. I promise."

The Indian nodded and slowly crept back toward Andra and Achilles. "Come on. We have to leave."

Andra merely stood there. "What! We can't just leave Damien to die out there!"

"He's going to be fine," Seneca replied.

"No I'm not leaving."

Seneca sighed. "We don't have time for this. Excuse me, Achilles right? Could you grab her arm there."

The two boys slowly dragged the girl away kicking and screaming causing the Guardian to turn and see what was going on. Already there were several people trying to come to Andra's aid.

Daggone it Andra! The Guardian focused his magic directly at the trio. A pair of hands reached out to grab Achilles, but stopped in mid air only inches from his shoulders. People ahead of them were moved out the way by some mysterious force.

"What in the world?" Achilles exclaimed before giving the Indian a look. "Did you?"

"No. Damien must have created some kind of magical barrier around us. Come on we need to hurry. He won't be able to protect us and himself for long."

Good they're all right. The Guardian resumed his stand as the Four Horsemen attempted to surround him. *Curse Andra, because of her I had to use more of my magic than I wished to. Between that girl and this crowd of idiots I'm beginning to wonder how I'm even still alive. I could attack, but because of the concentration I have to maintain to keep the wall around these people.*

I might not muster enough to get the job done. There might be a way though.

The Knight of the Order gripped his staff, waiting for the right moment to spring his trap when a light caught his eye along with a feeling of déjà vu. "You've got to be kidding me."

The armored knight had made his return. Same red armor. Same horse.

This time however Damien Parker took advantage of the interruption. He summoned his magic and released it upon the horsemen. Magical energy enveloped upon them like a net. The steeds were urged on, but the brutes didn't respond. Instead they stepped back.

A horse neigh drew all their attention as the charger raced toward them.

War glanced at the Guardian and back at the charging knight before turning to retreat. The other three followed the armored specter as a dark mist appeared in front of them. The demons barely made it to the mist when the charger met them. At the collision, a wave of bright light flooded in all directions. When the light dissipated only the Guardian stood in the street. For a few minutes the Guardian stared forward, ascertaining whether his foes were really gone.

Gone ... but not destroyed. He turned and headed toward the rendezvous point where Seneca and the others would be waiting.

Chapter 22

Andra Alexander's impatience brewed like a gumbo on a hot stove as she sat on the hood of her red Mustang. Every few seconds she would glance back and forth hoping to catch sight of him.

"Where is he?" she exclaimed with a snarl which left Achilles wondering if she was concerned about their classmate or just wanted him alive so she could kill him. Her body language and words seemed to confirm the former, but her eyes had a look he himself had seen before and experience told him that there was a strong possibility of her purpose being the later.

The Indian, Seneca Maza, apparently a friend of Damien, was leaning against a nearby building. His eyes closed as if in deep concentration, his body seemed rigid and lifeless. Had it not been for an occasional hard breath, Achilles would have wondered if he was dead. *For all I know he could be dying.*

At Andra's words, his eyes slowly opened and locked directly on the girl's face. "He'll be here," he replied.

"You're awfully confident," Achilles chimed.

"You would too if you knew what he was."

Achilles was just about to inquire on that very subject, but Andra threw a tirade that cut off his chance.

"How do you know? How can you be sure he's all right? We just left him there! How do you know he's not dead?"

"Because I'm right here."

Achilles almost jumped as a green cape suddenly appeared and unwrapped to reveal Damien Parker. Andra jumped off the hood and started toward him, but Damien turned and with a step was by Seneca's side just as the boy slowly slid down the wall into a sitting position.

"You all right?" Damien asked.

"I'm … I'm fine. I just need to rest for a bit."

"There's a bench nearby. You can rest there." The two slowly made their way to the bench followed by Andra and Achilles. Seneca slowly settled down on one end of the bench while Damien knelt on the ground beside him.

"Is he all right?" Achilles inquired. He noticed that Damien was no longer in his armored costume, but in a dark pair of jeans with a dark green polo shirt and a dark leather jacket.

"He's just woozy. I'm guessing Famine must have touched him at some point during the battle. Same thing happened to me during my first encounter with them."

"First encounter! You mean you've faced these things before?"

"Damien Parker what the hell is going on?" Andra yelled. "You put on a light show against some creatures that for some reasons give me the ultimate heebie-jeebies!"

Damien sighed. "Have you ever wondered how some things happen in the world that leaves you wondering how in God's name did that happen? How some tragedy or miracle happens to occur in what as seemingly an eminent triumph or doom?"

Achilles gave his friend a distressful look. "Yeah, what's that got to do with anything of this?"

"Everything. There are things that attempt to cause chaos wherever they can. They need for people to feel pain and suffering in order to exist. They feed off it. Standing in their way are people like me – like us."

Both of them gave him a look. "Like us?"

"Yes. You see there are other forces on this planet besides those that we apply to our laws of physics. Turns out physics is just the first layer of the cake."

Achilles started to back away in disbelief. "No, no, no, no! You're trying to tell me that we're part of some real life X Files plotline!"

"In dumb man's words, yes."

"That's crazy!"

"Is it? You'd be surprised at the amount of things in the world physics seem to fall short of explaining."

"How many times have things been a question of fate," Andra added softly.

"Exactly."

"Why you? Why us?"

"I don't know. I really don't know. All I know is tonight I need your help or a lot of bad things will happen. A lot of unnecessary bad things."

Achilles merely sighed before collapsing onto the pavement. "So what do we need to do?"

Damien gave a sly smile. "Actually it would help if Seneca had something to eat to help his body counter Famine's attack. Here's five bucks."

Achilles took the money, glanced back at Seneca resting on the bench before his eyes returned to Damien. "Okay I'm on it."

Damien watched as Achilles disappeared around the corner. "So," he said, not turning to face the girl. "How long you've been able to call that knight up?" He turned and her face was barely in his view when he felt her hand strike him with all the force she could muster.

"What was that for?" Damien demanded, rubbing the side of his face. *God she hits hard.*

"For lying to me, for trying to make me think I was crazy. You knew everything I saw in that alley was true and you deliberately made me believe it was an illusion."

"Andra it was for your own good. Think about it, if you went around talking about seeing knights and demons duking it out everyone would think you were crazy – even your own Pastor Greg."

Andra stepped up to him and Damien half expected her to slap him again. "Don't try to make excuses Damien Parker." She turned and started away.

"What did you want me to do? Say that the world is full of demons that you can't see or hear."

"But I **can** see them."

"That doesn't mean you have magic, that like me you're some warrior errand who has to protect everyone from bloodthirsty demons. Contrary to popular belief, these demons don't stop and cringe when you say a Hail Mary or the Our Father prayer. It just infuriates them – heck some of them get a kick out of it."

The girl turned but instead of fury, her face was a mixture of sadness and confusion. "You don't know how long I've been wondering if I'm sane or insane. Sitting up at night wondering if my whole world is an illusion of some kind. Damnit, I'm suppose to be superwoman!"

He grabbed her and softly pulled her in, his arms embracing her. "I know this is a hard pill to swallow, but you are capable of handling this." He chuckled for a moment.

"What's so funny?"

"The fact that you never answered my question."

"Oh yeah." She broke free of him and turned away. "It started about a week ago. I was jogging by myself as I had done countless times before, but there were these voices that I kept hearing and then I saw some kind of shadow ahead of me. Then I felt someone behind me – close behind me. I mean I could feel his hands descending onto my shoulders. I tried to scream, but couldn't. Finally, I just resolved to at least make it a struggle. Then the rider appeared, and then disappeared – but so did the shadow.

Then there was last Friday – the rider protected me from some monster that tried to attack me outside of Michelle's house. I had dismissed it as a delusion. How did you know about it?"

"That Sunday in the alley. It appeared after I had trapped you in my cape and a while ago when I was battling the Four Horsemen."

"Any idea what it is?"

"It's magic of course, apparently very protective magic since it only seems to pop up when you're in danger."

"You mean like some kind of magical automatic defense mechanism?"

"Yeah for the most part." He stopped himself; there were still things about the knight that perplexed him. *Is it automatic or can it be controlled and it's just been acting on reflex?* "What happened Friday night?"

"I just arrived at Michelle's house when this monster appeared out of the blue."

Why was it attacking her? Did it feel her magic? "What did it look like?"

"Like some kind of deformed vela raptor out of Jurassic Park. It leapt at me and I recall my mind bracing my body for an attack and then the knight appeared."

Could it be that it acts on her emotions? On her fear? Her determination? If so then it probably can be controlled. He sighed.

"What's wrong?" Andra asked.

"I wish Achilles would hurry back. The sooner he gets back, the sooner we can move." He went to check on Seneca when Andra asked a question that stopped him in his tracks.

"Does Serena know?"

"Knows about what?" *Don't play dumb Parker you know exactly what she means.*

"About this; about the magic?"

"Yes she does, in fact she can channel magic too."

Chapter 23

A laugh reeled from Andra Alexander as she hung up the phone and walked back toward the vehicles where the others waited. As her eyes looked upon Damien Parker, another peel of laughter rolled from her lips.

Andra's quick return only meant one thing – Serena wasn't home. Damien's face held a disappointing scowl. His mood was already distasteful from the fun Andra seem to have at his expense, his ignorance of Serena's whereabouts only added to his misery. Originally his plan had been to stop Andra and Achilles before the parade, return to Marrero, summon Serena and go from there. Seneca's summon as well as the appearance of the Four Horsemen wrecked that plan. Going back to Marrero would be at least 20 minutes and it was already two in the afternoon. *Four hours.* Four hours to find the two remaining pieces of the riddle and confront Magnus. *You know Magnus is going to have something waiting to delay you at every turn, whether it is Malagant or the four wannabee heralds of apocalypse.* However between himself, Seneca, Serena, Andra, and Achilles there was at least a possibility of hope even if they didn't find the last three of the seven "walkers"

"Are you still laughing at me Andra?"

"Yes," the girl replied with a chuckle. "Come on Damien only an hour ago you took on the four heralds of apocalypse single handedly like it was a game of hopscotch and now you're running from one man." She burst into fresh peels of laughter.

"Didn't I explain it to you? He hates me! One mention of my name and he would have said she was anywhere else but where she actually is! You won't believe the grief that man has caused me, he's a one man relationship wrecking crew! The sad part of it is though, I'm one of the good guys! He should be rooting for me!"

"To be honest I kind of envy the situation. I wish I had to choose between my father and a boy I was in love with."

"Why would any sane person want to wish that headache upon themselves?"

"Because," Andra answered softly, "It would mean my father was still here."

She knew they were looking at them, enticing them, pleading them. She couldn't blame them, it was Mardi Gras and they were on Bourbon Street and between her and Enrica, possessed enough curves and bust to make heads turn. Serena scoffed, these perverts were so sick they would get off on anything female whether she was beautiful or not. She glanced back teasingly and slowly slid her hand down her shirt, stopping at her hips. Her fingers grabbed and started to raise the shirt tail exposing the brown skin of her stomach.

The hooting grew louder with anticipation, but the shirt tail never reached higher than the rim of her stomach before she let it drop.

"Serena!"

The girl laughed as Sara glared at her with scolding eyes.

"It's bad enough Enrica's teasing them."

Serena laughed. "Oh don't even put me in the same class as Enrica."

Enrica Bradley's neck was full of beads, most of which she earned in the Quarter. Now that was a girl who teased. Enrica's standpoint was that toothpick models were paid so much money because it was the only way they could get a man. Real men wanted curves and if you didn't believe it all you had to do was observe good ol' Norma Jean and Halle. She lived by that creed and was a validity of the argument. Enrica might have violated the girl pride creed a few times to get some beads, but it was a rare occasion when she did. Rather she just used her hands, legs, head, back, and the laws of motion. In Enrica Bradley's world the key to a man's heart was through his imagination, especially sick, perverted ones. "Mardi Gras Law #1 Make a pervert use his imagination and he will give you the world." She said as they entered the French Quarter early Mardi Gras morning.

Serena glanced back at Sara, recalling last Sunday afternoon. "I never did thank you did I?"

"For what?"

"For trying to warn me."

"Ah it was nothing. Damien's the one who did all the rescuing, he's the hero."

Serena mentally sighed when she heard Damien's name. Three days ago she had thought of Damien Parker as just a normal teenage boy with a bright future, a future she knew she wanted to be part of. Now she knew that he was an extraordinary person with a tragic destiny much like her own. A destiny she wanted so much to cast aside. *How does he do it? How does he scope with all the stress, the pulling, the tugging ... the deception.* She paused her train of thought as she glanced down at her pager vibrating on her belt clip. With a simple sweep the pager was off her belt and in her hand in front of her face. *Speak of the devil ... I think about him and next thing you know you get a page.* She laughed as she scurried toward the payphone near the corner.

Damien Parker didn't need the caller id to tell him who was calling. "Hello Love."

"What's up?"

"Plenty, but no time to explain now. Where are you?"

"In the Quarter with Enrica and Sara."

Enrica and Sara? Could it be possible that ... Andra's the paladin, Achilles is the walking dead she desires. Seneca is the one who guards the land. All three of them were teenagers like himself. All of them acquaintances of his ... Sara's white, could she be the soul who guards fire?

You will die Guardian

The sleeper must awaken

Die Guardian Die!

To be ... or not to be --- that is the question.

You must die Child of Water.

To die ... to sleep

The sleeper must awaken

Is it I who waits to be awaken?

To find the silver and green, seek your heart's desire

   To sleep, perchance to dream.

      Die ...

         I am your heart ... that face?

            I am your heart ... that face!

            I know who they are now ...

                  the Seven Walkers.

                     But will it be enough? Have
I awakened yet?

"Damien!"

"Yes Love?"

"Did you hear what I just asked you?"

"Asked me what?"

He heard an impatient sigh. "Where do you think we should meet at?"

"Café Du Monde."

"Ok. How long?"

"We're on our way now."

"Ok so see you in thirty?"

Damien hung up the phone and rushed back into the sunroom where the others were watching the breaking news with his father. "Good God is that Charity Hospital?"

"Yep."

But that's only blocks from the French Quarter! Serena is in there!

"Come on you guys," Damien replied calmly we better get going. He turned and started for the door, the other three following.

"So where are we off to?" Andra asked.

"One last gathering before the final showdown." He immediately regretted the words almost as much as he blamed himself for the riots that were currently happening downtown. Those were not words that they needed to hear, but as he watched them get into Andra's car he noticed that they seemed a little more ... focused. He sighed. *They're so dedicated and yet they have no idea what they are getting into. I only hope I have what it takes to guide them because they deserve to see tomorrow and not dread it.*

He started the motorcycle and pulled off, leading his troops toward the abyss with Andra's Mustang right behind him.

Chapter 24

"C'mon y'all do we have to get to eat at Café Du Monde? We could have stayed in the Quarter and got some grub!"

"Good God girl," Serena fussed, "what you trying to do, kill us? You know all that fast food is bad for you. Besides you flirted with enough guys and I know for a fact that you don't want any of them."

"Yeah but you have to admit the girl still got the skills." Enrica countered.

"You sure you didn't have to lift your shirt up for some of those beads?"

"Serena I'm shocked! The both of you were watching me the whole time!"

"Not the entire time," Sara corrected. "There's a possibility that ..."

Enrica cut her off. "Don't worry Sara, I'll be happy to give you some pointers. Come on Serena let's go back."

"Girl no! I want some food and we have plenty of time to fool around in the Quarter." She didn't want to just leave them especially Sara and for all Enrica's carrying on, there was something bothering her. What she wasn't sure of. "Besides we're already three- quarters of the way there," she scolded as they neared Royal Street.

"Let's cut through Pirate's Alley," Sara suggested.

"Fine by me," Serena agreed but her voice dropped as she glanced around. Her instincts told her they were being followed, but she saw nothing. *Something is here following us.* She jumped as she felt a grip on her arm. Her tension loosened as her head turned to see the face of Sara Winters.

"Serena; you all right? You looked out of it for a second." Her large brown eyes were larger than usual and Serena could see the fear in them.

Serena forced a smile and patted the girl's hand. "I'm fine Sara, my stomach has me hearing things. Come on Enrica my stomach is killing me."

"We just passed the Old Coffee Pot!" Enrica whined.

"Girl I don't want any Old Coffee Pot, come on!" She prayed the terror in her mind wasn't conveyed in her voice. She led them around the corner of Royal Street, her pace fast and steady. The sooner they arrived at Café Du Monde the better she would feel. *Damien Parker, you better be there because something is here and it's hunting us.*

For Sara Winters Pirate Alley always revived a dying hope of possible romanticism. As she glanced up at the assorted balconies and their ironworks, she always found herself thinking of Juliet's balcony. This was the French Quarter she loved, a monument to dashing heroes, true love, and simplicit beauty.

She closed her eyes and inhaled. Despite all the craziness and despair, here hope existed. As long as buildings and atmosphere such as this existed, things like honor, beauty, and love would never die.

She opened her eyes as Serena Martin gave a sudden gasp, hardly her usual response to what she called Sara's deluded idealism. Usually she laughed. The ones who possess such traits often scoff them. However her vision cleared she noticed the dark shadow looming at the end of the alley, a dark voluptuous shadow.

Even worse was the sound that it emitted – terrible hisses and clicks that touched Sara's soul with a chill she had never felt before. *No, I have felt this before. In my dreams, my nightmares. Oh God please let this be a nightmare.* "Serena."

"Sara you see it."

"Yes."

Sara wanted to ask something else, but didn't as a terrible roar filled the alley as a monster stepped into the alley. Its body took up the whole width of the alley. Huge retracted wings covered its back and side. Its legs were like the tree stumps of an old oak tree her uncle had chopped down in the country near Baton Rouge. And its face – eyes that burned red as she had never seen before and hoped she would never see again. Its snout grinned to show sharp yellow teeth. Saliva dripped from them and evaporated as they hit the ground, creating a cloud of mist that only made the beast appear more horrific.

While the wolf-like creature frightened her; it was its rider that terrified her. First was its calm, confident manner in which it sat upon its terrible steed. Second were the assorted spikes and jagged edges of its armor. A dark joy emitted from it as if it could feel their fright and enjoyed the fact that it was responsible.

Sara was so terrified that she failed to hear a loud thud for if she had she probably would have died as the figure from her nightmare sneered from one of the balconies. Sara failed to see him, but Serena did not.

Malagant.

A hiss of hatred oozed out the demon as he eyed her. Pleasure filled his eyes for he knew she would die this day.

Serena noticed him, her eyes never flinching. They were cut off. She glanced back at Sara and Enrica. Both of them were scared. *What should I do?* She could probably take on Malagant alone, but with the other demon involved, she wasn't sure if she could hold out long enough.

She wouldn't have long to ponder because Malagant with a quickness that defied his size crouched and leaped off the balcony toward her.

Damien Parker closed his eyes, pondering on his next move. Serena still had yet to arrive and each passing moment only made him more anxious. *Should I try to go look for her or should I wait?*

Both choices could backfire. If he left and Serena showed up after he left to search for her, he would only be creating the same scenario he was currently in. *But what if she's in trouble? What if . . .* No he didn't dare think it.

He froze as a vibe flooded him followed by that same feeling that overcame him Sunday afternoon. Only this time the feeling was accompanied by a strong familiarity and a voice. "Damien … Please help me!"

Serena! He broke into a run heading straight for Jackson Square.

Andra glanced at Achilles who glanced at Seneca before following him. "Damien wait!" Andra replied as she avoided being hit by a car. "Where are we going?"

Damien's pace picked up as he entered Jackson Square, following the pavement to the famous statue of the general on a heading that took him to St. Louis Cathedral. He paused before gripping his staff in his hands and cautiously crept around the corner.

Resolve filled Serena Martin as she accepted her fate. Her body tensed as she again called for her magic. She could feel it swelling up, oozing its way to the surface.

Malagant is somewhere around here. She tried to calm herself as she backed Enrica and Sara down Calilido Way toward St. Peter's. Glancing behind her she noticed that the corner was only three feet away.

"Sara listen to me! I want you to go to Café Du Monde. Damien should be there waiting for me. Tell him …" She paused. As much as she wanted Damien to come for her, it was more important he stop the Maderan. "Tell him to go on as he planned, I'll catch up if I can."

"Serena are you crazy?" Sara inquired, "that thing will kill you!"

"Sara go!"

The words barely left her when the wolf-serpent suddenly appeared behind Sara. Serena quickly grabbed the girl and pulled her away. "Run both of you!" She turned to face the demon steed, its teeth gashing and snapping. She locked eyes on the monster's, her head burning with concentration as she unleashed her magic. *Work. Please work.*

The serpent reared, nearly buckling its rider. Serena stepped back to avoid the creature's feet and the boiling saliva dripping from its mouth as the armored creature brought the monster to bear. Something told Serena to lean close to the wall which saved her from being burned to a chard by a stream of fire.

As the orange red ribbon dissipated, Serena started to run. A yell caught her attention and she jumped back, avoiding Malagant's crushing descent. She shook off her dizziness as she surveyed the situation. On one side she saw the terrifying head of the wolf-serpent only inches from her and on the other, Malagant's sword arm was raised high ready to strike her dead.

So this is how it ends. Well so be it. Goodbye Mother ...Father ... Suddenly a strange joy filled her and Malagant stumbled forward over her into the wolf-serpent, his back covered with blue fire. Her weariness immediately raced away as she heard a familiar voice call her name.

Damien Parker had found her.

She scrambled to her feet and sure enough at the end of the alley stood Damien Parker, his purple cloak covering his shoulders. In one hand was the white staff that glowed as white and blue sparks flashed around it.

Sara and Enrica flanked him on one side and Achilles Harmon and Andra Alexander on the other.

What is going on?

"Will you come on!", Damien yelled.

Serena ran and collapsed into his arms. "What took you so long?"

Damien allowed a sly smile. "I was waiting on you and I had to gather a few friends."

A smart alleck until the end. She noticed his smile was gone. His face was now a stone countenance of determination. *He's the Guardian now.* She found herself feeling joyous and yet also sad.

"All of you into the Cathedral. Now!"

"I'm staying." Andra answered.

"What part of all don't you understand?"

"How do you know the other three aren't here?"

"I'm hoping they are. Now go! Trust me I got this."

Andra slowly stepped back. "If you die Damien Parker I'll kill you."

"Same goes here," Serena added.

The Guardian gave a soft humph. "I'm going to live just so I can tell both of you how conflicting that comment is." He watched as they all vanished around the corner. Out of the corner of his eye he could see Death and Pestilence leaping from the Cathedral garden.

Only three. I guess that'll have to do. Last time I held back. This time we really see what you guys are made of. He raised his staff and prepared for combat.

"So how long are we suppose to sit here and wait?" Andra inquired while Seneca gently moved his hands up and down the doors in close examination. "What are you doing? Is there something there I can't see?"

"There's a spell on these doors. A powerful one," the Indian answered.

"Do you think Damien's the one responsible for it?"

"Wouldn't surprise me," Serena replied. "Probably why he wanted us to go inside here."

"You think he's okay," Andra inquired.

"He took them on before and managed to come out of it alive," Achilles added. "I'd put my money on him."

"He'll live," Serena replied. "I've seen that look on his face before. I feel sorry for those demons right about now."

"All of this is crazy," Andra yelled. "I mean what started out as a date has turned into a save the world situation."

Achilles jumped. "Date? Who said this was a date?"

"What's wrong with you?"

"Trying to figure you out? First you want to kill me then when I almost die you visit me and next thing I know you're dragging me to a parade and calling it a date!"

Andra look at him in amazement. "You thought this was a prank didn't you?"

"Any reason why I shouldn't have; given our history?"

The girl turned away. "No. You're right, given our history."

A squeak caused them both to turn as sunlight shined in and a small shadow loomed in the light before it vanished. Seconds later a loud clank filled the sanctuary as the door opened and the Guardian stepped in before stopping the door with his body and letting it close softly.

"Damien," Andra whispered.

The Knight of the Order walked between the two toward the altar. Andra and Achilles followed behind him. "Is everyone all right?" he inquired as he observed them.

A chorus of fines and yeahs answered him.

He stopped at the front two pews, his eyes taking the image of each of them in. They were all here: Serena, Seneca, Andra, Achilles, Sara, Enrica, and himself. Yes that makes seven. Enrica possessing magic, who would have thought.

As he eyed them he recalled the vision in the Dreamtime – the children in the house. Achilles in his black jacket and jeans seemed to reflect the anguish in his eyes and face. Seneca's yellow sweatshirt and beige cargo pants gave him the appearance of a shaman. Andra in her John Ehret letterman jacket, red shirt and breeches had the appearance of medieval warrior. And with her light blue jacket and blue jeans combined with her baby blue eyes Sara was the perfect reflection of innocence and purity.

And then there was Serena, whose long sleeved white shirt meshed perfectly with her light blue jeans that a silver aura seemed to glow from her. Beautiful Serena. Yes we are the seven who walk together on the Eve of Penance. Whose walk would spell triumph or doom.

Chapter 25

"What about you?" Serena inquired.

The Guardian gave her a perplexed look. "What about me?"

Damien Parker. He's Damien Parker again. She really wasn't sure how she could tell the two apart. It wasn't something major like voice pitch or tone rather it was a matter of feeling. The Guardian was like iron, unbreakable and unable to be deterred. His voice like his manner was cold, calculating, and unyielding. Damien Parker was warm, soothing, with a taint of mischief and silliness.

The Guardian commanded, Damien Parker inspired.

"How are you feeling?"

"Oh I'm fine." He stretched his arms out and flexed, loosening some stiff joints.

"Will someone explain what is going on?" Enrica exploded.

Damien gave them all a glance. The question was on all of their faces with the exception of Seneca and Serena. "In the universe there have always been two forces conflicting with each other. Up, down, good and bad, yin and yang, heaven and hell, whatever you wish to call it. The things that you guys saw are Daemonites, commonly known as demons. They inspire chaos and mayhem because they need it to survive."

"You said there were two forces, so what's there to oppose these demons?" Andra asked.

"People who are able to use magic as it is mistakenly referred as. People who are able to see the demons and stop them. People like us."

"Us?" Enrica exclaimed.

"The seven of us here, yes."

"Come on Damien you trying to tell us that Andra, Achilles, Sara, and myself have magical abilities?"

"But you do Enrica. I'm not sure how all of your abilities operate but each of you have something to contribute to the big picture."

"Well I don't believe it."

"Do you?"

She wasn't sure if it was the tone in his voice that made Enrica feel uneasy or if it was the way in which he eyed her. *Does he know? How could he know he wasn't there. He didn't see.* "Yes I don't believe all this mumbo jumbo about demons and magic."

"Neither did I at first, but I keep seeing something when I look at you."

"I should hope so Damien, but remember you have a girlfriend already."

"Funny Enrica. I meant your powers, I 'see' the magic, it's been awakened. I'm not sure what it does, but it's definitely there."

No! God no!

"What about me?"

"With you Sara I feel nothing, which means your magic is likely still dormant. The magic has to have been used before I can sense it. Think of it like a candle, until it's lit I don't know if it is even there, but once lit I can see and feel its warmth."

"So whose magic is awakened?" Achilles asked.

"Seneca's, Serena's, Enrica's, Andra's and my own."

"What about my powers?"

"Just like Sara, still dormant."

"Not a lotta good are we?"

"Trust me your powers will awaken when they are needed." *I hope.*

"Putting a whole lot on a slim hope."

"That's a norm."

"Okay," Andra said. "We have special powers but what about those four horsemen? Are they really the heralds of the ..."

"No," Damien answered. "The horsemen were merely specters – creations of magic with a distinct purpose and skill, but still are only extensions of their creator."

"Were? So you managed to destroy them?" Achilles asked.

"No. They still exist, just not as horsemen. Three of them at least, I'm not sure if War's steed was destroyed."

"Why aren't Terror, Trembling, and Panic attacking anyone else. Why us?"

Seneca gave him a look. "Were you paying attention to anything he said? You possess magic, you're a threat to them and their creator."

"Look I didn't ask you Apache Chief."

"Quiet both of you!" Damien scolded before turning to Achilles. "Right now we're the only thing that can prevent the release of a berserker class monster that wouldn't mind unleashing terror, trembling, and panic on everyone in the doggone state!"

Silence loomed as they all took in the image of scenario presented.

"So what do we do?" Serena finally inquired.

"We go to St. Louis Cemetery, trap the main demon when he tries to release the berserker monster, kill it and go home."

"Sounds simple enough?"

If only it was, the Guardian thought. Magnus wasn't a fool. He knew that the Guardian would have to go to Marie Laveau's grave to stop the Maderon's release. Malagant and the Four Horsemen would keep attacking, delaying him and forcing him to use up all his magic against them. He had to admit it was a formidable strategy. Powerful as his magic was, the odds of him defeating all six demons were slim. He didn't want to consider if the Maderan was added to the equation.

No. Failure was not an option, not this time.

Magnus had only anticipated opposition from the Guardian and Serena. Seneca and the rest were wild cards, completely unanticipated. *The Great Equalizer, but only if the card is played at the right time.* Which wasn't now, for now it was convenient for Magnus to believe that he had anticipated everything.

"Time to leave. Follow me. Serena you behind me, then Sara, Achilles, and Andra. Seneca, you bring up the rear, let me know if you see anything behind us. Let's go."

They followed him through the rear corridor and through a twist of halls and corridors when their leader suddenly stopped, spun around and his eyes locked upon the door from whence they had came.

"What?" Serena inquired.

Damn persistent pest these demons are. He turned back to his companions. "All of you head straight down the corridor and through the door. Wait for me in the garden." His eyes diverted to Serena Martin who was standing with her hands on her hips, her lips curled, her right foot tapping the floor.

He knew there would be no deterring her and any attempts at trying would be futile. *The woman's too persistent for her own good.* "Seneca take the lead. Andra, Achilles you two are next followed by Sara and Enrica. Serena and I will bring up the rear."

Her hands fell from her hips, but her lips were still curled. However her eyes had their normal sparkle as she turned and followed the others. Occasionally she would glance back to see if he was behind her. *Yeah like I'm gonna do something that dumb.*

Seneca and Andra pushed the rear doors open to the sight of the evening sun basking on the statue of Jesus in St. Anthony's Garden.

"Perfect," Damien whispered softly as he trudged to the front. Although he was surveying the garden for signs of the Four Horsemen, he couldn't help but enjoy the beauty of the scenery. The fleeing winter had taken its toll but the garden had held its ground. Banana and Magnolia trees defiantly held their leaves and branches high despite the whipping the cold and wind had and continued to bestow upon them.

"Come on we won't have much time before they realize ..." *Too late.* Out of the corner of his eye he saw Malagant's shadow. The others wouldn't be too far behind. "Over the fence! Quick!"

They followed him to the fence but when they were halfway there the Guardian suddenly stopped. Seconds later Pestilence appeared out of nowhere but the Guardian didn't move. *He isn't alone.* He glanced around till finally he spotted Famine lurking behind the oak tree.

The Guardian suddenly sprung into action, sending lightning into the shadow near the end of the fence. Famine let out a chilling wail before emerging into everyone's sight.

"Get over that fence now! I'll hold them off."

"The rest of you go I'm staying."

"Serena I need you to go with them. The sooner
we all get out the garden, the better. They're trying to
delay us. Trust me on this."

She ran off reluctantly and the Guardian spun
around unleashing his magic into Pestilence, however at
the last possible second the apparition changed into a
cloud of gnats and wasps.

"What the ..."

The cloud hovered for a second before shooting
itself toward him. The Guardian crouched, wrapping his
cape over himself. The insects loomed over him, but
couldn't penetrate the protective shielding of the cape.

Sensing a possible moment, the Guardian rose to
his full height, magic fire lancing from his staff and hands
igniting the insects in a breeze of fire.

A loud growl caused the Knight of the Order to
turn as Malagant landed just in front of the rear entrance.
The Guardian again wrapped his cape around himself, but
this time he ordered the magic to cloak him in invisibility.

Okay they all should be over the fence by now. However
he was concerned about Death and War, neither of which
he had seen since facing them on the other side of the
cathedral. He started to make his way toward the fence
slowly as not to attract Malagant and Pestilence's attention
when his eyes noticed Famine – and Enrica. The pair was
eying each other. Enrica had her arms extended and from
the way she was cooing one would have thought she was
trying to lure a cat out of a tree instead of a face off with a
demonic apparition.

"Enrica," he hissed, dropping his cloud of invisibility to reveal himself in an attack stance. "Enrica, what the heck are you doing? Get back!"

The girl turned and looked at him as if he was crazy. "Get back? From her? Why would I do that?"

"Enrica that thing will kill you! Get back!"

"Oh Damien you silly boy she won't hurt me." She took a step toward Famine.

"Enrica are you crazy! Get back!"

Enrica wondered what Damien Parker was so scared of, she had started to follow Serena and the others when a noise caught her attention and she saw her. She was the same as she had been that day at the church. So innocent, so precious, so vulnerable. Her face seemed to hold so much pain and sadness.

"Oh little bunny. No one to take away your pain." She stepped toward the child, hoping she would recognize her. "Come here little bunny." She extended her arms, hoping the child would come to her, but she just stood there. Steadily Enrica crept closer and closer till finally Enrica enveloped the child in her arms, her hold strong and tight.

The child merely stood rigid till finally she started to cry and returned Enrica's embrace. Feeling the child's acceptance, Enrica began humming as she clung the child to her breast, relishing the moment and hoping she would never have to let go.

The Guardian started to reach for Enrica as she embraced the pitiful figure that represented Famine. A tragic wail filled the air and the Guardian, thinking that it was from Enrica, prepared to unleash his magic, but as he saw the girl's face he realized she wasn't feeling terror. *Mother use to have that same face when ... when she would rock me to sleep. She's ... she's happy? But why?*

He watched as Famine lowered her head over her shoulder like a baby on the shoulder of its mother. The Knight of the Order couldn't help but lower his head in reverence for he had to admit it was kind of touching. The moment was lost though when he noticed the bark growing upward, covering their legs.

"Enrica! Enrica! Get away!"

The girl however didn't budge instead she glanced at him and smiled, even as the bark reached her face and slowly entombed her and Famine in a magnolia tree prison.

Chapter 26

The Guardian vaulted over the fence but there was no one waiting for him. *No, no no!*

"Damien!"

He turned and sighed in relief as Andra Alexander and Serena Martin ran up to him.

"Where are the others?" he exclaimed.

"Hopefully they're ahead of us," Andra answered.

"What do you mean? What happened?"

"We were attacked you nitwit!" Andra growled.

Damien pulled his gaze away and his anger evaporated leaving only exhaustion and regret. His body seemed to sag under the weight of his role. "Let me guess War and Death."

"Well you're right on the Grim Reaper, but other I think was Pestilence. We had just made it over the fence when BAM! They just came out of nowhere!

Seneca managed to encase the Grim Reaper in a cube of ice before helping Serena fend off Bug Boy. Then we noticed Enrica was missing and Serena and I started back here to look for her when we heard this horrible wail and rushed back to the fence thinking Enrica was in danger, but then Sara screamed and we ran back to see Seneca trying to fend off some huge demon but before we could do anything else, they both just disappeared so we came back here."

Serena glanced around before giving Damien a worried stare. "Damien. Enrica …"

"Enrica... didn't make it," Damien answered.

Serena froze before dropping to the ground. Somehow she had known, maybe it was the look on his face or maybe it was something else, but she knew. She had hoped though, hoped that ... it didn't matter now. Enrica was gone.

"It ... It was. I can't really describe what it was." He stepped over and placed his hand on Serena's shoulder. "She didn't go out alone Serena. She took one of the horsemen with her."

The girl glanced up at him. It was a small consolation and they both knew it but they also realized the significance.

"She had the last word," Damien added.

"That's our Enrica," Serena sobbed, wiping tears from her eyes. She had experienced loss in her battles against the Abyss, but never like this. It was almost like someone had cut off her hand.

"Serena..."

"Time for that later. We both know it comes with the territory. Besides we got work to do."

The Guardian nodded before extending his hand to her. She gave him a soft smile before taking it and rising to her feet. He turned to Andra Alexander. "You still up for this?"

"To be honest no, but count me in anyway."

"Good because like I said earlier we're going to need you." He surveyed the scene around him before starting up Orleans Avenue, flanked on each side by Serena and Andra.

Sara couldn't understand it, granted the Quarter was always noisy during Mardi Gras especially at Bourbon Street, but something was different, something that made the whole world seem … louder. She sighed.

Here was the center of the "City That Cares Forgot." Here care was a luxury not a necessity, here problems were a trifle of ill significance.

Here the social norm was no regrets.

And even here I'm a deviant from the social norm. Boy was she ever a deviant. Before she had been an oddball among her peers, she was an intellectual, but not in that flashy cool way like Damien or Serena. She was the poster child of the intellectual square. That girl who started talking about the joy of mathematics only to look around a few minutes later and find herself completely alone.

She was neither athletic like Andra, willowy like Serena, nor curvy like Enrica; she was a complete turnoff. A complete turnoff who supposedly possess an uncanny ability to do magic. She wasn't an oddball, she was bizarre, one of those types that ended up in nuthouses and used to make psychiatrist famous.

God my head! A noise was jumbling her brain, no matter how hard she tried to close of her mind to it, the noises lingered. Even worse was the emotional rollercoaster she seem to be on. One instant she was awashed with joy and excitement, the next anxiety. Then she'd be flushed by bravado and vanity.

What the devil is wrong with me? Could this have something to do with the magic Damien was talking about? Whatever it was it was taking its toll on her, she was barely able to keep pace with Seneca and Achilles. They might have left her completely had not Achilles glanced behind him and saw her on the verge of collapsing.

"Seneca," Achilles yelled, "Something's up with Sara!" He ran back toward her. Already a group of college students was around her asking if she was all right. She waved them off as she saw Achilles run up to her before weakly reaching her arms out to him.

A couple laughed and gaily walked off, dismissing the matter as one who had too much to drink – a common occurrence in the French Quarter especially during Mardi Gras.

"You okay?" Achilles asked. "You look ...plastered."

"I'm fine," Sara sputtered. "I ... just need to ... rest a moment." She fainted in his arms.

"We have to stop and let her catch her breath," Achilles said sternly.

Seneca merely scowled. "She's lucky to be breathing after that stunt you two pulled. What were you trying to do? Get yourselves killed?"

"Hey it brought Serena and Andra time. Besides two less demons to face will make Damien's job a little easier."

"That remains to be seen," the Indian answered. There was a chance that he was right, but he had a feeling that something was behind them, which was why he was so adamant about them moving so quickly.

The sun was setting now. The Eve of Penance would soon be upon them. *Time to find out if all this was worthwhile or all for naught.* That thought recurred through his mind as he noticed the street sign ahead of him. He knew then that the end was near, at least for him.

And now Seneca Maza, we have a question for you.

The question had that changed him and brought him to this.

The race of man has strayed from the Golden Path. Indeed the Creator ponders if it is better that they perish.

At first he had been horrified, but then it was replaced with a deep sadness. Truth was they were right; men on the whole had lost their way. Each race of man had failed in their charge. The white man had abused fire till only destruction followed their wake. The dark man lost his soul in the currents of water – he was now a bitter and vengeful creature. The yellow man grew arrogant and hid his knowledge from everyone who could have benefited from it. Then there were his own people, the red men; theirs was the most tragic of all.

Maybe humanity doesn't deserve to live.

Then came the question. *"Do you believe these people are worth saving?"*

"Yes!"

Then came the real question. *"Are you willing to sacrifice everything for your fellow man?"*

"Yes!"

He had been surprised at how quickly he had answered. It was after that affirmation that they changed him. At first he thought he would die, then again maybe he did. *I died only to be resurrected, renewed -- only to die again.*

When you reach the dolphin behind the garden, the time to sleep, to die will be at hand.

Word play, not dolphin as in the animal, but Dauphin as in the street — the very street he was facing now. *It is time.*

The gasps and screams brought him back to reality.

"Damien what are you doing?" Serena asked unable to keep her frustration in check as she watched the Guardian glance around before entering the white panel doors of the Bourbon Orleans Hotel. The girl glanced over to Andra whose confusion matched her own. *What could have possessed him to come in here.* Finally she sighed and followed him into the hotel lobby.

"Damien an explanation would be nice."

Damien Parker started to answer, then stopped. *That daggone voice again.* Something was nagging him, a presence of some kind that was beckoning him. It had started not soon after they had started up Orleans Street, but he had dismissed it, eager to catch up with the others and reach the cemetery before it was too late.

They were crossing Bourbon when the nagging presence again rattled his brain, only this time louder.

What the hell could be doing this?

Far as he could tell it wasn't demonic; annoyed he turned around ignoring the confused faces of Serena and Andra and their constant inquiries on why he was leading them back the way they had came and their frantic reminders that Sara, Achilles, and Seneca could be in danger.

I'm well aware of all your concerns but if this godforsaken voice doesn't stop I'm going to go crazy!

As a result he was now standing in the lobby of the Bourbon Orleans Hotel.

Maybe it was from Seneca. Maybe they're here. Maybe I'm the next emperor of China.

Not surprising the lobby was nearly empty and with it being Mardi Gras the armored garb of the Guardian of the Cross brought little attention from the lobby personnel.

He felt a warmth on his arm. He glanced to see Serena looking at him, her face full of confusion – and frustration.

"What are we doing here?" she hissed.

Oh yeah she was mad. He was also glad she was whispering. His eyes surveyed his surroundings, hoping to find an answer to give her. As his eyes observed the nearby spiral staircase the figure of a woman came across his eyes before disappearing beyond his line of sight. She had been there maybe a second, but that was long enough for him to recognize who she was. *I should have known.*

He reached for Serena's hand and patted it gently before removing it with a smile. "Stay here." He started toward the spiral staircase.

Serena glared an indignant look. "Where are ..."

"Don't worry," he interrupted, his smile widening, "This won't take long." He started up the staircase, his green cape flying behind him like a tail.

A peacock tail for a pea brained fool Serena scoffed. With a humph she settled into a nearby Victorian chair next to Andra. They both sat in silence until simultaneously breaking it with a single scornful word: *Men!*

The Guardian entered the Quadroon Ballroom with a smooth wistful gait that a century ago would have marked him as a man of status. As a student of history – and as romantic he was familiar with the ballroom's story and its part in tales of romance, seduction, and manipulation that seemed too glamorous to be true. As a being of magic, he understood why Madame Fi La Reye would pick such a place to meet him, the Quadroon Ballroom had an even deeper history than even the most ardent of scholars acknowledged.

Heck even that crazy gala that Serena plans on dragging me to is based upon events that occurred in this ballroom. The gala ... Friday he had been worried stiff about attending the silly thing. Funny now it had become a mere afterthought. *I might not even be alive to attend the stupid event. Oh well.*

"Could you please explain why you insist on dragging me all the way back here especially when you know that each minute I waste here allows Magnus time to release the Maderan."

Madame Fi La Reye laughed as she stepped out the shadows and walked past him. "Do you know the purpose of the Quadroon Balls?" she inquired.

"If I recall correctly a whole bunch of rich Creoles and po' Quadroons got together to play matchmaker."

The woman chuckled. She was more vibrant and lively than she had been at their previous encounter – and he could have sworn she seemed to appear a bit – younger. "I suppose that's one way of describing it. The balls were an arena, a place of manipulation and strategy"

"You called me here just to give me a history lesson!"

"and arrangement," the woman finished as if he had not spoken at all. "You need to be reminded of what makes a successful arrangement."

"What? Money?"

"Trust."

"Can you guarantee that their magic will be enough if I trust them."

"No."

"Then you're asking a lot." He turned and started toward the door.

"I know that if you don't trust you will definitely lose the day."

The Guardian of the Cross didn't give a reply as he left the ballroom.

"Okay first he's decked out in black, then purple, then black again and his cloak goes from green to purple. What's up with all the color changes?"

Serena eyed the stairs before returning her gaze to the girl sitting beside her. "Damien explained it to me, different colors represent different power levels, kind of like belts in karate."

"Oh." Andra responded. "I understand now. So how many 'belts' are there?"

"If I remember right there are four: green, purple, black, and white. Green is the lowest and white I believe is the highest."

"Umm. So what about the cape?"

"I think the cape is more a fashion statement than anything else."

Have faith in yourself Serena Martin.

"Andra did you say something?"

"No," the other answered. "I didn't say anything."

Andra Alexander, take courage …

"Serena was that you?"

"No." Serena glanced around but there was no one in the lobby. *What's going on.*

"I would be what's going on."

Andra could only sit there dumbfounded. It was the woman who had talked to her Sunday before she ran into Damien.

"Who are you?" Serena whispered as she stood to face the woman before her.

"Serena," the woman replied, "have faith in yourself or else the day is lost." She turned to Andra who saw her in all her youthful vigor when her magic had been at its strongest. "Andra Alexander, the champion, take courage. Only fear can stop you."

Both girls blinked to find her gone. Awed, they stood there in amazement before Serena turned around to see Damien Parker. *I knew he was coming. But how?*

The Knight of the Order descended the staircase. "Ready."

The girls eyed each other for a moment before returning their gaze to Damien. "Yeah," they both answered.

The Guardian glanced around before eying the stairs from which he came, a suspicious curl formed on his lips. "Did anything happen while I was gone?"

Serena glanced at Andra, who Damien could have sworn gave a shake of disapproval. "Nothing. Can we go now?"

He nodded before opening one of the white doors and gesturing so that the girls would proceed.

"So what did she tell you?" he asked as they once again trekked up Orleans Street.

"What are you talking about?" Andra inquired.

The Guardian sighed "Fine. Go ahead and keep your little secret. But I'm telling you…" Suddenly a fierce wind engulfed him. It's cold breeze nicking his face like a thousand razor blades. The chill washed through him, but it was not uncomfortably chilly. Rather it was cool like the first blast of air conditioning that would strike one as he stepped a building on a late summer New Orleans day. Then it changed, becoming a gentle storm of heat baking him to the core of his soul where the heat burned at its fiercest.

With his next breath it was gone, but something else had gone with it, a raw power that had accompanied the wind. It was as if he had been caught in an explosion of some kind. *Oh God that is what it was?*

"Damien … Damien are you all right."

Voices. Serena. Andra. Yes. Damien Parker, that is who you are.

"Damien! Damien say something." Serena watched carefully as the Guardian slowly rose to his feet. *He's struggling to breathe.* "What happened?"

He shook his head, trying to clear all the remaining patterns and energies that had flooded through his mind. "It … It was an eruption of a great power. Come on we have to hurry. I have a terrible feeling the others are in great danger."

Seneca clearly watched as a swarm of insects merged to form the body of the creature Damien Parker referred to as Pestilence. The revelers on Bourbon Street slowly drew away in disgust as a horde of cockroaches crawled out the gutters and up the creature's body before meshing into some kind of body armor.

The time is at hand. He could feel a strange power burning in his soul, a power he had not felt since the Spirits had transformed him. *Yes it is time.*

He glanced at Sara who was still cradled in Achilles' arms. *Such an innocent creature.* He found himself smiling as he started to walk toward the demonic apparition.

"No!" Sara screamed as she wrapped her arm around his leg. "What are you doing? You'll ..."

"Save people," he finished though he knew that wasn't what she had planned on saying. "Sara I need you to promise me something.   I need you to promise me something.. I need you to promise me that you will never change. You hear me, never." He knelt down so he could look her in the eye. "Never change from the person you are now. Promise me."

"I ... promise," the girl stuttered, tears already flowing down her face.

"Good girl. You take care of her Achilles, make sure you both get to the cemetery, Damien is going to need you." He rose to his feet and looked Sara dead in the eye, ignoring Achilles' gruff mumbles. Finally he turned and walked toward the waiting apparition.

"Come on Sara, we have to go," Achilles scolded. "He'll be fine. Trust me he can take care of himself."

Sara Winters didn't budge. *No he won't. He won't live, I've just seen it.*

A feeling of anxiety drew over him as he stopped a few feet from the specter shaped in one of mankind's greatest fears.

The horseman reared its deformed head back before with a chilling wail belched out a horde of hornets in Seneca's direction. The Indian however merely brought up his arms, ice and cold oozed from his fingertips freezing the hornets in midair only inches from his body.

The horseman wailed again as the hornets shattered on the pavement like glass sculptures. Another wrenching cry filled the air as the creature stretched its arms toward the heavens.

"Uhh oh," Achilles thought as he noticed the dark cloud gathering above them and watched with concern as it slowly descended, stopping just inches shy of the horseman's head. Another screeching wail pierced the air and the cloud dispersed in every direction, attacking everyone in its vicinity.

No! Spirits help me! The Indian clapped his hands together and chanted a word before parting his arms. Gusts of wind gathered the insects and meshed them back into a single cloud while people took cover in whatever building they could. The insects tried to fly above the winds, but couldn't.

Seneca's face was lined, his mind racked by the deep concentration his gambit acquired. Focusing, he sent fire into the wind currents, igniting the insects and creating a wall of flame that encased Seneca and Pestilence within.

"Your move," Seneca uttered, awaiting Pestilence's next attack, but he had not anticipated on the specter moving so quickly.   The horseman dispersed his body and sent it at the Native American who was barely able to summon a gust of wind to help shield him as he dodged out the way.

Panting Seneca watched as the insects merged back into Pestilence. The Indian's temper flared, along with it, the fires that crackled in the winds surrounding them. Pain racked him in his side and along his back. Worse fatigue and weariness wheezed his strength; he also realized he was having trouble feeling his legs and arms.

He cursed himself for being so careless and allowing Famine the chance to poison him earlier. *Here I am nearly worn out and Pestilence hasn't even broken a sweat.   I can't die like this.   Not as a failure!*   He concentrated all his magic into his hand. *Come on! Come closer. Closer. Yes!* He delivered a punch, hardening his hand into stone the second it crashed into the monster's midsection.   However to his shock the monster didn't seem fazed.

"Damn you! Die!" He channeled fire through his hand, hoping to ignite the monster in a ball of fire. Instead pain filled him, forcing him to recoil his arm. He noticed the moving lumps in his skin, lumps that were slowly moving up his arm.   In sheer panic the boy slammed at the lumps with his fists, however to his horror his efforts had no effect as the lumps continued advancing up his arm.

They're in me! Ohmigod! They're inside me! I can't get them out! Wait maybe that is what I need to do; get them inside me.

The Indian concentrated, summoning the winds around him and sending them towards the monster known as Pestilence, ripping and pulling at the creature until it dispersed into a cloud of insects.

He could feel the venom of the insects corroding his heart and lungs. *Spirits just give me the strength for this one thing.* He concentrated, gathering all of Pestilence in the winds and clustering the monster into one tight knot. Here goes. He opened his mouth and inhaled, sucking in all the winds and the insects encompassing the terrible monster. His body jerked as if he had been stabbed a thousand times all at once and a terrible chill filled his body. *Focus ... Focus* He turned his attention to his body, willing skin, muscle and bone to become stone. He could feel his life force ebbing. Yes he would be dead soon, but he still had some magic left and it would be enough. He thanked his grandmother, wishing she could see this. She would be so proud. He smiled peacefully as the fire of his exploding soul coursed within the shell he had created, burning Pestilence in a cleansing internal firestorm.

So this is what it feels to be one with the earth. It's ... wonderful. His last thought before the final cinder of his life flame extinguished.

As the winds and flames miraculously died away, all they could see was a life-size statue of a teenage boy. The beige statue seemed to shine as if a star was shinning from within the statue itself. Just as the beauty and awe of the sculpture washed away, the crowd drew closer to observe the work of art but a gust of wind blew causing the statue to fall backward onto the pavement where it shattered on impact.

Chapter 27

Sara's screams filled his ears, but Achilles couldn't move as the statue of he who had once been Seneca Maza fell and shattered on the pavement. In the moment he forgot about St. Louis cemetery, he forgot about the other horsemen. All he could do was replay Seneca's death over and over in his mind.

After what felt like an eternity of seeing Seneca shatter to pieces, Achilles glanced down at Sara Winters and his mind remembered the charge the Indian had left them.

"Come on Sara," he replied lowly trying to conceal his own grief. "We have to go."

He heard her scream again and wondered if it was in defiance of his request or in defiance of the sacrifice she had just witnessed.

"Sara," he repeated this time in a sterner voice, "we have to go." He wrapped his arms around her waist and lifted her off the ground. The girl thrashed from side to side, kicking wildly as Achilles tried to drag her away. "Sara there's nothing we can do. He's gone!" She smashed the back of her skull against his nose, causing the boy to utter a loud 'ow' before releasing her.

"Sara," he growled but as he watched her run to where Seneca's shattered remains lied, his voice lost its force. She just knelt there, scooping the dirt in her hands like it was sharp glass. *Remember your promise.* It came out of her as a whisper followed by a long sigh.

"Achilles!"

The boy turned. Could it be? Yes it was them, Damien Parker, Andra Alexander, and Serena Martin. Relief surged from him as he saw them running up to him.

"Achilles, Sara! Thank goodness you all right," Serena replied before she stopped not at the sight of Sara, but the look on Damien Parker's face. A face that showed exhaustion and dejection – a face that had seen one too many deaths.

"Where's Seneca?" the Knight of the Order asked, hoping, praying that Sara Winter's face was not a confirmation of death.

The silence from Achilles along with the twisted look on his face said more than his words ever could. The Guardian lowered his head and closed his eyes in condolence. "How?" he asked finally, his voice a low soft whisper.

"It was one of the horsemen – Pestilence I think, but he beat him Damien. He beat him! However not without …"

"He died like a hero." Sara interrupted as she approached them, her hands full of fragments of the Indian's remains. Enclosing them in her fist she buried her face in Serena's chest.

For a while they all stood there in silence and as she eyed Damien Parker Serena realized she had never seen him so vulnerable.

They continued up Orleans, the Guardian leading the way, behind him Serena, Sara, and Andra with Achilles bringing up the rear.   As they approached the 720 block of North Rampart Street, the Guardian paused and glanced around for a few minutes before turning to face his companions, his face reflected the combat of decision.

Part of him wanted to go south down Rampart Street, take Conti and cross Basin there.   It would take them straight to the cemetery gates.   But he already knew why he wouldn't go down Rampart, because of a maxim from Sun Tzu's Art of War: The route to victory is the road of deception.

They would be expecting him to go through the front gate.   No what he needed to do was what they wouldn't expect.

They would never expect him to go through Louis Armstrong Park, which was why they were going that way.

"Isn't the cemetery that way though?" Sara replied pointing in the south direction.

"If we go that way we're gonna get ambushed."

"Hun?"

"They're gonna be expecting us to go that way."

"How do you know?" Andra inquired.

The Guardian gave her a look.   "Because that's what I would do if I were in Magnus' place. We go where they wouldn't expect us to – around the Marginot Line."

"And what if you're wrong?"

Again the Guardian gave her a look. "Not likely, but either way it won't be long before it all comes to a

standstill.   Personally I'd rather it be us doing the
assaulting than vice versa."

Andra had to admit she was tired of being on the
defensive. "Ok Damien, lead the way."

The Guardian led them north up Rampart till they
were across from the main gate to the park. "Ok, here's
the plan. Serena you cross first. Sara, you and Achilles
will go next, then Andra and myself."

They all nodded in concurrence. Serena crossed
first, sensing nor seeing any kind of danger she positioned
herself by the gate and watched as Sara and Achilles came
across. A minute later Andra and Damien Parker crossed.
The Guardian lifted his staff to the chains around the gate
and a spark flashed before the chains dropped to the
ground and he and Achilles pushed the gate ajar enough
for them to all enter. Together the five entered and
snaked their way through the park; the Municipal
Auditorium loomed over like a sinister fortress.

Here the dark taint in the magic could be felt at its
strongest as they trudged toward Congo Square. Although
Municipal Park frequently held lavish concerts and plays,
the area in truth was one of the tragic aspects of the city.
Littered with the homeless, winos, and crack heads and
ruled by thugs, the area was more a harem for minor class
demons than a monument of the city's greatness. Damien
had considered themselves fortunate that a police car had
passed just before they crossed scaring away a group of
fellas who had been loitering by the gate.

Leading the way, Damien was aware of the eyes
watching them cautiously as they made their way through

Congo Square. Though they outnumbered them, the imps recognized the magic of the Knight of the Order and the brown haired girl who accompanied him and desired no part of either.

Their magic however didn't deter them from observing, hoping for a mistake that could allow them to feed, to enjoy the rapture of their pain and fear.

It had been their bravado that had first warned Damien of something. Something else was here, an equalizer of some sort – only that could explain the confidence the imps had in their blantant showing – especially in his presence. The only thing that currently was close to fulfilling that role was …

He was already in battle mode, ready to strike with his magic when the sensation told him to turn. Andra who was immediately behind him followed his gaze.

All she wanted to do was run, forget about the demons and the magic. She had seen it before, but those two times had been from a distance. Now as she eyed the armored behemoth eying her with its horrible red eyes, terror filled her.

I could run. She glanced at Damien Parker, his face calm and cool, his purple cape now back behind him fluttering gently in a soft breeze. He's the Guardian. He can deal with this. She wasn't meant to handle this. This was way out of her league.

Andra Alexander … champion … take courage.

I could run. She turned her gaze to Serena, her face framed with determination. She turned back to the

Guardian, his hands clinched on his staff, eyes filled with defiance, awaiting the monster that dared to challenge him.

Wasn't he afraid? Wasn't she afraid? How did he keep facing monster after monster? Why would he face them?

Because no one else would, the same reason you captain the team because no one else can; because no one else will take the responsibility. Sacred or not he was all that stood between hordes of demons and unwary people. No she couldn't run; she wouldn't run. For some reason the Creator had selected her to be what Damien Parker was – a protector, a paladin against the night.

Only fear can stop you.

No fear. Ohmigod

She could feel it stirring deep within her, something tempered, yet primal. Everything about her that was civilized told her to suppress it. No embrace it. What if I'm wrong? Don't fight it; embrace it! She ceased fighting and embraced it, allowing the instincts to surface as they exploded through her, a rush of energy and determination fuelled by a drive to survive – to win. A desire she realized was more familiar to her than she originally believed. It was then that she completely surrendered and then it happened.

Andra suddenly felt herself being stripped from her body. A blinding light came upon her and as her vision cleared she saw herself standing petrified in the middle of Congo Square.

The neigh of the horse instantly caused her to turn and she saw the armored demon, her enemy waiting.

It was then that Andra realized she had become the red knight. She could feel herself being wrapped and twisted in a whirlpool of memories – memories of battle, memories laced with death.

The Red Knight reared her horse as she noticed her surroundings. In front of her was a girl she knew to be the Lady Andra, the Mistress of the Sword whom she served. On the other side of her was a Knight of the Order – a Guardian of the Cross to be exact. It had been a long time since they crossed paths.

From the corner of her eye, she saw what had to be her foe. Rearing the horse the Knight drew her short sword and charged toward the armored specter.

The monstrous wolf-serpent reared before charging. The demon raised his spike-covered shield as the two juggernauts collided. The Knight's sword banged into the demon's shield with a clang and the force of the attack knocked her to the ground with a deafening thud.

The Knight stood up readying her sword for another attack. The demon once again charged, but the Knight stood her ground. The ferocious wolf-serpent closed in, its rider raising his shield to deflect the attacking blow.

As the creature reached the point of trampling over her, the Knight sidestepped gracefully and stabbed her sword through the serpent's neck. The dead steed and its rider collapsed onto a shrub.

The giant behemoth arose from the ground and grabbed its mace.

The knight drew her broadsword from the sheath on her back and awaited the giant colossus. The demon hurled his mace down on the paladin but the knight parried the blow with her sword. The force of the attack however send her sprawling backward. The demon again went on the attack, the knight once again managed to deflect the attack, but this time just barely. As the knight staggered back, an unfamiliar feeling began to surface – fear.

The Guardian and Serena had sent all the minor demons scrambling when he noticed the Red Knight being forced back.

"No!"

He glanced over to where Andra Alexander was standing. The girl was trembling, her face pale with terror.

She's afraid. The Knight is being forced back because Andra is afraid.

He started to feel afraid himself. Seneca and Enrica had managed to defeat Pestilence and Famine. The Red Knight was currently battling War which left only Death, Malagant, Magnus and maybe the Maderan. If Andra lost he could probably defeat War, but that would he have enough magic left to face the Magnus and the Maderan?

Serena's magic was formidable, but odds were she wouldn't be a match for Malagant or Magnus. Would Sara and Achilles realize their potential before it was too late. Too many what ifs, then again it was always too many what ifs. With a yell he ran toward Andra. She had to win. He refused to lose another friend like he had lost Seneca.

"Damien what's wrong?" Achilles asked as he noticed the Guardian heading toward Andra Alexander.

"It's Andra! We have to restore her confidence or she'll never survive against that thing." He stopped as a tingling sensation raced through him. That could only mean … He ducked and the scythe whistled over his head.

"Achilles help Andra." He clutched his staff and went on the attack.

Andra was scared stiff. This was too much, she didn't have enough of what it would take to win. She heard a voice, a familiar voice. One that usually filled her with annoyance, but now it calmed her.

"Andra," it said, "You have to focus! You can do this, you're Wonder Woman for crying out loud."

She felt a warmth and glanced downward. Sure enough Achilles Harmon's hand was held in her own.

"I'm right here beside you."

Suddenly she blushed, at least internally she hoped. A new feeling filled her, a feeling she wanted to explore, but that meant she would have to live.

The Knight blocked the assault of the mace, but this time it was not in desperation. Memories of past battles ran through her mind, calling upon them she spun, avoiding the attack and placing herself behind the armored nightmare. With a mighty swing, the broadsword descended down and across the demon warrior's knees tearing through metal, bone, and flesh.   The giant juggernaut staggered almost falling to its knees. The broadsword was raised again, but this time it sliced through the neck and seconds later a headless body slumped to the ground.

As Andra came to she found herself watching the Red Knight with awe as a halo of light surrounded her. A smile crept upon her face as she caught one final glimpse of the armored champion before she was consumed by the shinning radiance. Red and gold armor gleamed and reflected the light giving the appearance of a miniature red sun shinning in the night. Andra closed her eyes, unable to bear the blazing splendor.

When she opened them the knight was gone as well as the light that surrounded it. She looked downward and noticed that Achilles' hand was still clasped in hers. She turned her head to see him rubbing his eyes with his free hand. Finally the hand dropped back to his side and he eyed her, his face displaying that smart-alleck grin that had become his trademark feature, at least in her eyes. Before that grin always left her with a desire to slap him. She never had a better opportunity to indulge herself than she did at that moment, but she didn't do it. Instead she kissed him.

Part of him wanted to push her away, but the dominant part of him was shocked. He barely had a chance to meet her kiss with his own before she pulled away.

"What was that about?"

Andra smiled. "We'll talk about it later. Where's everyone else?"

"I'm not sure. Damien was on his way to talk some sense into you, but then he ordered me to see to you and started off in another direction."

"Oh." Andra hoped her disappointment didn't show in her voice. "We better find them." She turned and jogged off.

"Andra wait!" Achilles yelled before running after her. "Will you wait up! Remember I'm not on the track team."

"No but you're on the baseball team though," she answered before stopping.

"That was last year! And don't think you can avoid answering the question."

"What question?"

"That kiss back there?"

"What about it?"

"Ok maybe a better question would be where should we go from here?"

"What are you talking about?"

"At first I thought it was a prank, but I'm beginning to think that you like me. That you're attracted to me."

Andra sighed. There was no sense in allowing this to linger if he only came to see about her because he had been ordered to, but before she could say anything Achilles continued.

"And I think I … maybe attracted to you."

Andra wanted to smile but managed to resist the urge. No sense in letting Achilles know too much.

"Well?"

"Well what?"

"Am I right?"

Andra gave him a sly smile. "What's wrong Baby Boy? Never been kissed before?" She blew him a kiss, never seeing the scythe as it sliced into her side.

Chapter 28

"Andra!" Achilles scrambled to where her body had fallen, completely ignoring the hooded figure that stood near him, its scythe ready to slice him into oblivion. Before the last horseman could swing, a ball of lightning slammed into it, shoving it back. Its last sight before being blinded by the light of the magic was the form of the Guardian accompanied by two human females.

"Ohmigod Andra." Achilles gasped as he noticed the severity of the wound. Serena and Sara pushed him aside, their med class training kicking into high gear.

"Andra! God, Andra!"

The Knight of the Order could only look his friend in the eye with a face of remorse. He wasn't an expert on wounds, but Serena was due to her classes and he had seen the look on her face and knew instantly that even if they got her to the hospital she would never make it.

Enrica, Seneca, and now Andra. It couldn't have been meant to turn out like this. Will I lose Serena too before night's end?

"Achilles."

Andra. The boy rushed to her side. He could see the dread in Serena's face. He knew she had some medical training – two years of it. Damn.

"Achilles."

"Yes Andra."

"I'm so sorry."

"Sorry for what?"

"You were right."

"About everything we argued about? I already know that."

"No," she moaned, "You were right about us."

The Guardian readied himself as Death made his return. His eyes noticed the rising moon. It's nightfall already? "Achilles we have to go." Why must I be so heartless. I know good and well if it was Serena lying there.

I would tell you to go.

He eyed Serena. Yes it did come from her. For the second time tonight he had been able to sense her thoughts, but why not before? He would have to ponder on that later, right now … "Achilles we have to leave?"

Achilles couldn't hear him, all he could hear was Andra's voice, and all he could feel was her hand as it swiftly grew cold as her last words oozed from her. "I think I'm in love with you."

Then Achilles Harmon just snapped.

The Guardian had never heard a yell like the one he heard from Achilles Harmon before the boy launched himself toward the horseman known as Death. "Achilles! No!"

Death readied his scythe to cut down the usurp challenger. The Guardian readied his magic but knew he wouldn't be able to stop Death's swing especially with Achilles charging into his line of attack. He watched angrily as the scythe arched downward then a cheerful yell erupted as Achilles twisted his body at the last possible moment resulting in the blade missing him completely and allowing the boy's shoulders to plow into the specter knocking it to the ground.

Achilles quickly rolled away and positioned himself. He could feel his heart racing, his breathing hard and rapid. Rage was churning inside him like a piston. He turned to the sound of his name, his eyes locking on those of Damien Parker.

The Guardian held in a gasp. Something had awakened in Achilles, something magical. Already he could see the golden glow emanating from his right hand, but it wasn't that he was concerned about. There was another power, a darker, more savage power that was churning, fighting its way to the surface. Even his eyes reflected the conflict of magic within him – one eye glowed yellow like the sun, the other seemed a reflection of madness, changing from blood red to purple to yellow.

He can't control it. He can't control the magic.

"Achilles!" he yelled.

The boy hissed as again his eyes locked on the Guardian of the Cross before turning back to Death.

"Achilles!" Sara yelled, starting toward him.

"No!" the Guardian yelled, stretching out his arm to block her.

"What do you mean no!" Serena exclaimed.

"Achilles is not in his right mind; he's lost himself to the magic."

Serena gasped. She had heard of how magic could cause madness. "Then we have to snap him out of it."

"If you go near him he'll attack you. He has no recollection of friend or foe."

"Then what do we do?"

"Nothing. Right now he sees Death as his enemy. He's powerful enough to hold his own."

Serena glanced at the enraged boy and then back at the Guardian. "Even if he defeats Death what's to stop him from becoming something just as bad?"

He said nothing at first, but after a moment he answered. "Trust."

Serena flinched. She knew Damien Parker, she knew how he hated not being able to control a situation, that he trusted them enough to even suggest leaving them showed, showed that he's the Knight of the Order. "Come on Sara we have to go."

Sara Winters gave Serena Martin a chilling stare but as her eyes fell upon Damien Parker her face became deathly pale and her breathing shallow. The Knight of the Order merely turned and started off down the path. A path that Sara now realized was a rendezvous, a rendezvous with Armageddon. She slowly started up the path behind him.

Serena glanced back at Achilles before glancing at Andra's body one last time as regret filling her. "I'm sorry Andra. Now I know we could have been friends." Her face then became a mask of determination as she turned to the south where St. Louis cemetery lied and in her mind a silent promise was made. *All right then let's get on with it.*

From the corner of his eye he watched as the others slipped into the coming night before eying the figure in front of him. Death ... or at least a facsimile of it. Death ... destroyer of life. He glanced at Andra's body. *Destroyer of love.* Did he say that? Why would he say that, all that mattered was that it was standing there and ... *it possesses power! If we can destroy it then we can destroy anything, even ... the Guardian.* What was he saying? Damien Parker was his friend. He glanced at his hands; he could feel the power in his left hand, a power over life itself. Was this the magic that Damien was talking about? Could he control it? *Yes you can control it and if you wish we can control anything ... and everything.*

What the heck was he saying? He winced, his shoulder felt like it was freezing and burning at the same time. The same shoulder I hit the Grim Reaper with. Speaking of the Grim Reaper.

His attention returned to the specter of Death just in time to see the scythe coming toward him. Crap! No time to duck. In desperation he reached to grab the handle of the scythe and succeeded. Achilles summoned all his strength, pushing as hard as he could to hold the blade back from his body when he noticed the glow aura on his left hand as its grip tightened on the metal handle. Even more surprising he could have swore he could feel his hand actually going through the metal and was shocked to find it was.

What the ... The scythe suddenly exploded into pieces knocking both combatants back from each other. Achilles stared at his hand. What in the world did I do? He eyed Death before with a yell he charged into the horseman, ramming it into a nearby tree. The horseman pushed back forcing Achilles back but the boy straightened himself and managed to halt the horseman's progress, ignoring the chilling cold that raced through his body.

Achilles couldn't help but note the irony. Here he was face to face with an embodiment of all he's been seeking since his parents died. The thing he thought could take the pain away for good and yet as he eyed this apparition whose eyes stared back at him, he didn't see relief he only saw the source of his pain.

You ... you took my parents. He glanced at Andra Alexander's dead body. *You took Andra. I was a fool wanting to embrace you, but I have a present for you. Here my anger, my sorrow, my loss.* He focused hoping that the power of his left hand would disintegrate Death the way it had his scythe. But nothing happened; rather he could hear the specter laughing. Death was laughing at him. Achilles grew angry, angry that he had desired death, angry that he had failed, angry that he would never get a chance to find out why Andra had meant to kiss him.

"No Damnit I'm not gonna fail! This can't be it, there's got to be something else! There's gotta be!" And he felt it a power he had never felt before, even more powerful than what he had felt in his left, this power seem to wrap around him, uplift him.

"I'm not finished yet!" With a yell he reached into the hood with his right hand and wrapped his fingers around the bony neck that lied within. The hood dropped away revealing a fiery skull. The horsemen struck Achilles' right shoulder hoping to break the chokehold, but Achilles held fast. It's afraid. He's afraid! They both yelled; Death's was one of fear, Achilles one of determination. Their screams filled the night as the specter slowly dissolved leaving only tattered remains of a cloak and hood that clothed the last horseman of the apocalypse.

Achilles Harmon could only laugh as he collapsed onto the ground. His laugh grew louder as he noticed the numbness on the left side of his body. He slowly crawled to where Andra Alexander's body was sprawled on the ground. He reached for her with his right arm and grabbed her hand. His laughter subsided as he gripped the dead girl's hand and as the last moment of his life came upon him, he couldn't help but find the humor of the realization that had dawned upon him, the realization that he was in love with Andra Alexander. Who would have thought?

Chapter 29

The trio ran out the park led by Damien who ran across Basin Street stopping on the median before cautiously stopping as he awaited Sara and Serena. He glanced down Crozat Street at the end of which he could see the brick wall encasing St. Louis cemetery.

Urging them on Damien had just passed the visitor center marker when by chance he glanced up before screeching to a halt.

Serena and Sara both froze as he glanced around the night sky before turning around to face the median before turning back toward the cemetery just as mass of shadow landed a few yards in front of him. Lights from the white building and nearby street lights illuminated the shadowed mass and as Sara saw it she let out a terrible wail.

The behemoth smiled menacingly to her reaction as it straightened its wings before glaring at Damien Parker. "Guardian!" it hissed. "Back with another pet I see. What's wrong, scared to face me alone?"

Damien laughed. "You're one to talk Malagant being that every time we've faced each other either you been knocked on your back or running with your tail between your legs." He stepped forward and Malagant's smile slowly faded.

"Let's see if I have this figured out correctly. You think that after being softened up by your four henchmen that you would actually have a chance against me." He took another step, the white staff in his hands gleaming.

"What's wrong little girl?" Malagant hissed, his eyes turning toward Sara. "Scared?"

Sara recoiled in horror and fell to her knees. Serena rushed over to her side. "Sara it's going to be okay," she replied rubbing her friend's wrist. "Trust me. Malagant's bark is worse than his bite."

"No! No it's not!" Sara stammered, her eyes locked on Malagant's red eyes. A detail that didn't go unnoticed by the Guardian.

"Leave her be Malagant," Damien ordered. Serena noticed he had not raised his voice yet there was a thunder in his voice that caused chills to run up her spine. "If I recall correctly," he continued, "you're suppose to be talking smack to me. What's wrong? Noticed I'm not as worn down as you were hoping?"

The demon tried to ignore him, attempting to keep his eyes locked on the white girl. He raised his blade arm, a sinister smile on his face. He started to step forward but backpedaled as Damien Parker positioned himself right in front of the girls, but the Knight of the Order didn't stop there. He kept advancing until the two were practically nose to nose. Malagant was about a foot and half taller, but Damien appeared taller than his 5' 11" stature and from Serena and Sara's viewpoints the two seemed to be inches from being eye to eye.

Malagant considered attacking. The Guardian had not yet summon his magic. One good swipe could kill him before he would have a chance to defend himself. However the more he looked into the boy's eyes, the more he dismissed the idea. While Malagant didn't want to admit it, he knew full well that one good swipe had to be a very lucky swipe as well and something told him that the boy wanted him to attack. No, he would wait.

"Damien wait!"

Damien said nothing, his eyes remained locked on Malagant.

"Damien you don't have time for this. There's another matter that needs your attention."

'Trust me Sara, this won't take long. Will it Malagant?"

"Damien trust me! The longer you wait here, the more likely the darkness will be released."

The Guardian shifted his head slightly, enough to see Sara Winters out of the corner of his eye without giving Malagant an inch of freedom. True he could easily defeat Malagant, but then again Malagant's role wasn't to destroy the Guardian, only to delay him while Magnus released the Maderon. Sara was right. Afternoon had become evening; evening was fast becoming night. He had minutes now instead of hours and he had to make them count. Still. "I can't leave him, he'll just attack us from behind."

"He won't be behind you."

Damien nearly dropped his guard. There in her voice, a strength that he never noticed in her voice before. Could she have found her magic? "And who's going to stop him?"

"I will."

Serena eyed her friend in surprise. The conviction in her voice, she had expected it from Andra and Enrica, but none of them were here. Sara.

"Sara you don't know what you're saying, but she is right Damien, you go on. I'll deal with Malagant."

"Serena!" Sara hissed before her voice dropped to a whisper, "You can't. You have to go with him. He needs you."

"He's a Guardian!" Serena answered, failing to notice that her voice too had become a whisper. "He doesn't need anybody!"

"Serena if you don't go with him all this will be for naught."

Serena's eyes glanced to where the demon and the knight stood. "How do you know this?" she whispered.

Sara grabbed Serena's hand. "I've trusted you ever since I first you. You inspire me, you make me laugh, and you bring out the best in me. I've never asked you for anything other than your friendship. Please give me this one thing. Trust me I'll be fine."

Trust, earlier Damien had used that very thing as the justification for leaving Achilles to face Death alone. She had wondered on the validity of the choice until now. Now she understood how he could do it. Part of it stemmed from a lack of an alternative. Most of it though stemmed from comradery, the one thing that distinguished the Knights of the Order from the Abyss. A creature like Malagant could never trust a fellow demon to aid him. Such a choice was a request for destruction, but for them, for those who sided with Order, friendship and trust gave them a power that something like Malagant would always desire, but could never possess.

Serena glanced back at Malagant, then at Damien before returning to Sara Winter's face.

"Now you and your boyfriend go save the world," Sara ordered, "Isn't that what we magic people do?"

Serena didn't answer, instead she started forward, her hand locked in Sara's until distance forced them apart. Moving close to Damien, she placed her hand around his right arm, looking him dead in the eye. "We're needed elsewhere Damien. Sara can hold down the fort. We have to stop Magnus remember."

Damien turned to face her, recalling his last conversation with Madame Fi La Reye. *You must trust if you are to win the day.* He returned his gaze to Malagant before slowly stepping around the demon and started toward the cemetary.

"Coward!" Malagant hissed as he turned to pursue.

"Come back!"

The demon hissed in frustration. He tried to continue his pursuit, but his body refused to move. He commanded his body to move forward, but every time he did his mind would hear the same words. *Come back.*

Slowly the demon turned and trudged to where Sara Winters was standing. This can't be happening! How can she be doing this? "You will pay for this girl!" he bellowed.

Sara was just as shocked as Malagant. She wasn't sure what made her give the command or why she believed it would have any effect. *Do I truly have magic?* That question kept repeating in her mind as the demon stepped in front of her.

"I can move," Malagant hissed to himself. He glanced toward the stonewall where Serena Martin disappeared over the top into the cemetery. He knew he should pursue, but his injured pride demanded retribution. With a hiss he punched Sara in the face, sending the girl flying backward onto the pavement.

"Fool!" the demon taunted. "Did you think you could defeat me! I am Malagant!" With a leap he was upon her. In desperation Sara tried the magic again.

"Stay away!" she commanded.

However Malagant never deterred, he grabbed the girl by the hair and yanked her off the ground. She stared straight into his pupil less red eyes.

"Fool! Did you think you were protecting anyone with your foolish actions? You did exactly what we wanted you to do!"

Sara knew he was lying. She watched as the demon eyed the blade that stood in place of his left hand before raking it across her midsection. Sara screamed as the blade ripped through cloth and flesh.

Malagant flung her to the ground. Sara grunted as her arm twisted into an unnatural position upon her collision with the pavement.

"Stupid child, my task was not to kill the Guardian! Magnus sent me to kill you."

A half truth. Sara grimaced as pain filled her whole body. Her mind struggled to retain consciousness. Even the thought of movement brought pain. She moaned in agony as again Malagant jerked her off the ground by the hair.

"Yes you will die," Malagant sneered before stabbing his sword hand into the girl's right shoulder causing the girl to scream as the metal pierced flesh, muscle, and bone. "But not quickly; no." A twist of that same hand led to another chilling wail. "And definitely not without pain." He pulled her close as he whispered the last two words.

Sara winced as the demon slowly pulled the metal out of her shoulder. Tears flowed down her face as she noticed the sneering face of the demon.

"What's the matter Sara? Isn't this what you wanted? Don't worry you'll be joined soon enough by your friends and their deaths will be far more painful than yours!" He threw her to the ground. "Why are you crying Sara? Does it hurt?" He kicked her in the midsection and Sara's breath left her with an abrupt grunt. "The joy of killing sacrificial lambs. So innocent." He kicked her again, this time in the head. Sara rolled onto her back.

Malagant straddled her, lowering his face to meet hers as his talon hand caressed her face. Sara never felt more defiled.

"I could take such joy from your suffering," he replied, his hand moving down her neck before resting it over her left breast. His grin widened as he felt the rapid pulse of her heart. "Enough for months and months of enjoyment … but alas it is not meant to be."

Sara moaned then screamed as claws squeezed and dug into her flesh, her already fading life-force plunged as her heart felt a chilling yet also searing grip around it.

"And now I will feast upon your heart!" But as the demon tightened his grip and pulled on the organ, pain shot through him. This time it was Malagant who screamed as fire raced up his arm, enveloping the demon who tried to free himself but couldn't. His screams grew louder and more frantic as the fire slowly and painfully devoured him. His last words were a hysterical scream before his dark demonic heart exploded into ashes.

Sara opened her eyes but despite all her efforts her vision remained blurry. Her body ached but it was no where near the pain she had experienced only minutes ago. *Was it minutes ago?* How long had she been out --- hours, days? Was she even alive?

"Sara."

A voice. A soft calming voice. Was it real or just a …

"Sara. Sara."

No it was real, but what did it mean? She willed herself to focus , sending every ounce of strength she had left to a single purpose. Slowly like a fading dream, the fog of blurriness dissipated and the form of Seneca Maza stood before her. While he appeared no different than he had been before leaving her and Achilles to face

Pestilence, there was an uncanny vibe that ascertained something ... unnatural.

Seneca smiled as he read the whisper of his name from her lips. "You did well Sara. You refused to give up despite all that had been done to you. You sacrificed yourself so that the others would have the strength to finish. Come now it's time to rest." He extended his hand toward her.

"I can't move Seneca," she managed to utter.

"Nonsense! Just relax and stop thinking about it."

Sara relaxed and found herself able to move. She grabbed Seneca's hand and he pulled her to her feet.

"What about Damien and Serena?"

"Shush," Seneca answered. "Don't worry about such trifles, just relax and rest. Everything is all right. Everything is all right."

Sara gave him a look before she closed her eyes and exhaled.

Chapter 30

Damien Parker landed on the top of the stonewall before reaching down to grab Serena's hand.

"Will you climb!"

Serena pulled herself as far up as she could and with a tug of strength Damien managed to pull her along side of him. "Still think I shouldn't lose any weight?"

Damien eyed her before eying the cemetery. From up here it seemed so organized and arranged. "Nah I still think you shouldn't lose any weight." He followed her gaze. Behind them Malagant was slowly moving toward Sara Winters like a mummy from one of those horror movies of the 50's.

"Damien were we wise to …"

"She'll be fine," he assured before leaping down into the cemetery.

Serena gave Sara one last glance before hoping down behind him. "Where are we going?" she asked following him as turned and started down the alley.

"The tomb of Marie Laveau, the Voodoo Queen."

Serena could see various demons lurking in the shadows. She also found herself feeling sick to her stomach though she wasn't sure as to why.

"Damien are you feeling okay?"

Damien paused for a second, wondering what had suggested such a question. "I'm just a little queasy. It's because of the misbalance in the magic. I'm sure you feel it."

"Yes that was why I had asked."

"We're almost there." He zigzagged between a couple of tombs before zipping straight ahead at that infamous pace of his.

Serena raced behind him trying to keep up, but crept up behind him as he stopped in front of a tomb. Time and weather had tarnished the once white marker. Now it was a collage of brown, mildew green with traces of white that had been too stubborn to wear away. Compared to the tombs around it, this one gave the impression of a pauper's resting instead of the Queen of Voodoos.

Despite the worn, battered look, however magical energy pulsed from it, rippling through Serena to the core of her being.

Damien glanced around in anticipation. He could feel the hatred, the fear. It hung over the area like a storm cloud. Was he too late? Had the Maderan already been released? No he would have known, not sure how but he would have known.

"Damien Parker."

Damien turned as Geryon Magnus stepped out from behind Marie Laveau's tomb. "Give it up Magnus," he warned.

The demon sneered. "Now why would I want to do that? You feel the taint in the magic just like I do. So why would I give up when everything is going in my direction." He seemed to grow taller and more menacing with each word.

He reached over and touched the side of the tomb, a purple glow illuminating his fingers spread until filled the entire side was covered in an eerie aura. Seconds later a crack formed in the wall and a dark blue light exploded from within.

Damien watched as sparks within the light danced, circling each other till a form was patterned. A flash of light temporarily blinded him and as the brightness faded Damien could only stare in disbelief at the monstrosity that appeared before him. From the face and body shape, one would have merely thought the creature to be a giant supersized gorilla. However the long, golden blond hair extending from the rear of the crest ontop the creature's head had never graced any gorilla he had ever seen. Four bony spikes protruded from each muscular arm, much like thorns on a rose stem. Glowing green eyes glared upon them, but what stood out most were the hands --- hands that seemed too big even for the massive behemoth possessing them. Hands that possessed long, razor-sharp fingers glimmering in the night like knives. Then there were the legs, two powerful hind legs that could probably send the beast 14 feet up with ease.

He had newfound respect for the Voodoo Queen as he wondered on how she had ever imprisoned such a monster. *That thing's gotta be at least 8 feet tall and at least twice as wide as Shaq!*

The Maderan let out a dreadful roar before dropping on all fours. It obviously had felt the magic within him and knew immediately what he was.

"Serena I want you to go behind that tomb over there and stay there no matter what! You hear me stay back!"

"Are you crazy? Why?"

"Do you trust me?"

Serena eyed him, then the monster looming before them before her gaze returned to Damien. "Yes but ..."

"If you trust me, if I ever meant anything to you; do as I say just this once!"

She moved away about two tombs behind him, but not before her eyes locked on to him with a look and Damien Parker already knew this discussion would resume later – if he lived to see later. He gave her one last glance before turning toward the Maderan. Above him the purple sky was littered with twinkling stars. *So it comes to this.* He stepped forward surrendering to the magic as its weaves surrounded him.

Serena stared in awe. She had never seen Damien Parker so immerse as the Guardian. His armor was bulkier, thicker than the body armor he had sworn during his previous encounter with the servants of the Abyss. The white staff pulsed with light as the Knight of the Order closed on the Maderan.

Damien didn't circle the creature, instead the two stared straight at each other. The Maderon's eyes a whirlwind of rage, the Guardian of the Cross' gleamed with determination and defiance. The Maderan charged, the Guardian sidestepped jabbing his staff into the creature's side, magic sparkling from the butt of the Knight's weapon.

The Maderan roared and with lightning reflexes stopped and readjusted its attack, catching the Guardian completely off guard with a quick slash of his spikes before closing in with amazing speed. The Guardian desperately parried each attack of its claws with his staff. Attempting to avoid being backed into a corner, he leaped over the creature and prepared to attack but the creature again moved with incredible speed as it spun around and connected with a jump kick to his midsection knocking him back into the wall vaults.

In a berserk frenzy the Maderan flew onto the Guardian, claws and spikes raking in fury ripping into the armor and the magic shield the Knight of the Order had barely been able to erect.

Serena prepared to charge to his rescue but the Guardian stopped her with a look.

The Maderan lifted its head, howling as if mad, again attempting to seethe its claws into the Guardian's flesh. The Guardian again parried the attacks with his staff. Midway through a parry, the Knight of the Order released his right hand and channeled his magic through it. Energy flared and flickered as it raced through the creature's body, but the monster still continued its assault. The Guardian increased the intensity of his attack; the Maderan howled and nipped at the forks of magic that assaulted it before leaping back.

"Is that all you got," the Guardian sneered. The Maderan loosed a frightening wail before suddenly disappearing into thin air – to the untrained eye that is.

The Guardian calmed himself and concentrated on being one with his surroundings. He already knew the Maderan was going to attack, the question was from which direction would the attack come.

He turned around just in time, moving just in time to avoid the sharp claws and spikes, but creature quickly adjusted itself leaning a broad shoulder into the Knight of Order, pounding him with a power that any NFL fullback would envy as the Maderan rammed him into a tomb. Green eyes locked defiantly on the winded Knight of the Order and snarls of triumph hissed from its lips. Serena desired to run to his aid and nearly gave in to it – that is until she heard what appear to be laughter indeed the Guardian of the Cross was laughing. "You're not the only one with some speed", the Guardian informed before with amazing speed the Knight of the Order maneuvered along side the creature unleashing bolts of magic that caused his foe to screech in pain before retaliating with a backhand that sent the Guardian flying into another tomb.

The monster wasted no time and was upon the Guardian in a single leap, again the Guardian loosed his magic, pounding the creature this time in the side, knocking it back. The creature howled before launching itself back at the Guardian, claws raking. The Guardian sidestepped, but not before the creature caught him with its claws penetrating the Guardian's armor, rearing through flesh.

Serena noticed the grimace on his face, but the Guardian failed to scream instead he laughed. The creature again lunged for the Guardian this time with more fury than before. The Guardian leaped back before swinging his staff, the Maderan leaned back, avoiding the attack, but the Guardian simultaneously unleashed a magical fury that caught the creature by surprise, knocking it back to the end of the alley.

The Guardian wasted no time delivering another magical attack. White lightning seeped out into the creature that howled in maddening fury, forcing itself to its feet. The Guardian twirled his staff as he settled into an attack stance. The wounded monster took the attack head on, paring attack after attack before again lashing out in a frenzy. The Knight of the Order swung his staff, fire flaming as it crashed into the monster's midsection. Another blow crashed into the monster's neck.

Lightning lanced through the air, wrapping itself around the Maderan. Energy crackled and burned yet the creature stumbled forward, howling and gnashing, his body simmering from the heat of the Order's magic.

My God, Serena thought, how can it keep pushing itself like this? She watched as the Guardian stood there, willing his magic forward, pounding the Maderan as it twisted and writhed yet continued to push forward.

Slowly he approached, magic continuing in a steady current till finally the two opponents were nearly face to face. The Guardian quickly stabbed his staff into the monster's throat before unleashing another storm of magic. The forks of power seemed to pulse through the both of them, both screamed – the Maderan in a voice of agony laced with madness and frustration, the Guardian in determination.

Suddenly an explosion of light and magic rippled through the cemetery with the force of a hurricane blinding Serena and knocking her to the ground.

As Serena Martin came to she quickly rushed to where the two combatants had stood. Damien Parker, the Guardian laid still on the pavement, nearby about 15 feet away, a large pile of black ash simmered. Serena rushed toward him cradling his head, praying that he was alive. Relief flooded her as his eyes slowly opened. His breathing and his pulse were shallow and blood flowed from the wounds inflicted by the Maderon's claws, but he was alive.

"The Maderan," he sputtered.

She nodded toward the pile of black ash slowly dispersing in the wind. She started to smile, but her joy faded as she noticed that his shallow breathing and pulse was fading, which puzzled her. *It's like he's dying. Granted the wounds are bad, but they're not that terrible.*

"It's the Maderon's claws, they're laced with poison."

"We have to get you to a hospital."

"It's a berserker, an anomaly of magic. It feeds off fear and madness, even its own. It kept pushing itself because it went mad over its inability to feed off my fear till it started to feed off its own frenzy. That's why I wanted you to stay back. I was pretty sure I could keep my emotions in check, however I couldn't chance the Maderan attacking you and . . ."

"And making you lose control." She smiled, here he was lying in her arms dying and he still managed to say something sweet. "We can still get you to a hospital. The doctors …"

"Too weak to move." He chuckled. "Don't worry maybe I'll … enter … the Resurrect Sleep." He knew the chances of that were slim; he had used a lot of magic in that battle maybe too much. *I can't die like this. Can't leave Serena. Mustn't leave Serena.*

Serena Martin nearly started to cry as Damien Parker slipped into unconsciousness. "Damien wake up! Wake up! Damien!" She cradled his head, sobbing, never noticing the red orb that swiftly approached her until it had enveloped her and whisked her away leaving Damien Parker's body lying in the cold dark night alone.

How long had he been walking he wasn't sure, but he knew he was tired and his heart lifted as he saw the house. The candle burning in the window he knew was meant for him.

With relief he approached, glad to be at the end of his journey.

"I see you finally heading indoors."

He turned to see a familiar face yet he couldn't quite tell from where. "Yes it'll be nice to rest for a change."

The stranger merely glanced up toward the sky. "A storm's a coming. A terrible one."

"Yes." He had seen his share of storms, terrible ones. A part of his life he hoped to put behind him.

"Well I have to be off."

"Where are you off to in this terrible weather?"

"Where I'm needed. Here, there. This place and that. You know."

For some strange reason he did. "Good journey to you."

"Till we meet again."

The comment for some reason left him at ease but he dismissed it, content to watch the man walk toward the oncoming storm clouds till finally he disappeared.

The rain was already pouring as he opened the door and closed it. He stopped in surprise as he saw them all standing around the table.

"How did you know?"

"We've been waiting for you." Her face seemed to be the moon, the stars and the sun all at once.

"But why? For what reason?"

"So that you can know who you really are."

"Who I am?", his voice low and full of confusion.

"Speak our names," she cooed softly.

"Speak your name," another voice commanded.

The storm outside raged. Water seeped between the cracks in the door. As water ran around his shoes he found himself recollecting memories – and names: his name, their names.

"Speak our name," the prince commanded.

"Speak your name," she again cooed.

Thunder boomed, shaking the house.

He eyed the dark boy tall and conflicted. "Damien Parker."

The boy smiled.

"Knight of the Order." This time his words were aimed at the armored female who drew her sword and saluted in response.

"Guardian of the Cross." This time to the girl in blue who smiled.

He turned to the girl in the green tunic. "One of the Nestari!" She shyly bowed and stepped away.

Lightning flashed across the sky, thunder again boomed. The water now rose past his ankles, almost to his knees yet he kept going.

"Caretaker of the Nexus!" The Indian bowed.

Rain drummed on the rooftop. Thunder roared as he finished the name.

Then there was her standing there, beautiful and terrible all at once. "Child of Water," he replied softly. She didn't move instead she placed both her arms around his and smiled.

"The Suriana Uchawi!" he finished strongly to the Prince who bowed before again standing, but now he seemed taller than he had been before, his voice rivaled the thunder as he spoke.

"The Child has spoken his name."

"He now knows who he is," the Indian added.

The water by now was up to his waist as the door burst open and water poured in, flooding the house, chilling him almost to the bone. No one moved as the water rose above their heads, burying them in wetness and cold. Just as the water rose above his head, the Lady leaned her face close to his.

"Now you are ready to awake."

As the water drowned him he closed his eyes and relaxed, giving himself over to the inevitable. And then he woke up.

Chapter 31

As the orb dissipated around her, Serena stared blankly around her. She was no longer in St. Louis Cemetery, gnashing and howling hissed all around her. She noticed the Guardian of the Cross was missing, she also became aware that she was being watched.

Serena quickly embraced her magic as she eyed the demon Magnus standing no more than a few feet away. Around her she could see eyes and shapes looming, she was surrounded.

"Where am I?" she demanded. "And what have you done with Damien Parker?"

Magnus said nothing, instead he smiled before stepping toward her. She waited as he took another step and another before unleashing her magic in a flurry she had never used before.

The assault took Magnus by surprise. His eyes widened in shock as his body took the full brunt of her magic. He staggered back before falling to a knee. However a moment later his face lift to reveal a disappointing smile. "Is that all you have? A pity I was expecting more." With a fluid motion he straightened, a red aura flared around him before lifting his arm and with a sight effort his fist flicked open.

The force of the demon's magic dissipated any defense Serena could muster and send her crashing into a wall of rock.

She tried to move but all her efforts were for naught as she hung there suspended helplessly against the wall.

Magnus' eyebrows narrowed and with the same simplicit effort he slowly closed his hand. Simultaneously the wall cracked and crumbled in various places until a stone cross remained.

Magnus lowered his hand and a sinister smile crept upon his face as he stepped up and admired his handiwork.

"Did you truly believe you could defeat me Serena?" he implied softly as he reached up and stroked Serena's cheek. "Oh how naïve you are child."

Revulsion and disgust filled her with his touch. She wanted to scream but she knew all that would do is amuse him. *Damien where are you?*

Suddenly a glimmer of hope shot through her as she glanced over Magnus' shoulder. Although he was a good distance away she could see his trademark features well enough: the armor, the cloak, the white staff. There was no doubt about it, it was the Guardian.

Slowly the Knight of the Order made his way closer and Serena noticed there was something weird about him. At first she thought it might have been the color of his armor which was void of the usual colors she had seen him in. Instead his armor was a dark red, his hat and cloak black. However it was more than that, there wasn't that uncanny enigmamatic feeling that she had grown accustomed to, rather the vibe from him was inexorable.

Still he was the Guardian and he was here. Let's see what smart alleck here has to say now.

Magnus smiled at her and to Serena's disgust he continued to stroke her face and hair.

God Damien hurry up!

"Ahh Serena," the demon jested, "you cringe with my touch. Why?"

"It's because you are disgusting and vile!" She wanted to struggle, but didn't. *Just keep looking at me a few seconds more.*

"Ah Serena, torturing you will give me such pleasure. I will enjoy hearing your screams day and night."

"Someone may have something to say about that."

"Oh yes I almost forgot about Damien Parker. I believe he should be right behind me now. Stop!"

To Serena's horror Damien obeyed.

"What's wrong Serena, you seemed shocked? Allow me to explain. You see Damien Parker is an illusion of my creation, designed to keep you out of my way and off guard."

Serena merely hung there dumbfounded. "But what about Malagant, the Four Horsemen and the Maderan."

"All an elaborate ploy. There was no Maderan in St. Louis Cemetery, it's just a myth, a myth I used to my advantage. You shouldn't feel so bad you stupid child, all this was a result of events I set into motion months ago. Did you think it was by chance that Damien Parker came

and swept you off your feet. The last year has been a
dramatic piece under my direction."

"But why?"

"Because of this." His hand opened to reveal six
jewels that glowed like miniature stars. The jewels flew out
of his hand and hovered above his head like planets
around a sun. "For eons these seven seals have kept us
imprisoned here. All that could end this excuse that is
known as Order is mine!" He laughed. "To think of all
the creatures that fool would trust such power to – the
Order trusted it to you! Such a fool to gamble on such
pathetic creatures, to give them such a Pandora's box and
not expect them to unleash the evil within it."

He gently stroked Serena's hair. "I'm sure you
noticed I said seven and there are only six here. Ah how
proper for the last and most powerful jewel to be trusted
to such a beautiful creature such as you."

Serena glanced at the figure that now stood along
side the demon. Disbelief, anger, sadness all flooded her.
A whole year – a lie. Everything that had been between
her and Damien had been a charade. It was too much to
bear. If it was true then dying would only be a comfort.
She closed her eyes hoping it was all a bad dream, but
everywhere she tried to put herself Magnus' laughter and
words followed. Worse she started recalling all the
moments they had spent together. That night at the
homecoming dance, the first night they went to the Jazz
Bistro. She remembered being the envy of every girl in
school that Valentine's day as they all noticed her stuffed
teddy bear and two roses. The way he would kiss her,
never abrupt or rough – always soft and comforting. The

caress in his voice as he talk to her – even over the phone it was there.

She never really told him but he had won her just by the words at Homecoming, "I think you're something special." The sincerely in his voice told her that he would love her for all it was worth. How could that be a lie? As she pondered the question another set of feelings came over her, a rapport that was familiar and warm and with it a soft soothing voice carrying a single message: "I love you Serena."

Damien. A spark generated in her heart. It was him, her Damien. "You're lying!" Serena exclaimed, struggling with a ferocity she failed to display before.

"Stupid child you've lost! Give up!"

"Everything you told me about Damien Parker has been a lie!" She freed herself with an unexplainable effort, lashing out her magic at Magnus.

Magnus didn't try to defend himself, instead prepared to take her assault as he had earlier, but his eyes filled with a painful surprise as the magic assaulted him – this time with a strength far greater than what she had attacked with before. The demon stumbled back clasping his head with his hands and loosing a dreadful wail. He tried to step toward her, but the ribbons of magic confined him as his countenance distorted and changed, revealing the true evil that lied beneath. A dark ugliness that writhed and struggled as if it was horrified by the stark reality of its own vile appearance.

Serena moved in, her intensity doubled, her resolve certain. Magnus had haunted her, tortured her, and caused her to doubt what she should have known to be a certainty. Now it would end. She stopped though as she noticed the sky which had suddenly turned pitch black and the earth shook with a tremendous force and the ground parted. The gnashing and howling ceased as the demons cringed and cowered as a white light appeared between Serena and Magnus. The light's radiance continued to grow, shinning brighter and brighter. Within the core of the shinning hew a shape slowly revealed itself – a long sword held in an up stretched arm of an armored figure flanked by a billowing cape. A figure encompassed in all white.

Magnus hissed, Serena watched in awe as the sword slashed through the air into the demon's heart, sending the servant of the Abyss screaming as it descended into the dark chasm bellow.

The girl was still in awe as the Guardian glided smoothly across the ground, power and radiance searing and sparkling off his form. She backed away a step before stepping forward to meet him. He stopped about a foot from her, his ephemeral form floating in front of her. Serena wondered if he even recognized her. His eyes and face no longer displayed any of the features that distinguished him as the boy she was in love with.

"Damien?" she whispered.

An eternity seemed to pass before the stone countenance broke into a slight smile and his eyes sparkled with a familiarity she never took for granted. Her fear diminished, she stepped up to embrace him, but just as her arms were about to wrap themselves around him, Damien Parker's body flared with a blinding light forcing Serena to shield her eyes. When the blinding nova died Serena found herself back in St. Louis Cemetery – next to the tomb of Marie Laveau.

The tomb of Marie Laveau was no longer cracked where the Maderan had freed itself from the Voodoo Queen's prison. As she rounded the corner, the creature's remains were still where she had last seen them though by now only an outline of charred cement stood as the only reminder of the Maderon's existence. Damien Parker was also missing. Serena wasn't surprise however a slight spell of disappointment lingered. She had hoped he would be standing there or sitting somewhere nearby, an assurance that all was now well.

Ohmigod Sara!

It took a few minutes for her to find her way out of the cemetery and back to Crozat St where they had left Sara to fend against Malagant.

Please let her be alive. There's been too much death today. Enrica, Seneca, Andra, Achilles. I've already lost one good friend, I can't afford to lose another.

She arrived to find the street empty. No body, nothing to indicate a struggle had taken place. *Good. Hopefully she's alive.* Most likely if Sara was alive she would have gone to check on Achilles and Andra. She re-entered the park, unconcerned of the potential dangers of Louis Armstrong Park. She came upon the area where they had left Achilles in his struggle with Death, but there was no sign that they had even been present. Determined she continued backtracking, screaming the names of her friends, not caring if she attracted a mugger or not, but despair finally took its toll as she walked back toward the gated entrance where she fell to her knees in tears, lifting her eyes to see the twinkling stars and peaceful heavens. A bitter scream was at the tip of her tongue, but froze as a silver ball of light hovered high in the night sky before stretching and tearing into five smaller spheres, each a different color: red, blue, black, yellow and green. They descended slowly in front of her stopping about a foot from the ground when the intensity of their auras brightened and Serena couldn't believe her eyes as five familiar figures emerged from the radiance and stood in the entryway into Louis Armstrong Park.

Andra, Sara, Achilles, Seneca, and Enrica. All alive and well.

Serena bee lined straight to Andra and Sara, embracing them in a long hug. She grabbed Enrica next, squeezing as hard as she could till the girl complained about not being able to breathe.

"Being that last I saw you, you were shattered all over the pavement," Achilles chided to Seneca before turning to Andra. "And you ... you were ..." he didn't finish instead he embraced Andra in a fierce hug.

"I think it can be said that the good guys won," Seneca assumed.

"You did well Serena," Sara chimed. "You saw through Magnus' deception and didn't give up the faith. Damien would be so proud of you."

Serena's face hardened as she noticed that Damien was still missing. "Sara do you know where he is? Seneca tell me you know where Damien is!"

"It's all right Serena," Sara replied softly, holding the girl close. "Shh it's all right. The nightmare is over." She pulled back and placed her hands on her friend's shoulders. "So now it's time for you to wake up."

Serena gave her a confused look. "Wake up?"

"Yes. Wake up Serena."

Chapter 32

"Wake up Serena."

Serena awoke with a start, surprise washing over her as her eyes wondered. She was in her room, but how did she get there?

"Come on Baby, time to get ready for the gala."

She gave a soft moan as she rolled out of bed still in … *my clothes are exactly the same as what I wore to the Quarter.* "Mother what time is it?"

"It's 8:45 dear."

8:45? It was possible, but how did she get back home?

"My you must have had a time at the parade with your friends. Your father found you on the porch swing in the backyard. He carried you all the way upstairs."

"When was that?"

"I don't know, about 6:30?"

6:30! It was 5:45 when Damien took on the Maderan.

She showered and fumbled into her dress, a long and gregarious procedure. She made her way downstairs, eying the telephone.

Call him.

She picked up the phone, slowly dialing the numbers while glancing upstairs every now and then. An argument with her father was not something she needed right now. *Please be home.*

"Hello."

"Hello Mrs. Parker, it's me Serena. Is Damien there?"

"Why no, I thought he'd be with you. He said something about some ball you two were suppose to be going to."

Serena kicked herself. She had assumed that his parents would know, his parents were so understanding and he always was close with his parents. It seemed obvious they would know. "Yes maam he was with me earlier, but he took off. Something about a surprise for this evening, but that was late this afternoon." She couldn't tell the real reason for her call. *I'm calling because I think your son maybe dead.*

"No we haven't seen him since this morning."

"Thanks." She fought the urge to cry, closing her eyes she hung up the phone. She had barely placed it on the hook when the phone rang. Serena quickly answered it, already aware of whose voice she would likely hear.

"Serena?"

A sigh of relief breathed from the girl. Sara Winters was alive. "Sara ... are you?"

"I'm all right. I'm just ... confused. Last thing I remember was lying on the concrete following ..." she paused a beat and her voice was a shrill as she continued. "Next thing I know I'm lying in the playground near my house."

Her story left Serena even more puzzled. Sara mysteriously taken home? But how and who? The thud of a closing door caused her attention to flicker. "Sara I'll call you back later." She hung up the phone just as her parents descended the stairs.

"Who was that dear?" her father inquired.

"It was Sara. She was calling to see if I had made it back."

"What's wrong dear?" her mother asked, "You seem sad."

"Nothing. It's just that it looks like Damien Parker won't be able to escort me tonight."

The mother eyed her daughter before embracing her in a hug. "I'm sorry baby."

"So am I," Serena whispered. "So am I."

Apparently Victor Morris' date had to cancel. *Right* Serena scoffed as the pair entered the hall and descended the stairs to the main floor. She detested these silly gatherings and repeatedly vowed that if she had a daughter she would be spared the agony of balls and debuts.

The only enjoyment she had was when her father danced with her. While she didn't agree with his insistence on choosing her husband, he was her father and she understood that he was only concerned with her well being. If only he understood that he had instilled with better sense than what he often perceived. Her father would like Damien Parker if he stopped seeing him as the smuck across the tracks and saw him for who he really was. *A magical being. One whom I'll never see again.*

The thought of him vacuumed away all the pleasantry of her father's company. So numb were her senses that she failed to see Victor standing behind her father until he spoke.

"Excuse me. May I cut in?"

The look that formed on her face made it obvious that she'd rather watch paint dry than dance with him, but neither her father nor Victor Morris seemed to see it. It didn't surprise her; her father was blinded by parental duty, Victor was just plain stupid.

The older man stepped back allowing the younger to step in and wrap and arm around her waist while holding her hand in the other.

Suppressing her anger and annoyance she stomached enough to sit her through two dance numbers before his endless bragging and attempts to grope her proved too much for her goodwill. Citing thirst and fatigue, she managed to lure Victor away to get a drink and wasted no time escaping to the far corner of the floor. For the longest time she remained there, admonishing the beauty of her silver gown. She and her mother had spent weeks working on it and she had been looking forward to Damien seeing her in it.

She sighed as she caught sight of the starlit sky. A streak caught her eye – a shooting star. *I wish Damien was here.*

No one noticed as he entered but then he wasn't expecting any attention. He could count on one hand everyone he knew here. He was dressed in a simple tux, all white with the exception of his bowtie and jacket lapels which were black and his cape which was dark purple. A gold mask covered most of his face exposing only his lip and chin.

While his dress was simple, his presence was anything but simple. His stride whistled with regality and guest wondered on him as they parted with his passing and questioned on him as they resided.

She never noticed him walking up to her, being lost in her thoughts but as he stood there she could feel something imposing about him. Her eyes noticed the butt of his white cane and rose slowly till she finally saw his masked face and outstretched hand.

"Milady, may I have the pleasure of a dance?"

Her first impulse was to dismiss him as she had been doing every other suitor, but there was something about him. She took his hand and rose to her feet before slipping her arm into the crook of his.

He escorted her to the dance floor before releasing her hand and placing his arms around her waist and pulled her close with a gentleness that seemed strangely familiar. As the music played she drifted in his arms to a rhythm so powerful that all the anguish of earlier seemed a distant dream. She glanced at the masked face, eyes hidden beneath the gold mask, but something told her that they were watching her with concern.

She wasn't sure why but she eased closer to him, embracing him and for the first time all night she relaxed, whirling and drifting where his steps commanded. Neither spoke but to Serena the silence seemed to be a music in and of itself and the pulse of his heart were all the noise she needed, that is until he spoke.

"You look good."

She pulled back from him, staring as his hands reached for his mask and pulled it off to reveal the face of Damien Parker. Serena started in disbelief as something seem to lift within her and she found herself smiling. Shyly she lowered her face to hide her joy. She might have been ecstatic to see him but she had learned from her mother that a woman could never let a man know how much of a hold he has over her heart – such knowledge only led to trouble in the long run. Besides if Damien Parker thought he could place her on an emotional rollercoaster and expect her to jump into his arms and kiss him just because he was smiling well he was about to find his expectations far off the mark.

She was about to demand an explanation when she realized her feet – and his were dangling about six inches above the floor. Instinctively she pulled up and embraced him tightly, her face so close to his her nose tickled from the breeze of his breath.

Damien merely smiled. "You smell good too."

Staring into those dark eyes she forgot all about the womanly code of ethics, she didn't care if her father saw or if the world came to an end. All that mattered was the tenderness of his lips as they touched hers.

For a brief moment their lips parted. Neither said anything, merely staring into each other's eyes, never noticing nor caring about the eyes that stared upon them. Finally the girl buried her face in his shoulder, eyes closing,

and her breath soft. She felt an additional warmth and
knew that his cape had been draped around her. She could
feel his heart racing, his arms snugly around her. She
smiled for she knew that everything was all right – despite
the ongoing war between the Order and the Abyss,
everything was all right – for now even if it was just for a
moment. It was a moment both relished as they floated
above the dance floor enticed in a rhythm and music that
only they heard.

He merely stood by the tree, watching her as she stared into the water. They were in City Park, the gala with all its pretense and illusion had become annoying to both of them.

He exhaled a soft breath as he gazed at the reflection of the moon and stars in the surface of the lake. She had demanded an explanation and he had tried to give her one. Truth was the whole thing was just as complex and confusing to him as it was for her. Last thing he remembered was entering the Dreamtime, he awoke from the Dreamtime much as he had countless times before only he wasn't in the cemetery – exactly where he woke he wasn't sure, but it was on a plane he had never experienced before and likely never would again – even now the experience left him in awe. Words were too limited to explain what had happened, no matter how many times or in how many ways he tried the explanation would always fall short of adequately describing the experience.

His eyes lowered in response to Serena's voice.

"So how did it feel?"

"How did what feel?"

"Having all the power in the world coursing through you."

"To be honest it felt great, but also scary. There I was able to see anyone, do anything; able to solve all the problems of the world." He paused for a moment and for a second his face seem twisted with a great pain. "Yet I found myself contemplating and accepting acts that I would have never condoned before. Embracing concepts that contradicted everything I ever believed in."

"So you gave it up?"

"Barely." Never had such a small word expressed so much. She would never know how close he had been to refusing that choice and keeping it, but what shamed him even more was how in that instant eternity he had to be deterred into making what should have been the obvious choice, for there with him beyond the fringes of what was and what could be, was something older, wiser if not more powerful than him, it was the force that had humbled him, allowing for him to act, to let all that power go and that bothered him. For all his dedication and commitment he had been found wanting and that was a crushing blow to the vanity within him, which only bothered him more. So much that he couldn't even tell Serena. He turned to her as he felt her soft hand on his shoulder and his anguish slowly mellowed. Her dark brown eyes sparkled and her smile was illuminating --- a face of absolute faith.

"You gave it up. You're not a monster."

"Maybe. But I saw things Serena. A future, the future I'm not all together sure. Worst I think ..."

"You think what?"

"I just have this feeling that...before I gave it up I did things. Caused a ripple that could affect things to come."

"What did you see?"

"Achiles, Andra, Sara, Enrica."

"And what about us?"

His eyebrows raised. "What about us?"

"Did you see anything about us?"

"That's one of the weird things. For everyone else the sight was linear, flowing and for the most part precise. With us it was jumbled. Like someone took all the movie previews of an actor and actress and shot them through my mind in no particular logical order."

"So what did you see?"

"A little bit of everything."

"And?"

He glanced back at the water and after a few minutes of silence finally spoke. "Serena I'm different from the other Guardians. For them channeling the magic was something they could do. After their ability was exhausted they still had the possibility of a life. For me the magic is who I am. As long as I have it it will be battle after battle after battle and once its gone so am I." He stood there for a long time before turning around half expecting her to be gone, to give him up so she could have real happiness, but she was still there.

"Are you deaf? Did you hear a word I said Serena? I'll never have a normal life! You have the chance of having one. You're able to use the magic, but you're not bound by it. Not bound to the crusade like the Nestari are. I can't ... I can't ask you to share that kind of life."

"Shut up!" She was upon him in an instant. "You're right Damien Parker. You have no choice in the life you were given and while you keep saying I have a choice I don't think the thought is fully clicking in that head of yours."

Damien nearly tripped over a low branch and for the first time realized he had been backing away.

"Aht! Don't even think about opening that mouth of yours. A life with you may not be the life my parents want for me, but guess what it's my life! For better or for worse Damien Parker you're stuck with me!" Her voice softened. "You want me … and believe it or not I want you too."

Damien Parker, Guardian of the Cross merely stood there watching her, waiting for whatever unexpected additional act the woman would shock him with.

Serena leaned in closer to him and smiled as her fingers gently reached up and stroked his cheek. "Isn't this where you're suppose to kiss me," she said softly.

It had the appearance of a question, but he knew better. The woman is insane and not just her, the whole gender was insane. Nevertheless he kissed her softly on the lips.

Their lips finally parted and she gazed at him, her face beaming with a smile that wise men feared. "You're glowing."

"Oh and how am I glowing?"

"A bright gold aura is surrounding you."

"And what does that mean?"

"Why are you asking me? You're the one who's one of the Nestari!"

"You're the one who sees me glowing!"

"Seeing the glow doesn't mean I know what it means!"

"Maybe it's because …"

"Because of what?"

"Kiss me again and we'll see."

"With pleasure."

Epilouge,
Another Ending ... A New Beginning

Somewhere on an unknown island in the South Pacific, air twisted and crackled as the mouth of a Portal diverged. A moment later a tall dark figure stepped through and stood alone as the Portal closed behind him on top a ridge summit.

The view from this point was the best on the entire island, from any direction one could see the green grass and trees angling downward till it met the reef which formed a beautiful teal blue ring extending nearly 30 meters from the island where the ring darkened into the dark blue of the Pacific.

His eyes drifted down the westward side where he could see the rooftops of the city below glistening in the noon day sun, looking onward his eyes were barely able to gaze upon the giant metallic sea fortress in the harbor shinning like a beacon. Down there awaiting his return were his people, his charges. His.

Ironic, prior to all this he never considered being king, president, or whatever else heads of state are referred as. All he had hoped to be was a simple man whispering simple words to whoever was on the throne, and now he was this.

He eyed his left hand before staring up at the clear sky. *Hidden by the glare of the sun, this sun, are the stars. But there are places that lie even beyond the stars. Beyond everything and anything I could ever comprehend. And I've been there … and I've been changed. What have I become? An angel? A god? What?*

No, he was none of these things. He knew exactly what he had become --- a king, a protector, a guardian. Whether he liked it or not it is who he is, what he has always been. He had just refused to accept it because he was terrified of the consequences, but no longer. Now he was ready. He closed his eyes as the cool sea breeze caressed his face, the salt in the air filling his nostrils. Sighing he opened his eyes and started down the mountain toward the city below where his destiny awaited.

www.ingramcontent.com/pod-product-compliance
Lightning Source LLC
Chambersburg PA
CBHW020821180626
46814CB00001B/54